Envy

Envy

A Seven Deadly
and Four Novel

by

Tim Beeden

First published in Great Britain in 2022

Cover by: Jack Staples

For Nate.
May you dance to the beat of your own drum forever more.

CURIOUS PLACES

THE GRUMBLINGS
PROPHECY STRETCH
UNDEROVER LANE
LOOSE DRAWERS EMPORIUM
MAUDES HOUSE OF DUBIOUS REPUTE
THE HANGING TUMBLER
THE BURIED STIFF
SQUIRE'S ROW
COBBLE CLAP CORNER
HA'PENNY BEND
STAGGING PASS
FAILSAFE HOLDINGS
SERMON'S CROSSING
LOOSE CHANGE TRAIL

FUNNEL TWITCHEL

GRINDERS CLEARING

INNARDS LANE

PATHETIC TREE

BROKEN ALLY

GAMBLE POINT

DRINKLE STREET

RAT AND VAT INN

LOWER CALVER

THE MAP OF
THE BACKSTREETS

CHAPTER 1

Close encounters

C HARLIE LIGHTFOOT SKIDDED around the corner—fiddle under one arm, bag of coins under the other—and hurled himself down Drinkle Street as fast as his legs could carry him, which at that moment, and given the circumstances, was just about fast enough.

But only just.

He risked a glance over his shoulder as he reached the end of the street and decided his legs might need to carry him a little faster. Through the perpetual gloom of the overhanging buildings and the type of rain which seemed determined to become mist, he could just make out the three odd-sized men who were intent on catching up to him.

And catching up to him they were.

Charlie burst forth from the end of the street as a large stone clattered against the wall where his head had been seconds earlier.

"Ha! Missed!" he shouted.

"It was supposed to!" shouted one of his pursuers. "It was a warning shot. Meant to scare you!"

Well that bloody worked.

Up ahead, three of the most notorious routes through the

Backstreets met at a crossroads known as Gamble Point. As in, pick one, take a gamble and see what happens to you.

Something always happened no matter which you picked; it's just that some of the things that happened were worse than others.

Charlie picked the centre prong of Broken Alley and put shoe leather to cobblestone.

From somewhere behind, he heard the muffled shouts of the three odd-sized men.

"Which one did he go up?"

"Dunno."

"How many streets are there?"

"One, two, three."

"And how many of us?"

"One, two, three."

"That's handy ain't it?"

"Why?"

"Good lords above! You are proper thick!"

"Thanks. I been lifting rocks."

"Not thick like that, numpty. Thick in the head!"

"Oh. Wait… is that one of them insults?"

"What do you think?

"Sorry to break in to your chat and everything, but shouldn't we get after him? He had a lot of coins in that—."

And that was as much as Charlie heard as their words became the grunts, scuffles and wallops of things turning physical.

As he moved on, he smiled. It really wasn't fair. He knew the rambling streets, alleys, dead-ends and general hotch-potch construction of the Backstreets better than just about anyone in the city of Calver. Once he'd given the odd-sized men the slip, there was no way they'd catch him.

Charlie shook the coins in his bag and once again smiled. The odd-sized men were right—he did have a fair few coins in there. Not bad for a morning's work. It was market time and that meant plenty of people in and around Lower Calver. He was wondering whether he should drop the coins off with Auntie, then head back out again, when he turned one of the many corners of Broken Alley and slammed straight into a wall.

Charlie fell down on his backside, his fiddle skittering off in one direction, the bag of coins spilling its contents in the other.

The Backstreets were an ever-changing entity – Broken Alley wasn't its original name but it's adopted one after so many extra buildings, twists and turns had been added – but he was pretty sure the last time he'd passed this way, there hadn't been a wall where there now was one.

As he started to stand up, the wall spoke.

"If I was you, I'd stay down there. Arse on the cobbles and all that."

Charlie looked up.

Way up.

A huge man loomed over him. Everything about the man was flat. And wide. Indeed, his face was so flat and so wide it seemed as if his features were trying to run away from one another.

From behind the giant stepped an all too familiar figure.

"Hello Dodge," said Charlie.

"Wotcha Charlie," replied Dodge.

Charlie eyed the massive man. "See you've got yourself a new friend," he said.

"Oh yes, Charlie. Do you like him?"

"As a wall, I'd say he's second to none."

Dodge's lips parted revealing only a few small, spaced out teeth. It was not a nice smile. It would *never* be a nice smile.

"He can do other things, you know," said Dodge. "Show him, Mr. Lunk."

Mr. Lunk turned around. This in and of itself was a major achievement and seemed to take into account the gravitational pull of the nearest moon. He reached out a massive hand, grasped the door of the nearest building, and with the merest tug, ripped the door and its frame free, leaving crumbling brickwork behind.

"*What in the—!*" came a confused and incensed shout from inside the doorless house, as the owner emerged from his new hole. He strode angrily into the street, and took one look at Mr. Lunk—the door still clutched in the giant's meaty fist.

"Never mind, keep it," he said, before turning around and hurrying back inside. Had he still a door, Charlie thought, he'd have probably slammed it shut and double bolted it.

And then left by the back door.

"Good innit!" said Dodge, skipping from one foot to the other.

"Very impressive," replied Charlie.

"It's quite a bit more than impressive. It's fantastic! Think of the possibilities!"

Charlie didn't like to think of the possibilities of someone like Dodge being around someone like Mr. Lunk.

"Well, I suppose if you're thinking of getting into property development, I can see how your new friend might prove pretty useful," Charlie said, starting to stand.

Dodge moved in front Charlie and scowled.

"You're making fun of me Charlie Lightfoot. That's what I'm thinking. In the past, too many people made fun of me. Not now. Not anymore. With my new friend Mr. Lunk, I think a lot of people who used to make fun of Reginald Herbert Dodginton might have cause to think otherwise."

Charlie lifted himself from the cold cobblestones and brushed himself down.

He'd known Dodge all his life. Growing up on the Backstreets, Dodge had always been around. He always seemed to stay the same age; always seemed to somehow survive, scurrying from one place to another. Charlie knew him well—he knew what he'd done and what he would do to survive. He was pretty low level, but that just meant that he'd mastered how to be low.

"You know me, Dodge," Charlie said, taking in the looming form of Mr. Lunk. He tried not to think about how easy it would be for the man to tear his arms off, and forced what he hoped was a pleasant smile. "Laughs and jokes—Mr. Easygoing, that's me. I didn't mean anything by what I said. Look, how long have we known each other? We're proper Backstreet lads, aren't we?"

Dodge spent a moment studying Charlie, his head tilting first one way, then the other. Then another nasty smile split his rat-like features.

"Course we are, Charlie! Course we are. Proper Backstreet lads, that's us." He leaned in towards Charlie conspiratorially. "Although, there's a few round these Backstreets who Mr. Lunk and I are going to pay a visit to. Settle a few scores and all that!"

More than a few, I'd wager. Bet there's plenty who've wronged ol' Reginald Herbert Dodginton in the past... or at least that's the way you see it.

Of course, Charlie said none of this. What he did say, as he dusted himself off, retrieved first his fiddle and then his coins from the floor, was: "Well, it was nice to see you again, Dodge. Always good to bump into an old friend. And, Mr. Lunk, it was... nice bumping into you too."

Mr. Lunk considered Charlie for moment, his face expressionless. Then, in a creeping wave of understanding, his stony features slowly drew towards each other, and he laughed.

"Har, har. That was a joke and it worked and it made me laugh. Har. Har."

Charlie edged past the giant, a nervous smile plastered across his face and held in place by willpower alone.

"Hang on a minute there, Charlie," Dodge said.

So close.

"Sorry Dodge," said Charlie, feigning disappointment. "I'd love to talk but Auntie's expecting me. Duty calls."

"Yeah, well, I can't exactly let you go now, can I?"

"Erm, I think you can," Charlie said edging away.

Dodge calmly took another step forward, blocking Charlie's path.

"No, I can't, Charlie. And unless you want to find out

what your fiddle sounds like when you don't have the arms to play it, I'd suggest you stand perfectly still."

Mr. Lunk navigated himself around in a half circle to face Charlie. His features had since gone their separate ways and the smile had vanished.

"You see, Charlie, as much as it pains me to do so, now that I've got Mr. Lunk, I've got a reputation to build. You'll help me build a reputation, won't you Charlie?"

"I don't like where this is heading, Dodge," said Charlie, ignoring the question.

"Don't worry, Charlie-boy!" said Dodge, giving him a gentle slap on the cheek. He smiled smugly. "Blimey, you should see your face, it's a right picture! Okay, seeing as we're old chums and everything, I won't let Mr. Lunk lay a finger on you. Honest."

Charlie knew when people like Dodge used the word honest – especially at the end of the sentence – it was only in the vaguest sense.

"That's good to hear, Dodge, it really is. I—"

"However, as I've mentioned, I've got a reputation to build as well as an empire."

Charlie gritted his teeth.

"I don't think there's much room for an empire on the Backstreets," said Charlie. "Bit crowded as it is, don't you think?"

"Still, I've got to give it a go, haven't I?" said Dodge. "And you must feel some sort of duty to help a fellow Backstreets lad, yes?"

"And how do you suppose I do that?"

"By handing over that bag of coin," he said, eyeing Charlie's earnings. "It doesn't look like much, so I'm sure you won't miss it."

"I think I will," said Charlie, clutching the bag tighter. "Besides, I worked bloody hard for these coins. Some blokes already tried to take them away from me."

"But Charlie, old pal of mine, you aren't thinking big enough. Imagine if your small investment was the very thing to kick-start my empire. I'd be forever in your debt. Technically speaking of course."

"What if I don't see the business opportunity?" asked Charlie defiantly. "What if I decide I'd like to keep a hold of my hard-earned coins? What then?"

Charlie knew he was pushing it. Whilst Dodge was hardly the worst the Backstreets had to offer, he was still wary. You had to be around here. Always.

Dodge smiled that smile again; the one which hadn't told the rest of his face what it was doing.

"Charlie, I really thought you'd have a little more sense, I really did," he said, his disappointment far from genuine. "Well, since you asked, I'll tell you what might happen when you fail to spot a fantastic business opportunity such as this one. Now, I promised I wouldn't let Mr. Lunk lay a finger on you, remember that? I even used the word 'honest' and that's pretty much an iron-clad guarantee, as you know I'm a man of my word. The problem is... if Mr. Lunk were to decide – of his own accord, you understand –that he couldn't help himself and *had* to lay a finger on you, well... I'm not entirely sure I could stop him."

If you weren't looking closely, you probably wouldn't have seen it, but Charlie was looking closely. He'd grown up looking closely.

So Charlie *did* see the little nod Dodge gave Mr. Lunk.

The massive man began to lumber towards Charlie—flexing fingers which looked like tree trunks.

"Now hang on a minute, Dodge!" Charlie said, backing away. "You'd do this to me?"

"Not me, Charlie," Dodge said innocently with an odd glint in his eye. "Mr. Lunk makes up his own mind. Once he has decided on a course of action, it's like trying to stop a wave from crashing upon the shore."

Mr. Lunk reached out and, in a motion much faster than Charlie thought possible for a man his size, grabbed a hold of Charlie's head as if choosing a melon from a market stall.

"Okay, okay," said Charlie, waving his hands in front of him. "C'mon, Dodge. Tell him to stand down, I've got an idea."

Dodge studied Charlie in that way of his again, his head tilting first one way, then the other.

"Mr. Lunk, as much as I am unable to stop you in your current line of action, if you wouldn't mind – and remember this is your decision and yours alone –releasing your grip?"

"Eh?" said Mr. Lunk, turning his giant head to look at Dodge.

"Just let him go, would you?" Dodge hissed.

Mr. Lunk dutifully let go of Charlie's head. If he was unhappy at doing so, it certainly wasn't shown upon his face, which remained as impassive as ever.

"So what's this idea?" Dodge said. "And it had better be good."

Charlie brushed him self-down again, stalling before an

idea actually came.

"Why take all my coins now?" Charlie asked.

"Because I want them," Dodge replied.

"But you're not thinking like a businessman."

"I don't want to be a businessman," Dodge said. He stood up a little straighter. "I want to strike fear into the hearts of people, and I want to get rich while I do it."

"And that sounds like a great thing to aspire to," Charlie said gently, "but what would happen if you took my coins now?"

"I'd have your coins," Dodge said.

"You would, that much is true," Charlie continued, "but I'd go out of my way to make sure we never crossed paths again. If there's anyone who knows these streets better than you, Dodge, it's me. You caught me off guard once but that'll never happen again. No more coin."

"Where are you going with this?" asked Dodge.

"What about a partnership?"

"What, me and you?"

"Exactly," said Charlie, hoping his sales tactics were good enough. "I give you some of my coins now, and next week I'll give you a few more. And then the week after that. And so on."

"And why would I agree to that?"

"Because it makes sense. You're guaranteed weekly coin."

Dodge reached up and pinched Charlie by his cheeks. "You know," said Dodge, "I could just take your coins from you every week. I know where you live."

Charlie smiled as the smaller man released him.

"That you do, Dodge. But if you're planning on knocking

on Auntie's door each week demanding money, you're going to need more than Mr. Lunk."

Dodge paled at the thought.

"Oh… I don't think that would be necessary. Not necessary at all. I'd… probably just grab you as you made your way home."

"Listen Dodge. I'm trying to suggest more of a long-term business relationship rather than you skulking around the Backstreets trying to rob me every day. Anyway, I thought you said there were others round here you needed to pay a visit to. Won't you be a bit busy to be hanging around, waiting for me to show up?"

Dodge thought it over and glanced up at his partner. Mr. Lunk remained unmoving.

"So… let me get this right," Dodge said, moving back to Charlie. "Each week you give me some of the coin you earn—"

"Yes."

"—leaving me free to go about constructing my empire with Mr. Lunk at my side. Or rather, in front of me."

"I'd say so."

"And how would we set up such a transaction?" Dodge asked.

"How's about, every Friday, just after happy hour ends in the Rat and Vat?"

"And if you don't turn up?"

"You have *my* permission to give *your* permission to Mr. Lunk to pop my head like a pimple."

"And what do you out of this deal?" asked Dodge again.

"Aside from still being able to wear a hat when it rains, not a lot, I'd say."

Dodge wrung his hands, still contemplating.

"All right then," he said after a moment, and then stepped aside. "The more I think about it, the more I like this new agreement." He clapped Charlie across the back. "You do understand the whole threat of violence thing didn't sit very well with me, don't you? I mean, I thought I'd try it out—it'll be my main tool going forward—but my heart sank when I saw it was you who'd bumped into Mr. Lunk. I'm glad you're such a quick thinker, Charlie, I really am. Me and Mr. Lunk look forward to a long and prosperous future dealing with you."

Dodge put his hand out and Charlie shook it, but just as he was about to let go, Dodge pulled him in close. And Dodge up close was not a good thing.

"But remember, Mr. Charlie Lightfoot, it'll take more than quick-thinking if you decide to double cross me. You will remember that, won't you?"

"Of course, Dodge," Charlie said, pulling his hand free. He reluctantly reached for the bag clutched beneath his arm and pulled the drawstring, but before he could get any coin from inside, Dodge had snatched it from his hands. He tipped a sizable share into his and threw the bag—now significantly emptier than before—back to Charlie.

"Well then, that's all lovely!" he said, smiling again. "Say goodbye to our first business partner, Mr. Lunk."

"Goodbye, funny man," Mr. Lunk said without as much as a look at Charlie.

Dodge clapped Charlie on the arm a final time and began to walk away, with Mr. Lunk following slowly in tow.

"Every Friday, just after happy hour ends in the Rat and

Vat," he shouted back over his shoulder, "I'll be waiting!"

Charlie let out a breath he didn't realise he'd been holding and made his way back home on legs which were only somewhat steady.

CHAPTER 2

Musical Knives

B Y THE TIME Charlie made it home, it was starting to get dark. The moon, or the glimpses of it he could see between the overhanging buildings, peered dimly through the passing clouds, scattering its glow across the cobbles. Unfortunately, it also scattered its glow across the many things that populated the cobbles of the Backstreets.

"Evening, Morgan," Charlie said as he stepped around a lumpen, vaguely human-shape lying in the street.

"Blargh," Drunk Morgan replied.

"Everything okay with you?" Charlie asked, more out of habit than anything else.

"Blargh," Drunk Morgan again replied. He tried to stand but gravity and vast amounts of cheap alcohol conspired to defeat him.

"Don't bother yourself in getting up," Charlie insisted, as he fetched a coin out of his bag and tossed it to him. Drunk Morgan caught it, winked at Charlie and beckoned him closer.

Charlie cautiously bent down, fighting his way through the curtains of stench.

"Tell you something, young Lightfoot," Drunk Morgan

said. "Things seem to be getting interesting for you, don't they?"

Charlie pressed another coin into the man's hand. Drunk Morgan slipped it into his pocket. It left an imprint of the King's head embedded in the dirt of his palm.

"What might you mean by that?" Charlie asked.

Drunk Morgan shook a filthy finger. "Most folks don't really pay me much mind, what with me often to be found lying prostrate in the gutter somewhere."

"You and me both know that's so you can look up at the stars, Morgan."

Drunk Morgan chuckled.

"When they're not paying me any mind, their lips get loose. They say you're starting to make a bit of coin for yourself, now you're playing out of the Backstreets. Some-one—don't ask me who, my booze-riddled brain will surely forget on purpose—but yes, someone said you've even made it into some of the establishments that line the King's Pass."

"You know how people like to talk," Charlie said.

That explained the three odd-sized men lying in wait for him.

Drunk Morgan lay back down on the cobbles and tucked one arm beneath his head.

"As far as I'm concerned, and it's not worth much but, keep doing your thing. I wish you all the very best young music man. Just keep an eye out."

"Thanks Morgan," Charlie said and flicked a third coin the man's way. Drunk Morgan caught it and tucked it into his coat.

Charlie moved on. The moon glow was starting to look less poetic by the minute.

⇉⇉⇉⇇⇇⇇

THE BURNT TANKARD was particularly depressing that night and, as Charlie entered, a wave of apathy crawled towards him.

There were only three customers in the inside. Two were regulars and barely lifted their heads from their stout as Charlie made his way towards the bar. Trev, as usual, was behind the bar.

Trev was always behind the bar.

For as long as Charlie could cast his mind back, Herbert Gore – or Trev as he was better known – had been a permanent fixture behind the bar of the Burnt Tankard. No-one actually knew why he was referred to as Trev, it was just one of those names a person seems to wear, whether they like it or not. It wasn't even clear if he owned the place; the kind of people who drank the Tankard's lukewarm ale didn't care much about ownership. Or personal hygiene, for that matter.

In their own way, they did care for Trev though. Because he was always there for them. And because he poured their beer without the mindless chit-chat which tended to get in the way of the serious drinker.

"Alright Trev?" Charlie asked. "Fancy a discussion about the recent changes in the King's cabinet?"

Trev was built like a piece of old leather—thin, worn and weathered. He turned towards Charlie, arms still folded and shook his head. Right, left.

"Nope," he said.

"Thought not," Charlie said. "How's life treating you Trev?"

Trev shrugged. Shoulders up, shoulders down. Yet in that shrug, he managed to encapsulate all that was good in his world and having done so weighed it against all that might bring him down and, in the end, judged everything was just about even.

Or maybe it was just a shrug.

"Auntie in?" Charlie asked. This was the only time anything even remotely resembling emotion broke into Trev's world, like a ray of sunlight poking through a gap in the curtains. He raised one corner of his mouth in an almost-smile and nodded twice. Up down, up down.

"Yup," he confirmed.

"Right-ho then Trev," Charlie said, lifting the hatch at the end of the bar, "nice talking with you. I'll leave you to the early evening rush."

Trev looked out into the room and the three bedraggled men slumped over their tankards and shrugged. It was a shrug which suggested that whilst those in front of him may indeed represent a sorry trio of humanity, there was at least some element of profound reality in their doleful existence.

Or maybe it was just a shrug.

Charlie closed the hatch behind him, moved through to the back of the Tankard, which was little more than another room used to house a few barrels of beer, and left by the back door.

A small courtyard separated the Burnt Tankard and Auntie's house. Across the courtyard a washing line stretched – always full of clothes, night or day.

Auntie's backdoor was unlocked, as usual, and Charlie let himself in. It led into the kitchen—one of two rooms downstairs. Up until he'd met Auntie, Charlie hadn't really thought much about kitchens; it wasn't something young boys tended to spend a great deal of time pondering. Now, he could hardly picture Auntie without thinking of her kitchen. It was where she spent most of her time and a place which seemed to encompass her entire 'Auntie-ness'.

Shelves lined three of the four walls, each one stacked with jar upon jar. In the centre of the room stood a large table, scuffed and worn but scrubbed within an inch of its life—the very epitome of its owner.

Charlie felt almost any problem in life could be solved with the words,

"*Here, have a cup of tea and sit yourself at the table.*"

He placed his fiddle by the door, took off his thick patchwork coat, and tossed it and his bag of coins onto the large armchair by the stove. He approached the table and sat down.

"That you Charlie?" came a shout from the pantry. "Or is it my lover-boy come to whisk me away for a night of shenanigans at the palace?"

"It's me Auntie," Charlie replied. "And what would you know about shenanigans?"

Auntie bustled into the kitchen, arms full of vegetables. Auntie did a lot of bustling. She dropped the vegetables on to the table, opened a nearby drawer, and brought out a knife. As she spoke to Charlie, she began to chop.

"You youngsters think you've got the inside track on shenanigans"—she stopped midway through dicing a carrot to within an inch of its life and pointed the knife at Charlie—

"but let me tell you something, Charles Lightfoot—my

generation not only invented shenanigans but we also had a heck of a lot of fun working out how to do them best."

"And I thought you were nothing more than a prudish old lady," Charlie said in mock surprise.

Auntie stopped, leant forwards, and fixed Charlie with one of her many stares.

Auntie had a pantry full of stares.

"You watch your tongue or it's liable to flap its way right out of your mouth. And if it doesn't, my knife will surely help it."

"Sorry, Auntie," Charlie said. "I didn't mean anything by it."

"Pah!" Auntie said, commencing chopping. "Being prudish is a matter of opinion. What give some cause to stuff their shirts with moral indignation, others find a hoot." She pointed her knife at Charlie again. "But call me an old lady again and I'll chop your fingers off and plug up every orifice in that scrawny frame of yours."

The rest of the evening passed as they normally did when Charlie stayed at Auntie's—they argued, they ate, Auntie busied herself with an array of seemingly endless tasks, and eventually Charlie fell asleep in the big chair cosseted by the warmth of the stove.

>>>><<<<

CHARLIE AWOKE TO find that Auntie had covered him with a knitted blanket before retiring herself. He knew, even though it was still dark, that she wouldn't sleep for long. Auntie seemed to require only the smallest amount of sleep before she was up and busy again.

Charlie had no idea how she did it—he'd once asked her and she'd just told him that her generation had been through times when getting to the end of the day was a blessing. Times when the Backstreets were far worse than they were now. She said she'd simply got used to being busy and using up all of the hours in the day.

To Auntie, the very notion of slowing down and taking life easy was as preposterous as telling the sun to take the day off and not bother rising the next morning.

Each day would see Auntie visiting a variety of people hidden away among the twists and turns of the Backstreets. Most would receive food of some description – whether they wanted it or not. Charlie had yet to work out how Auntie had come to fulfil the role—as he often called her—of Matron of the Backstreets. She pretended to hate it but Charlie knew she took a certain amount of pride in the name.

As a result, Auntie knew everyone and therefore everything that happened on and around the Backstreets. This was no mean feat given the sheer amount of people who called the Backstreets home.

And, of course, this is how Charlie had met her.

Auntie had taken him in as if he were one of her own, and Charlie hadn't resisted. He had no idea who his parents were. He'd heard rumours that his father might be a Sergeant in the King's Guard, and others that he was a bum who'd gambled and whored his life away. Charlie never really wanted to find out truth. His mother had left him on the doorstep of a butchers shortly after he'd been born, and as far as Charlie was concerned, that was that. He'd spent his childhood in and out of various houses; a lot of households in the Backstreets were pretty fluid. He'd spend a while in one place before he was taken somewhere else. Then, as he got older, he ended up not really having anywhere in particular to stay.

And that made life interesting.

Any port in a storm soon became Charlie's motto. He'd slept just about everywhere most people could think of and a few placed they couldn't possibly. As he moved into his teenage years, he'd won a fiddle from a man whilst playing Catch 'em, and decided to teach himself to play.

He'd seen one or two people playing instruments on street corners on the odd occasions he'd ventured into Lower Calver – some a fiddle, some a whistle and, on one occasion, a strange stringed instrument. It's tone-deaf owner had played so badly that a passing member of the King's Guard had snatched the instrument mid-strum and brought it down upon the performers head with such force that he'd ended up wearing it like a necklace.

But what struck Charlie more than anything, and what made him practice day and night, was when most of the musicians played, people would, on occasion, drop coin into their hats on the floor.

To Charlie, this was a revelation.

He practised until his fingers bled. Then he strapped them up and practised some more. He made his home at all manner of houses until his incessant screeching became too much and he was asked to leave. Soon he ran out of places to stay, but it didn't matter—Charlie had become a man possessed. He knew that if he could just get good enough, people would surely drop their coin in his hat.

It was around this time, after getting caught squatting in the attic of a butchers shop, that Charlie stumbled across Blind Watchem.

Quite literally.

The butcher had just launched Charlie out of the back door, his feet only just skittering across the cobbles, when he'd crashed into someone heading in the other direction. Charlie had just enough time to spin around and grab his fiddle as it came sailing out the back door after him, before he toppled over and clattered to the floor.

"Steady as she goes!" said the person. "You'll have me over!"

"Sorry about that," Charlie said as he stood, dusting himself down. "Are you okay?"

Charlie looked at the man he'd banged in to. He was about half Charlie's height and a true concoction of crumpledness.

"Why I'm as right as rain, thank you very much for asking. Unless, of course, it's that drizzly type of rain."

"Erm," was as much as Charlie could muster.

"Erm is exactly right, young chap. Erm indeed. Wait... what were we talking about?"

"I was apologising for banging into you," Charlie said.

"Oh, think nothing of it," said the man. "I certainly won't. Now what do you say you and your lovely fiddle buy me a drink by way of an apology?"

"I'd love to," said Charlie "but I don't have any coin."

"Ah! A little cash-flow problem. The river which once floweth is now dry. What a sorry tale. Never-you-mind.

Come with me. And bring your fiddle. We'll need that."

He led Charlie to the nearest pub—the Ruined Stones—sat him down at the only empty table, and headed towards the bar. The Ruined Stones was a place Charlie had never been. In fact, at that age, he hadn't been in many pubs at all. Not because he was too young, goodness no—drinking was encouraged at just about any age. He hadn't been in many pubs because he'd never really seen the need to. One of his darkest secrets was he never really saw the appeal of it.

This was an opinion he kept buried deep.

On the Backstreets, anyone who turned his nose up at a jar of ale or cup of spirits was eyed with suspicion. So Charlie generally steered clear of places like the Ruined Stones, which, given he rarely had any money, wasn't a difficult task.

Now sat inside, he surveyed the scene before him. Most of the room was male, with the odd female patron dotted in between. Most sat sullenly hunched over their beer, talking in low whispers, although one table seemed to have taken sole responsibility for filling the room with noise.

There were four men sat at the table and they were chatting in voices clearly meant to be heard by others, often erupting into brays of raucous laughter, occasionally slapping each other on the back. The slapper would often undertake this task whilst the slappee was attempting a sip, sending ale spraying across the table, and resulting in further guffaws of laughter.

Just as Charlie was about to turn his attention back to Blind Watchem and where he might have wandered off to, one of the seated men caught Charlie's gaze.

"What you lookin' at, boy?" he shouted over at Charlie.

A host of responses rattled through Charlie's mind, most of which he discounted immediately for fear of them resulting in a good slapping.

"Sorry," Charlie said, smiling his best smile. "Thought I recognised you. You look a bit familiar but I see now that I was indeed, mistaken."

The man looked back at Charlie, then to his friends.

"Not a problem—" he said.

And relax.

"—unless, of course, the person you thought you recognised is an ugly bastard. Is he an ugly bastard, smiling boy?"

And tense.

"Not at all," Charlie said rather quickly. "Quite the opposite really. Fine looking chap. Some would go as far as to say he's rather handsome."

"You saying I'm handsome? That I'm 'fine looking'?"

"To be honest, I don't really know what to say to that. What would you rather, yes you are, or no you're not?"

The man leapt to his feet, sending his chair crashing backwards.

"All I know is that you've got a smart mouth on you, boy. One minute you're saying I'm fine looking—which, in my book, makes you one of them funny folk—the next you're trying to wheedle out of it with daft questions." He cracked the knuckles on his right hand. "How about I come over there and smack you about a bit until you learn it's not a good idea to piss off the big man."

Charlie looked at the man. He was at least a head smaller than Charlie.

There are certain moments in a person's life when, after

saying something, they wish they could freeze time, scoop the words back in their mouth, and then close said mouth lickety-split.

"Look, I don't want any trouble," Charlie began. "I don't normally come in here and the last thing I want is to upset people." He looked at the man and his friends. "Wherever this 'big man' is, I'll gladly apologise to him."

One of the friends, who happened to be mid-gulp, sprayed a mouthful of beer across the table, while the other two tried to stifle their own giggles.

The short man turned a strange shade of crimson.

"*I'm* the bleedin' big man, you little shit!" he roared.

Again, thanks to the ignorance of youth and a mouth which seemed to delight in running away with itself, words came out of Charlie's mouth before he could stop them.

"But... you can't be more than five foot five... and that's on a good day," he said, genuinely bemused.

The big-short man's face bled to a colour more akin to an angry bruise.

"It doesn't mean I'm *tall*!" he hissed through gritted teeth. "It means I'm important round these parts. The big cheese!"

"Ohhh," Charlie said. "Now that makes more sense. Because you are quite short, you know."

The face turned a dangerous cardiac purple.

"*Why you little...*"

The big short-man snatched up his half-empty tankard and launched it at Charlie who quickly ducked down as it hurtled past his head.

"I'm going to teach you a little bit about manners," said

the big-short man as he began to push forward in Charlie's direction, "and watching what your mouth says."

"No you're not," came a voice from across the bar. It was Blind Watchem, who made his way over to the table, a small carved tumbler in each hand.

"Excuse me?"

The big-short man, now standing just a foot away, managed to fill the question with a heavy dose of who-do-you-think-you-are-pal?

"Firstly," said Charlie's crumpled companion, "you are just about the last person this boy needs as a guide when it comes to manners. Second, you cannot teach him to watch his mouth given that it's physically impossible. And third—and most importantly—your winky's hanging out."

The big-short man stopped mid-stride, a confused look screwing up his face as he worked his way through the words, and, as he reached the end, his eyes fell to his button fly.

As he did, Blind Watchem picked up Charlie's fiddle, turned it so he held it by the base and, when the big-short man looked up again, jabbed it into his face. It was only a short jab but the crack of breaking teeth was unmistakable.

The big-short man howled in pain as he crumpled to the floor, and his three friends stood up in alarm.

"Now then fellas," said Blind Watchem, as he lowered the instrument. "It's hard to get away from the fact I've just cracked your chum in the chops with the hard end of a fiddle, but do you really want to hurt an old man like me? One pop from you and I'd probably mess myself. Hardly seems fair."

The men considered this for a brief moment before

deciding fairness wasn't a concept they were too worried about.

"Oh, and I've got these." The old man produced two short-handled daggers from somewhere on his person. "Watch, boys—you'll get a kick out of this."

He flipped the daggers into the air where they spun end over end and came back down deftly into his hand.

"Ta-da!" he said.

One of the men clapped until he saw the look his other two friends were giving him.

"Thank you, young man," the old man said. "Although, quick tip, if you want to learn that trick, make sure you're wearing steel-toed caps while you practise."

He threw one of the daggers at lightning speed, which embedded itself in the floor mere inches in front of the big-short man.

"Speaking of messing yourself," he continued, "probably best you take the big man home. Steady as you go."

And with that, he turned, sat down, and took a sip of his drink.

Charlie sat beside him as the three men scooped up their friend and made for the door.

"Have a drink," Blind Watchem said. "It'll put hairs on your... something. I forget what. Or where. Either way it'll warm your cockles. Or chestles."

"That was amazing!" Charlie said, dumbstruck, and still looking back at the door as the four men shuffled out.

"Not really, but it's kind of you to say. Just takes lots of practice but once you get the balance right, they're pretty easy to throw."

"Not the knives. Well... actually, yes, the knives, but also, the whole thing! How did you learn to do all that stuff?"

"Ah, well now my boy, the answer to that's simple. I used to be a musician. But before I go any further"—he stuck out a dirty hand—"Blind Watchem, at your service."

Charlie took the hand and shook enthusiastically.

"Now give your fiddle a wipe. It's still got teeth in it."

CHAPTER 3

Ride the Lightning

MOST OF CHARLIE'S formative years were not spent chasing girls, drinking alcohol, or getting up to all manner of tomfoolery. They were spent with an old man learning to play the fiddle.

Shortly after their first meeting, Blind Watchem agreed to meet Charlie by the edge of the Backstreets. Once there, the old man took Charlie out onto the King's Pass, down the hill and over to the edge of the marketplace at the bottom of Lower Calver. Charlie helped Blind Watchem onto a bench and, together, they looked back up the King's Pass.

"Tell me what you see," Blind Watchem said.

"Thankfully, quite a bit now that I've had a few days to recover. What was that stuff you gave me at the Ruined Stones?"

"Ah, my dear boy," Blind Watchem said, a smile creasing his weathered face. "The drink of the gods—well, those gods who have very little shame that is. It's called Rye. That particular blend was called Old Gut-Rot. Far from one of the better ones but gets the job done. Did it affect you much?"

"In my seventeen short years I've barely touched a drop of alcohol. You made me drink three measures. What do you think?"

Blind Watchem laughed "How long before your sight returned?"

"It took until mid-morning. At one point I thought I'd gone blind. Turns out I'd fallen asleep with my head in the guzunder."

"And how do you feel about drinking now?"

Charlie's stomach gave an involuntary flip.

"Wasn't much of a fan in the first place. Now, I don't want to touch the stuff ever again."

Blind Watchem shifted in his seat until he was looking directly at Charlie.

"I sincerely hope that remains the case. That heavenly drop of wonderfulness ruined me…"

Charlie sat and looked as Blind Watchem fell to silence. He didn't know what to say. Then, suddenly, the old man slapped him on the back and turned to look up the King's Pass.

"So, young Charles, what dost thou seeth beforeth thee?"

Charlie followed Blind Watchem's gaze.

"Well, I can see most of Calver," he replied.

"That's a start, which is as good a place to begin as any. Go on…"

"There's Lower Calver," Charlie continued, tracing the route with his forefinger, "which climbs upside the hill."

"Tell me of it," said Blind Watchem.

Charlie dropped his hand. "Why? You know what it's like."

Blind Watchem tutted. "Such questioning! What is it with you youngsters? Just do what I say and respect the fact I am old, three-quarters alcohol, and still not dead."

Charlie's brow furrowed but he couldn't help but let a smile escape. "You know, you say some pretty odd things," he said.

"I've been told so," said Blind Watchem. "Now tell me about Lower Calver."

"It's… the biggest bit of Calver. And, obviously, it's the lowest part of the Great Hill. Erm… it wraps around almost half of the Great Hill and spread downs onto the flat land at the base of the hill where we're now sat."

"Boring!" Blind Watchem shouted abruptly.

A woman preparing her fish stall over to their left tutted and threw a dirty look.

"A thousand apologies, my dear lady," Blind Watchem said, grinning as he doffed his hat. Then, in a whisper, said, "Imagine being her fella. Face like a smacked bum and she stinks of fish all the time. No wonder she's sour."

Charlie ignored the comment. "What do you mean boring?"

"I mean you're telling me things anyone with eyes can see," said Blind Watchem. "How is that anything other than boring?" His gaze flitted to Charlie's fiddle, sat beside him on the bench. "Do you want to be a musician?"

"Yes," replied Charlie.

"Why?"

"So I can make some serious coin."

Blind Watchem shook his head. He slowly removed his oversized cloth hat and clutched it in his gnarled hands. He got off the bench, turned and dropped down on one knee in front of Charlie.

"Dearly beloved," he said in hushed tones. "We are gathered here, at this time, and in this place, to mourn the loss of this boy's immortal soul. He lived a hard life on the Backstreets of Lower Calver but that is no excuse for his distinct lack of appreciation of the arts…"

"Erm, what are you doing?" Charlie said, looking around to see if anyone was watching.

"Holding a funeral for your lost soul," Blind Watchem said, without looking up. "Oh, holy and quite often unnecessarily vengeful gods, please go easy on him! He knows not what he does!"

These last lines, Blind Watchem shouted at the top of his voice. Stall holders stopped as they unpacked their goods ready for the market to begin. Some stood and stared while others simply shook their heads and went about their work.

The price you paid for setting up shop in Lower Calver.

"Get up would you!" Charlie hissed, trying to haul the old man to his feet. "People are starting to stare!"

Blind Watchem vaulted upright, spun on his heel and bowed towards the marketplace. Then, he snatched up Charlie's fiddle, spun it around in his hand, tucked it under his chin, twirled the bow in his other hand, and began to play.

Charlie sat, open mouthed as Blind Watchem—the old man he'd met only a few days ago, who said and did the strangest of things, and who now stood dancing at the edge of the marketplace on a cold morning—was transformed.

He drew the bow across the strings as if caressing the body of a lover. So graceful were his movements, that Charlie quite forgot anything and everything he'd seen of Blind

Watchem so far.

This was something else.

The man in front of him produced a sound so beautiful all of the nearby stall holders stopped what they were doing and wandered over to hear him play. Right on cue, as the last reached the back of the semi-circle that had formed around him, he looked up, smiled and launched into a performance so frenetic that his bow became a blur.

He stomped his foot in time to the music, dipped and twirled as the notes rose and fell; somehow wrapping himself and those around him in the glorious sound he made.

But just as he reached a fizzing crescendo, the bow slipped from his hand, flew past Charlie and skidded to a halt at the edge of the semi-circle of stall holders. Blind Watchem's fingers twanged into the strings of Charlie's fiddle, snapping two strings with a screech. He fumbled the instrument and it slipped from his grasp. Charlie leapt forwards and caught it just before it hit the ground.

The stall holders had already begun to turn away. The spell had been broken. No-one clapped. And there certainly weren't any coins.

Blind Watchem sat back down on the bench as Charlie fetched his bow.

"I'm… sorry," Blind Watchem said. He looked downcast, forlorn; no longer the twirling minstrel Charlie has seen only minutes earlier, but more like the strange old man he'd bumped into a few days ago.

"You were fantastic!" Charlie said, sitting down beside him.

"Right up until I wasn't," Blind Watchem replied. "The

worst part was, I knew it was coming. Could feel it coming but still couldn't stop. Once the music gets a hold of you, you've got to ride the lightning. Even if it means you end up getting burnt."

He patted Charlie on the knee.

"I'm old and I drink too much. You're young and don't. Back when I was young, I played—boy, did I play! I've played everywhere there is and some places there aren't. When I look up on the Great Hill, I see the streets of Lower Calver with the King's Pass winding up it. Just like you. Only I also see the street corners which became my stage… once I'd worked my way out of the Backstreets, that is. And I how worked."

He seemed to drift for a second into memory before jumping back on point.

"I was always talented, but on the Backstreets, talent buys you a hand full of nothing. You name a pub anywhere on those worn-out cobbles and I played it. I worked hard at my craft, and, in the end, I had them eating out of the palm of my hand."

He gestured down, tracing the path in the distance as Charlie had.

"Then I moved on to Lower Calver. On the streets, at first, but I soon made my way indoors. You see, the folks of Lower Calver aren't so different from the folks who call the Backstreets home. I played every gig I could get. Once word got around I could hold a crowd, Middle Calver was the next step."

"You've been in Middle Calver?!"

To Charlie, the thought of passing through the gate

house in the wall which separated Lower and Middle Calver was, well, unheard of.

Blind Watchem laughed.

"Charles, I've been through all the walls. In and out. Up and down."

Charlie looked back down across the marketplace and away from the Great Hill, to the highest of the three walls which ringed the bottom—the one which separated the city of Calver from the rest of the Kingdom.

Plenty of people ventured out through that wall; it happened every day. People came in, people went out, across the Bloodwastes and on into the surrounding towns and villages. It was easy to imagine Blind Watchem heading out that way and travelling around, playing his fiddle.

Then he turned to look back up the hill—past Lower Calver, up to the gatehouse and into Middle Calver. He had no idea what it was like up there. Sure, you could see the houses, which were much bigger and finer than those down here, but what it would be like to spend time up there was a mystery to him.

He looked higher, to the third and final gatehouse, which separated Middle Calver from Upper Calver—home of the King's Palace.

Blind Watchem nodded. "That's right," he said, as if following Charlie's thoughts every step of the way "Lower Calver, Middle Calver—all the way up."

"You've played at the palace?!" Charlie couldn't hide the disbelief in his voice.

"It's a hard thing to forget. Trust me, I didn't confuse it with the Ruined Stones. Although, there are far more similarities than you'd imagine. Plenty of differences too.

He ran a finger across his chin.

"The patrons at the Palace were far less reserved. Must be something to do with being rich and the complete lack of responsibility in their daily doings. Or maybe it's the altitude up there. Who knows?"

Charlie sat, neck craned, looking up at the palace. It perched atop the Great Hill, gleaming in the morning light. Two walls, lots of buildings and a whole host more separated him from it.

"I want to learn to play like you," he said.

And he found that he did. Truly did. He'd only known Blind Watchem a few days but in those few days he'd offered Charlie a glimpse of a world which, up until now, he hadn't known existed.

"Why? So you can get out of the Backstreets? Maybe make it up to the palace like I did?"

"Partly, yes. I can't lie about that," Charlie said. "I never really thought about it much before but I realise I want to get out and explore. I want to see places and experience things."

"Well," said Blind Watchem, and slapped Charlie across the knee, "that's a start."

"But I think it's more than that," Charlie continued. "Just now, when you played… I've never heard anything like it! It was like you stopped being you. You weren't the, erm… interesting old guy who got me drunk the other night."

"Well said," Blind Watchem said. "Excellently careful choice of words too. Although, you should know, I've been called far, far worse."

"I don't really know how to put it but when you played just then, it wasn't you, was it? It was as if the music took over and you were only there to help guide it. Does that sound odd?"

"Not at all my dear boy!" Blind Watchem said, jumping up, suddenly animated. "Remember, you've got to ride the lightning!"

"I think you did just that," Charlie said, also getting to his feet. "For a while at least."

"In that case," Blind Watchem said, "I suppose it was worth snapping two strings and making a tit out of myself."

Charlie smiled. "Will you teach me how to play?" he asked.

"Of course I will, dear boy. Why do you think I've let you hang around me these last few days?"

"I thought I was the one letting you hang around with me? Respect your elders, and all that."

"Bugger all that," Blind Watchem said, tugging his cap back into place, "I've got far better things to be doing than contributing to your sense of worth."

"Oh…" said Charlie, feeling foolish.

"Come on," Blind Watchem said as he reached for the fiddle. "You've got to get ridiculously good before you can even think about anything to do with lightning."

"And how do I do that?"

"Practice."

"For how long?"

"Years, my boy," Blind Watchem said pushing the instrument into Charlie's hands. "And even then, you'll only be half as good as I was. But don't worry. You'll probably give up before that point."

"Marvellous," Charlie said.

And so began his apprenticeship.

CHAPTER 4

Practice makes... your fingers bleed.

A ND SO, THROUGHOUT his remaining teenage years and
into his early twenties, Charlie practised. He played
whenever and wherever he could. To the people of the
Backstreets, he became a constant presence, playing his fiddle
on the many street corners and busier thoroughfares.

At first, nobody would consider parting with any coin
and his coat, which he'd piled at his feet, would remain
empty. It was a tough gig; trying to get anyone who called the
Backstreets home to part with their coin was like trying to
sell them a piece of the sky, but Charlie didn't mind. He was
out there playing. He managed to survive by helping out in
all manner of places. To Charlie it didn't matter. Any type of
work which kept him fed just gave him more time to play.

He'd meet up with Blind Watchem every week, usually in
the back room of some pub.

The old man would put him through his paces, forcing
him to play ever harder snippets of music, each one with its
own unique sound. He'd remain seated for most of the
session, sipping rye and telling Charlie what he was doing
wrong, occasionally rising to snatch the fiddle and bow from
Charlie hands to show him how it should be played. Then

he'd flop back down in his seat and wave for his student to continue.

Charlie would leave those sessions with his hands, arms, shoulders and neck throbbing but determined to be better next week. A life on the Backstreets had taught him there were far harder things to be done than playing a fiddle.

It was about a week after his twenty-second birthday when he realised he might be getting half-decent.

In truth, he didn't know when his birthday was; Auntie had asked him once and when he couldn't tell her, she'd been mortified.

"We can't have that," she'd said, folding her arms in a pose which Charlie knew meant business. "A birthday gives a person a purpose. Something to aim for. Even if it's only to survive until the next one. I'm going to bake you a cake—it's your birthday today, I've just decided."

Only Auntie could decide when your birthday was.

A FEW DAYS later, he'd been messing around with a tune whilst lounging in Auntie's big chair by the stove when she came bustling in from the other room.

"That's not half-bad, Charlie," she said, busying herself near the sink. "Might be that old sozzled Watchem has managed to teach you something. You sound like you're getting quite good."

Charlie sat up. This level of praise from Auntie—the kind which wasn't hiding between a couple of thick layers of warning—was rare.

"You really think so?" Charlie asked.

"Oh yes," Auntie said, washing her hands in the water pot and drying them on her apron. "I was just saying so to my friend Ida. You remember Ida—husband with a roving eye and a son with ideas above his station? Well, she agreed. Said, 'He's gone from that Lightfoot boy who screeches his way around that fiddle like a cat stuck in hot tar to that Lightfoot boy who don't sound half bad.' And then, I said, 'Thank the gods for their small mercies. I was afraid that if he didn't get any better quick, then someone'd lynch him. Possibly me.' She agreed to that too."

Nobody had told Charlie he was good at anything before. Of course, Auntie had always encouraged him to go out and make something of himself but he had a feeling that to her, that meant stay out of trouble and try to earn your keep. He felt a smile creep across his face. This time, it stayed there too.

"Now don't you go getting like Ida's boy. I won't tolerate ideas above your station," said Auntie noticing the smile. "You keep your feet well and truly on the ground. You're getting good, there's no two ways about that, but don't let it swell your head or I'm apt to pop it. You tell me one thing Charlie Lightfoot, how did you get to be half decent on that fiddle of yours so quickly?"

"Hard work, for the most part" Charlie said.

"Imagine that. You worked your way to getting better. Who'd have thought such a simple recipe existed? If you could let the rest of your generation know, that would be just fine with me."

"Yes, Auntie," Charlie said, getting up and pulling his coat on. "Anyway, I'm off out to see Blind Watchem again. I think I might like to try and play out on the streets of Lower Calver."

"That sounds nice dear," Auntie said, seemingly preoccupied preparing a stew that looked large enough to feed most of the Backstreets. "Oh, and one more thing before you go," she said turning to face Charlie.

"What's that?" Charlie said.

She pointed her wooden spoon at him.

"You keep your feet on the ground, like I said, but make sure your head's ready for bigger and better things. You've got a chance to make something of yourself, Charlie. I sure as buggery don't want you moping around here into middle age. I've got a life to lead too you know. Now clear off and practise."

AND PRACTISE CHARLIE did. Once he found that he could play, even just the basics, the music took over. So he practised and he played.

Bolstered by the words of Auntie and Blind Watchem, he decided to try his luck outside The First Inn—a popular place to stay in Lower Calver.

He'd barely got three notes in when a very flustered doorman came bustling over from the entrance. His overcoat flapped behind him, and Charlie couldn't help but notice that it was fastened with silver buttons. Charlie had never seen such things.

"What are you doing?" the doorman hissed as he approached Charlie.

"Playing my fiddle, hoping people like it, you know?" Charlie said, smiling his brightest smile.

"Well, not bloody here you're not!" said the doorman has he gathered up Charlie's coat from the floor.

"Why not?" Charlie said, snatching his coat back from the doorman.

"Why not, he asks! Why not? I'll tell you why not young feller-me-lad," the doorman said, pulling Charlie over to one side. "First of all, this place is well-to-do. It is a proper establishment for proper people. You see in there"—he pointed up at the building behind him—"in there, we've got actual furniture in the guests' rooms. There are places you can hang your clothes! By the side of each bed, is a bedside table."

"A table by your bed?" Charlie said. "Wouldn't that take up a lot of unnecessary space?"

"Hah!" the doorman said as if some major point had been proven. "These aren't your normal, full-sized tables, oh no! These are small tables what actually look like drawers!"

"Tables that look like *undergarments*?! What kind of place is this?"

"Good lords above, which passing cart did you fall off?" the doorman said, shaking his head. "Not those kinds of drawers! The ones you put things in which slide out and stuff."

"Oh, *those* kinds of drawers," said Charlie. "Now that makes much more sense. Just one question."

"What?"

"Why do they call it a bedside table if they look like a set of drawers?"

The doorman pondered for a moment. He seemed genuinely flummoxed by the question.

"Never you mind! Anyway, as I was saying, this is a proper place, with proper furniture and proper guests. The management have made it very clear they don't want no riff-raff knocking about, and for you my laddie, that translates as clear off!"

Charlie felt a little hurt. "But I just wanted to play my music. It's quite good."

"I'm sure it is," said the doorman who was already ushering Charlie away from the First Inn and out onto the cobbles of the King's Pass. "Just bugger off and do it somewhere else."

Charlie had been moved on plenty of times on the Backstreets and in far harsher ways. A kick up the backside was the usual method. In Lower Calver he'd received a far gentler bum's rush, still, he'd hoped things would be different out here.

"Can't I play wherever I want?" Charlie shouted back to the doorman.

"I couldn't give a kits whisker, sunshine. Why don't you try your luck? See what happens," the doorman shouted over his shoulder as he returned to his place by the door.

SINCE THEN, CHARLIE had become a lot better at playing but also a lot smarter. Lessons learned on the Backstreets were invaluable, but as Blind Watchem had told him after his encounter with the doorman of the First Inn, 'every time you take a step up, you've got to learn how to avoid getting knocked down'. He'd also said that 'you can chop a tree down, but you can't stop a weed from growing' which didn't seem to help much, but it had been early afternoon so Blind Watchem was probably well on his way to being sozzled.

And now, a few years later and much the wiser, Charlie was earning actual coin on the streets of Lower Calver. He'd worked out where, when, and even what to play, and the closer he got to King's Pass, the jollier and jauntier his tunes became.

Visitors to the city seemed to like that sort of thing.

CHAPTER 5

The Bride, the Barrel and a chance.

A FTER A MORNING playing at the market and, given the takings were particularly slim, Charlie decided to head home, making his way back up the King's Pass.

Whilst walking past the Halfway Barrel, he spotted the inn's landlord and his son hauling barrels down through the trap door and into the cellar. He nodded as Charlie passed which, when you ran a place like the Halfway Barrel, could mean anything from '*Evening, what'll it be,*' to '*That's your last, clear off and be on your way.*' Charlie nodded back.

"Hang on, pal," said the landlord's son. He was about Charlie's age but close to twice as wide. "I know you, you're the bloke who plays the fiddle."

Charlie looked at the fiddle under his arm and raised his brow.

"Great powers of deduction, this one," said the landlord, patting his son roughly on the head. "Bartending might be a bit beneath him." He shook his head, rubbed his hands on the front of his apron, and turned his attention back to the barrels.

"No, hang on dad," the son said. "I've heard this guy play. He's not half bad."

"Then he's only half good," the landlord said, rolling a barrel and sending it down the ramp into the darkness, "which is better than most of the so-called musicians I've heard around here. Used to be, back in the day, folk knew how to play a fiddle. Now it's all about daft screeches and twiddly-twangs like you'd hear played for the stiffs up at the palace. All lar-dee-dar like but not much oomph, if you catch my meaning."

"Nah, this guy plays the good stuff," the son insisted, "the old stuff. Heard him down by Forchester Street the other day. That was you, wasn't it?"

"It was," Charlie said, already getting his bow ready. "Care for a tune?"

The Halfway Barrel was a proper pub. Everyone knew that. Words like gift, horse and mouth seemed appropriate.

The landlord shrugged. "You do what you like, lad," he said. "A decent tune might make the rest of this job easier but if you think I'm parting with any of my hard-earned coin, you've got another thought coming."

"Dad, we've spoken about this," the son said, turning to face his father, embarrassed. "We could do with a bit of entertainment inside. It'd draw a right crowd."

"This one thinks we should break with hundreds of years of tradition," the landlord said to Charlie, "tradition which, I might add, has stood the Halfway Barrel in good stead for centuries and made it the place it is today. Imagine what people would say if they came in for a quiet jar only to find some flounce screeching away in the corner. Present company excluded, I'm sure."

"The last thing I am is a flounce, mister" Charlie said. "I

come from back there." He thumbed in the direction of home. "Do you know what would happen to me if I flounced around the Backsteets on this fiddle? Well, you can probably guess. It wouldn't be pretty, sir. What's more, your son's right – I'm a fine fiddle player."

Why not? What have I got to lose?

"And whilst I can play that lar-dee-dar and twiddly stuff better than most who play at the palace," he continued, "I can play just about anything you like. Here's what I'll do, if it's okay with you. Name a tune. Any tune you like. If I don't know it, I'll be on my way. If I do, I'll play it for you while you load the rest of those barrels. There aren't many left so it shouldn't take long. How does that sound?"

The landlord folded his thick arms across his stomach.

"You're confident, I'll give you that. And you say you'll play any tune I choose?"

"If I know it. If not…"

"You'll be on your way," the landlord finished. "All right then. Play me 'The Bride of the Open Pastures'. If you know it, that is."

Charlie pinched his jaw.

"Wow, that's an old one. Not too well known either. Tough pick."

The landlord smiled smugly, but his smile froze as Charlie launched into the opening bars. It was indeed a tough song to play—it began slowly and almost too quietly, then burst into life mid-way through. It featured complicated chord work and the fingering required lightning speed to get right, but by the end of the song the landlord and his son were sat on a barrel each, feet tapping, hands beating out a rhythm on their thighs.

As he finished, Charlie let his bow and fiddle drop to his sides in a modest flourish, then bent over, his arms outstretched, bow and fiddle pointing straight out.

There was no clapping, no whoops of joy, and certainly no shouts for an encore. Charlie slowly righted himself, feeling more than a little foolish in the silence of the side street.

The landlord's son was sat looking up at his father who had stood and was now staring at Charlie with his arms folded.

"I haven't heard the Bride played like that since I was a boy living out in Heverton. My boy was right, you're not half-bad son. Can you play many more like the Bride?"

"Yes, I can," Charlie said.

The landlord furrowed his brow as if weighing his options, his arms folded.

"Go on, dad," urged his son, now standing himself. "Give him a chance. The locals will love it. It's proper music."

"Not a lar-dee-dar or twiddly bit in sight. I promise," Charlie said.

"Okay," said the landlord, and pointed at him, "you get fifteen minutes on Sunday night. Just after it gets dark. Take it or leave it."

"I'll take it," Charlie said eagerly.

"On two conditions," the landlord said. "If the locals don't like music getting in the way of their drinking, you're out."

"Agreed," said Charlie.

"And second, you never perform that daft bowing thing

ever again. Do that in the Halfway Barrel and, no matter how good you are, you're liable to end up with your fiddle up your arse. Got it?"

"Absolutely," Charlie said, feeling his cheeks flush. "No… flouncy bowing."

"Right then," said landlord, stretching his back, "me and this one have got more barrels to shift. We'll see you on Sunday. For my sins I pray to the gods this doesn't come back to haunt me. If it does, I'll never forgive the pair of you."

The landlord's son smiled. He strode over and shook Charlie's hand enthusiastically.

"The name's Arthur," he said.

"Charlie, and thanks for that."

"Not a problem. You just make sure you play well. The old man will only give you one chance."

"Hey, these barrels won't shift themselves," the landlord shouted.

"Coming dad," Arthur shouted back. He pumped Charlie's hand a final time. "See you Sunday. Don't let me down," he said, then ran back to help his father.

➤➤➤❮❮❮

OVER THE NEXT few days, Charlie worked on his songs for Sunday night at the Halfway Barrel. With Blind Watchem's help, he managed to get to a point where he felt happy with the songs he'd chosen. He decided to start with the Bride of the Open Pastures—a proven crowd pleaser—and follow with others Blind Watchem had gathered on his travels around the Kingdom. Songs like 'Where the Water Flows' and 'On a Harvest Morn' were of a similar ilk to the Bride and he felt confident playing them. Although, for each one he practised, Blind Watchem swore he was murdering the way it should be played.

The only cloud on his otherwise clear blue horizon was his meeting with Dodge and Mr. Lunk on Friday. He knew there was no way he could get out of it but, as the fateful day drew nearer, he realised he didn't want to get out of it.

Charlie had a plan.

CHAPTER 6

Things that go Lunk in the night.

CHARLIE ARRIVED AT the Rat and Vat early on Friday. He wanted to be ready and he needed to see what sort of condition the place would be in.

Happy hour was drawing to a close, which meant the place was nearly full. If the Burnt Tankard was at one end of the spectrum of when it came to the atmosphere in a drinking establishment, the Rat and Vat was way towards the other.

Located on the edge of the Backstreets, it was the kind of place where tourists and locals could mix without fear of one being stabbed by the other. The tourists got a taste of life in the big city on a very rough and ready level, and those from the Backstreets got to enjoy the company and free drinks of interesting strangers.

This was very different from its early days, when the Rat and Vat was a no-go place for tourists, given that any who ventured in for a taste of the down and dirty side of Calver soon found themselves down, dirty and often, down in the dirt. The then owner—a formidable woman by the name of Tessa Hardstruck—soon realised although the tourists were the minority, they spent the lion's share of coin in her establishment. Being a sound businesswoman, she employed a gang of useful gentlemen to work security, who were under strict instruction to deal in clear physical terms with anyone who tried to take advantage of a visiting tourist. It's hard to rob someone when all of your fingers are broken.

After that, the tourists returned, and in record numbers. The Rat and Vat was transformed into something closer to a beer hall: the tables long and wide; the benches old and worn; the beer cheap and frothy. Locals and tourists mixed without issue and business was good.

Happy hour was the hour preceding the closing of the gates of Lower Calver and thus sealing the city off for the night. Charlie entered and was hit by a wall of noise. All around him, folk were drinking, talking and generally having a good time. If pubs spoke their own language, the Burnt Tankard and the Rat and Vat wouldn't have a clue what the other was on about and would have to resort to a lot of shouting and emphatic hand gestures.

Charlie weaved his way through the crowds, sidestepping a serving girl who, through some strange law of physics, managed to carry seven tankards of frothy ale in one hand, and found himself a perch on the end of one of the smaller tables. Five of the six places around the table were taken up with what, at first glance, appeared to be mercenaries. They all wore some form of thick leather armour, and each had a weapon propped against the table. As Charlie sat, they finished their ales in unison and slammed the wooden tankards down on the table.

"Ahh, I love my ale!" the one nearest to Charlie shouted to no-one in particular. He seemed a little small for a mercenary but in this day and age, you never could tell.

"Not as much as I love fighting!" another said, belching loudly. This one wore spectacles.

"Well," said a third, "I love both ale and fighting, but I love the mercenary life even more!"

"Actually, Gerald," said a fourth, adjusting his helmet which was at least a size too large and had started to slide down over his eyes, "I think drinking ale and fighting pretty much runs the whole gamut of mercenary life and, as such, renders your proclamation redundant."

"I hate to disagree with a fellow mercenary," said the fifth who at least had the general appearance of a mercenary; he was large, had a nose which had been broken at least once and a face only a mother could love. This was all destroyed by the clearly blunt sword he was waving at his friend as he made his point. "but I think the point is valid as no-one has yet specifically mentioned killing. Fighting, yes. Killing, no." He waved the sword some more. "Anyone can fight, theoretically at least, but killing? Well now we're straying directly into mercenary goings on. As such, Gerald's proclamation, could in fact, be seen as valid."

"Fair point, Bertie, fair point. I rescind my earlier statement."

Charlie could hold his tongue no longer. "Excuse me for butting in, but are all five of you mercenaries?"

"Indeed, we are," said Bertie, waving his blunt sword skyward. "Just returned from a recent commission during which we had to chop off lots of heads and act generally quite viciously, I might add."

"Actually, we're not," said the one named Gerald, leaning

in closer to speak to Charlie in a whisper. "We're just a bunch of guys from Middle Calver. We all work in taxes. Did you really think we were mercenaries?"

"Oh, most definitely," Charlie said as convincingly as he could. "You had me fooled."

Gerald elbowed his friend on the right. "We are definitely going to score tonight, lads!" he said. "If we can convince this guy—and I hope you don't mind me saying, you look a bit rough around the edges—we should have no trouble persuading the ladies."

The five friends grabbed the next five tankards that came their way and toasted the night ahead.

Charlie turned his attention away and scanned the crowd. It was a good night to meet Dodge and Mr. Lunk; the place was busy and that meant it was less likely Mr. Lunk would try to relieve Charlie of his upper limbs. Not entirely impossible, but far better than meeting Mr. Lunk down a dark alley. Or even a well-lit alley.

There was clearly some sort of commotion happening at the front entrance. After lots of arm waving, head shaking, and a few heated words from the security, the men at the door parted as Dodge barged his way past them into the room, followed by the towering figure of Mr. Lunk. Dodge scanned the crowd, head twitching from side to side while the group of security guards followed, walking apprehensively in step with Mr. Lunk.

Charlie stood and waved Dodge over. Dodge turned to the guards, muttered something, then marched over to Charlie with a face like thunder.

Mr. Lunk and his security detail followed in his wake.

"Can you believe it?" Dodge shouted as he approached Charlie. "Myself and my colleague have been discriminated against."

Charlie looked past Dodge at the guards flanking Mr. Lunk. They were big, hard men who'd think nothing of bouncing your face down the steps as they threw you out of their establishment. Next to Mr. Lunk, however, they didn't seem so threatening, mainly because Mr. Lunk cornered the market—as well as the adjacent street—when it came to threatening. Simply by being wherever he was, Mr. Lunk took up the position of the most threatening person anywhere in the near vicinity.

The security guards watched him carefully, but Charlie had no idea what they'd do if the man actually started causing trouble. Dodge shifted his weight from one foot to the other, still clearly annoyed.

"They said we couldn't come in! Said we looked like trouble. That I looked 'proper shifty' and that my good friend Mr. Lunk looked like, and I quote, 'a right 'un'."

"They're here with me," Charlie offered to the doormen.

"See! I told you so!" Dodge said.

"Yeah?" said the biggest of the security guards. "Well, if you or the big fella cause any bother, you're out on your arses."

Mr. Lunk turned his head very slowly and looked at the guard who took an involuntary step back.

"There will be no trouble," he said.

"Well that's good then," the guard said, moving a step backwards. "Cos, you know. I'd hate to get rough with you and all that…"

"I'd hate for it too," said Mr. Lunk in his slow monotone.

With that, the security guards moved away, possibly a little quicker than they needed to.

"Like they'd be able to do anything," Dodge said laughing. "This seat taken?"

He pointed to Bertie's stool who, it would seem, had taken the opportunity to dash someplace else which wasn't right here, right now. He sat down.

"Mr. Lunk, would you care for a seat?" Charlie said, pointing to Gerald's seat, also now swiftly vacated.

Mr. Lunk turned his head slowly and looked down at the stool, which was slightly small even for Charlie.

"I think I'll stand," he said, turning his gaze back across the room.

The other members of the 'Middle Calver Mercenaries' made a hasty exit, mumbling something about giving the other two a hand.

"Friends of yours?" Dodge asked.

"Not really," Charlie said.

"Good. They looked like a right bunch of pillocks. What were they supposed to be?"

"Mercenaries. I think they were just out for a good time," Charlie replied.

"Looked like Middle Calver stuck-ups if you ask me. Suppose they think it's entertaining to come down to Lower Calver and rough it. Can't stand people like that—thinking they're better than us. Come down here for a taste of the real world then totter back up to their quaint little lives in their quaint little houses with proper beds and everything. Makes me sick." He spat onto the tavern floor.

"That's a bit strong, don't you think?" Charlie said.

"Is it really, Charlie Lightfoot?" Dodge rounded on Charlie. There was a look in his eyes Charlie didn't much like. "I wonder why you might say such a thing? Maybe now you're out playing on the streets of Lower Calver, you think you're ready to leave the Backstreets behind you. That is what I wonder."

"I just think they were out for a good time," Charlie said with a shrug. "Live and let live, you know?"

"You see, Charlie, that's where you and I disagree. Why should I live and let live? Where's that kind of a passive attitude gotten anyone in life? Absolutely bloody nowhere. I prefer to live and maybe let others live if they don't annoy me or get in my way. Which brings us nicely back to you, Mr. Music Man."

Dodge grabbed a tankard from a passing waitress and drank it down in a matter of seconds. He wiped his mouth on the back of his sleeve and belched loudly. Behind him, Mr. Lunk remained impassive. He could have been made of stone.

"I've been thinking about what you proposed," Dodge said, smiling. "Could be a nice arrangement. You go out and about, play your fiddle, earn some coin. Then—maybe not once a week, but let's say, once a month—me and Mr. Lunk collect our fee from you. We wouldn't take it all of course, as we want to protect our investment. As of right now, you can consider us your management."

Charlie guessed as much would happen. Given that the last time they met Dodge was prepared to have Mr. Lunk crush his skull, this development could be seen as a good one. And one that Charlie felt he could use.

"Oh, and if you think about turning us down," Dodge said, "or maybe doing a bunk—"

"Dodge," Charlie said, smiling, "you don't need to keep reminding me." He pointed a thumb at Mr. Lunk who was slowly scanning the room.

"I know, I know," Dodge said. He leaned in closer to Charlie, looked both ways and in a hushed voice said, "To be honest, I'm still trying to get the hang of this whole having a bit of power business. Not really used to it."

"Well, I think you've taken to it like a duck to water," Charlie said, managing to lie convincingly.

Dodge gave Charlie one of his sideways looks, eyes narrowed. He seemed to come to a decision.

"You know what? You're okay, Charlie Lightfoot. I think this could be the start of a beautiful way for me to make money."

"Glad I could be the one to help," Charlie said. "There is just one thing…"

Dodge shifted on his stool. "Oh, yeah," he said narrowing his eyes. "And what might that be?"

In for a penny.

"Well, it's just that in order for you to make the most from our business relationship you need me to make as much coin as possible, right?"

"Right," Dodge said.

"And I can't very well do that if there's other people who want to get in the way of the coin flowing from me to you, can I?"

"What do you mean?"

"Well, for example, I've got a gig coming up at the Half-way Barrel this Sunday—"

"The Halfway bloody Barrel!" Dodge said. "My, my, we really are going up in the world! How in the hells did you get in there?"

It was as if Charlie said he was playing at the palace.

"I played a tune for the landlord and his son. Was on my way back from the Market and I happened to come across them."

"See, it's that kind of luck that gets you places," said Dodge "Me, never had it. I've had to claw my way up the ladder. The Halfway bloody Barrel! You jammy bugger! Maybe me and Mr. Lunk should come along to make sure you don't mess it up."

"Oh, I don't think that'll be necessary," Charlie said, quickly. "And besides, it's not the biggest place in the Kingdom and you'll want as many paying customers in there as possible, right?"

"Fair dues," Dodge said.

"Anyway," Charlie redirected, "back to my original point. As my management team, you and Mr. Lunk will certainly want to protect your business interest—mainly me and the coin I earn."

"Absolutely," Dodge said as he snatched another tankard from a passing serving girl.

"Well, you remember when I first met Mr. Lunk?"

"Yeah, you ended up on your arse."

"Indeed I did. That was because I was being chased by three large and oddly-shaped men who seemed intent on separating me from my coin."

"Taking your coin after all the hard work you took to earn it," Dodge said looking incredulous. "The depths some people will go to! It never ceases to amaze me, Charlie, it really doesn't. That's why the Backstreets needs people like me and Mr. Lunk. Bring a bit of order to the chaos. Someone to run things."

Charlie chose not to mention the colour of a certain kettle and associated pots. "Running the Backstreets? That's a big ask."

"Dream big, Charlie Lightfoot. I've always been a go-getter. You've got to dream big. Then, if that fails, just go out and find yourself something big to help you go get your dreams." He nodded towards Mr. Lunk who remained as animated as a brick.

"Fair enough," Charlie said. "But if we could get back to my original point... if I'm being chased and harassed on a regular basis—and something tells me the three gentlemen I mentioned didn't happen to bump into me by chance—the amount of coin I can pay you won't be as much as if I wasn't."

"Message received loud and clear, Charlie. Loud and clear. Like you said, we've got to protect our interests. In this case, your coin. Don't you worry, from this moment on, I'll make sure everyone who calls the Backstreets home will know that you're untouchable. That you're mine."

Charlie winced at the last part but, for now, and until he had better options, decided to let it go. He was well aware he wasn't in the best position to bargain. It wasn't fair and it wasn't right but he knew to roll with the punches and get on with life, which was liable to try to give you a jolly good slapping at every available opportunity.

"Right then," Dodge said standing up. "I reckon that's us done. This place is starting to give me a headache. Too many toffs living it up with daft Backstreet folk who wouldn't know they're being looked down on even if they were two feet tall. I think next time, we'll meet somewhere else."

He shook a warning finger.

"Better get earning, Charlie Lightfoot," he said. "My services come at a price," and before Charlie could reply, Dodge had grabbed a handful of coins from the bag Charlie had put on the table, elbowed Mr. Lunk, nodded to the door, and added, "let's go."

Mr. Lunk nodded once and proceeded to cut a channel through the throngs of people, as he waded forwards through the Rat and Vat. Most lurched out of the way in time but those with their backs to the large immovable object heading in their direction were cast aside like driftwood. Drinks were spilt, stools knocked over, and people were trampled underfoot as Mr. Lunk made his way across the room – with a smiling Dodge following in his wake.

This presented those deemed as security with a dilemma. Under normal circumstances, a disturbance inside the Rat and Vat was an excuse to release some aggression under the guise of protecting the patron's well-being. However, in this case, said disturbance was Mr. Lunk.

"Think we should do something?" said one of the security team.

"And what might you suggest?" said another.

"Well, I dunno really, it's just… there's a disturbance."

"That there is. Can't deny that. Definitely a disturbance."

The two men scanned the room, all the while purposely not looking in the general direction of Mr. Lunk.

"It's just normally, we'd, you know, wade in and grab a hold of the disturbance—"

"Or disturbances if we're lucky."

"True, true. I do prefer it when there's more than one disturber."

"Is that a word?"

"What?"

"Disturber."

"Not sure. I suppose the person doing the disturbing's got to be called something."

The guard thought for a second. "I normally just go with knobhead."

"I prefer bellend myself, but I think if we're talking in general terms, you can refer to your standard person doing the disturbing as a disturber."

"Okay. I can go with that. Disturber it is then."

"Has the big lad gone yet?"

"He has."

"Oh good. As you were then."

CHAPTER 7

Night moves.

CHARLIE ARRIVED AT the Halfway Barrel as the sun began to set. He walked up to the door, fiddle tucked beneath his arm, half expecting the landlord to have completely forgotten about their deal and to turf him out on his ear.

This was, after all, the Halfway Barrel.

Come to think of it, what in the god's names was he thinking? Who was he, thinking he was anywhere close to good enough to play in a proper pub?

If people didn't like what he was playing or didn't think he was worth listening to out on the streets, they walked away. Inside the Halfway Barrel, it was the other way around. *He* was the one who'd have to walk away. All the practice, all the self-belief and arrogance of youth didn't seem to carry much weight when faced with a gig in a proper pub.

He almost turned and walked away. Almost.

What stopped him was a voice in his head. A voice which sounded strangely like Auntie.

"You bloody well get in there and play, you wet wazzock," it said. *"You've practiced, you've worked hard, and you've got yourself a chance. You better grab a hold of it so tight it can't breathe."*.

With a smile, Charlie pushed open the door and walked inside the Halfway Barrel.

LOOKING BACK, CHARLIE could remember very little of his fifteen minutes performing on that Sunday evening. Arthur had pushed a few of the tables back to give him a space to play but he still felt a little like an afterthought.

He did remember nobody really paid him much attention as he made his way over to his designated space, threw down his coat, and took out his bow and fiddle from the sacking he carried them in. Then he stood and waited. Was he supposed to be told to start playing or did he just launch into the Bride of the Meadows?

He didn't have to wait long to find out. The landlord made his way over, collecting a few wooden tankards on the way.

"I'm still not sure about this," he said by way of a greeting. "But seeing as you're here now, you best get on with it."

Charlie nodded and tucked his fiddle under his arm.

"Just remember," the landlord said, pointing a dishcloth in Charlie's direction, "if this lot don't like it, or folk start to leave, you're out. Understand?"

Charlie nodded. Truth was, he couldn't speak a word; his mouth had suddenly gone dry. Here he was, stood in front of maybe twenty people in the back corner of a dark pub yet, and it surprised him to discover this, he'd never felt so nervous.

He scanned the faces of the patrons. Most weren't even

looking in his direction. From over by the bar, Arthur gave a wave, a huge grin upon his face. And then, as Charlie nodded back and cast his gaze further, a small, wrinkled hand raised a cup of what was, in all probability, some form of rye, and Charlie knew it was all going to be all right.

And so, he played.

WHILST HE COULD remember very little about the performance, he knew it had been good. In fact, it was best he'd ever played and, for that very small moment in time, he hadn't been Charlie Lightfoot from the Backstreets of Lower Calver. It was nothing as dramatic as being transformed or even existing on another, higher plane—that would be both pretentious and plain wrong—but he had forgotten himself. He had committed completely to the music and he knew, above all else, that it had felt good.

Damn good.

Did he ride the lighting?

In his own small way, maybe.

Once he'd finished, people stood and clapped. Some even came up to him, wanting to talk about the songs he'd played; how they hadn't heard that particular song for such a long time; or how the way he played reminded them of something; or just how they thought he was a pretty good fiddle player and whether he'd be around next week?

"Of course he bloody will!" the landlord said, slapping Charlie on the back. "This is our new regular musician. Tell everyone you know that…"

"Charlie Lightfoot," Charlie offered.

"… that Charlie Lightfoot will be back next week with more of the same," the landlord said beaming.

Arthur came over from the bar, with a huge grin plastered across his face to match his father's. "That was great, Charlie, just great!"

"Thanks," said Charlie, "it was, wasn't it?"

"Yes! You were amazing! The way you played, you had them eating out the palm of your hand!"

Charlie felt a strange sense of unease creep over him as Arthur spoke. Even more so because he didn't think he'd ever be able to explain to Arthur that it wasn't *he* who'd been amazing but *the music*. He didn't feel he was being unduly humble or trying to misdirect—he had, after all, practised his arse off—but it was more that the music had taken over and that, *that* had been the amazing part.

"Just you wait until word gets out," Arthur continued, "the Halfway Barrel's got a fiddle player and he's amazing. The place'll be packed to the rafters."

"I'm not so sure it'll—" Charlie started to say.

"Just you wait Charlie—this is going to be the start of something huge, you'll see."

With another slap on the back, Arthur strode off, making a beeline for his father.

Charlie picked up his coat, tucked his fiddle under his arm, and made his way towards the door, receiving plenty of nods, a couple of pats on the back and a few words of praise along the way.

Outside it was getting dark; the lamplighters were already out, tallow in hand. He pulled on his coat and tucked his fiddle under his arm.

"Superstar Charlie Lightfoot. The man, the myth, the legend."

"Bog off, old man," Charlie said, as Blind Watchem laughed and made his way over from the lamppost he was leaning against.

"No, no. Credit where credit is due," he said. "You were marginally above average."

"Careful. That's the kind of praise that could go to a person's head," said Charlie, pulling his coat tighter.

"As your teacher, mentor and all-round spiritual guide throughout this tumultuous ocean we more experienced members of society call life, I feel it is my duty to keep you on an even keel. To wit, one half-decent gig does not a musician make."

"I know," Charlie assured. "Trust me, I'm not going to get carried away anytime soon. It felt pretty good being up there but, to start with at least, I didn't have a clue what I was doing."

"Ah, but you did. Or should I say, *the music* did. I'll wager once you started to play…"

"Everything just seemed to flow," Charlie finished.

"Of course it did," Blind Watchem said, taking a hold of Charlie's arm and steering him towards the Backstreets. "The music doesn't care if you're anxious, nor if your pet rat's died and you held a small but moving burial service for it in your backyard that very afternoon. The music is always just the music. Pure, real and ready to be set free."

"How much have you had to drink today?" Charlie asked.

"Enough to maintain the necessary balance of blood and alcohol that pulses through these tired old veins of mine. It's practically an art form getting the ratio spot on, but I've made it my life's work to get it right. Now, where were we…"

To the careful observer, the scene before them was one young man and one older man making their way home after a night in Lower Calver. Admittedly, the younger man seemed to be supporting the older, who leaned on him heavily, clearly a little the worse for wear after one too many sherbets.

But the careful observer might also be prone to an uneasy feeling.

A young man and a slightly wobbly older man out at this time of night, when most half-decent folk are tucked up in a warm-ish thing to sleep on (or under), well, that might lead to some not-so-nice consequences. After all, there's trouble wherever you go in Calver—it's just that trouble's got a pretty accurate way of finding you on the Backstreets at this time of night.

The careful observer might listen out for the familiar sound of heavy boots shuffling and scuffling. Because those heavy boots, more than likely, contained some heavy bodies, with faces containing all the right features just not necessarily in the right order.

And, upon hearing the sounds of said heavy boots filled by said heavy occupants, the careful observer might also nod their head knowingly, maybe even shrug their shoulders in what passed for some kind of sympathy, and head off to bed themselves.

Just before settling in for the night, the careful observer

might even hear the owners of the heavy boots mutter and mumble something along the lines of a quickly devised plan.

"Right, now's our chance."

"Fair enough. My legs are getting tired. It's the heavy boots."

"Tell me about it. Folks think what we do is a doddle. I'd like to see them have a bloody go at this."

"I hear you, my friend. I hear you. Right. I'll clobber the young one, you do the old one. Handing out a jolly good slapping is one of the few perks of the gig."

"Isn't it just? I—"

"Everything alright?"

"Strangest thing. I walked into this here wall. Could've sworn it wasn't there a moment ago."

"Let's have a… oh dear."

"What is it?"

"Well. On the one hand, you're right, this wall wasn't here a minute ago. Because this wall isn't a wall at all. It's a person."

"Oh dear…"

And then, were the careful observer still observing, they would probably be subjected to a series of noises—the underlying theme of which was pain.

CHAPTER 8

Squiffy Mushrooms.

"IF YOU DON'T slow down, you'll give yourself indigestion," Auntie said. She had her back to Charlie but, even across the kitchen, she could tell the boy was practically inhaling his pie.

"Sorry Auntie," Charlie said through a mouth full. "I need to get a move on or I'll be late."

"You know, ever since that gig at the Halfway Barrel, you've not stopped!" Auntie said, shaking her head. "You young folk, always rushing about. Here, there and everywhere. You want to slow down a bit."

Charlie decided not to point out the obvious to someone who survived on a couple of hours sleep a night.

"Where are you playing tonight?"

"I've got an early doors gig at the Summoner's Ladle, then there's a party I'm playing at in Middle Calver. Some councillor's event or something."

Auntie finished washing the pots, placed the last bowl on the draining board, flicked her hands twice, and dried them on her apron.

"A party in Middle Calver no less. Well, well, well."

She shook her head and smiled. Auntie didn't smile

often. She was too busy to waste time on such things. When she did, it always reminded Charlie of the times when the sun broke through the clouds on a thoroughly miserable day; often unexpected but with enough warmth to see you through.

Sat at Auntie's table, finishing off her pie, Charlie took in that smile for the brief gift that it was.

THE GIG AT the Summoner's Ladle went as it always did. Charlie played a more toned-down, softer version of his normal set; one which seemed to go down well with the early evening crowd. By the time the sky was flecked with the final remains of the day, he was hustling up the cobbled rise of the King's Pass, headed for the gatehouse which would take him into Middle Calver.

Over the past few months, he'd been playing in Middle Calver on a more regular basis. The first few times he'd asked Blind Watchem to accompany him—and the old man had obliged willingly. Through the wider, less cramped streets of Middle Calver, he'd regale Charlie with stories of his past conducts, pointing out places of interest with a running theme of nefarious deeds, outrageous parties, and the goings on that made Charlie question the truthfulness of the old musician's words.

Initially, Charlie found it hard to listen. Not because of what Blind Watchem was saying, but because he was trying to take in all he saw. It staggered him that Middle Calver was only separated from Lower Calver by a wall (albeit a very thick one), yet the differences were so huge he struggled to comprehend how the place he'd just come from and the place where he now stood were both classed as part of the same city.

One of the first things which struck Charlie was the space. As in, there was some. There were gaps between the houses, they even had enough land so as to be set back from the road. Not only that, they had these strange little walls and fences around them.

"Why do they need to have walls around where they live?" Charlie had asked. "Can't imagine there's that much crime up here."

"Pah!" Blind Watchem exclaimed. "You've got much to learn, young chap. Crime changes based on the folk perpetrating it. Back down there in Lower Calver, it's often and it's in your face. It pulls no punches and it doesn't claim to be anything other than what it is. Subtle as a brick, that's what crime is down there.

"Up here, it happens just as often only on a much grander scale. It's often dressed up—sometimes even disguised—and it's done behind a mask of somewhat respectability. If you ever have the good fortune to find yourself in Upper Calver, then you'll really start to understand what crime is."

"Sometimes I'm glad I'm from the Backstreets. Everything seems a bit more straightforward."

"A musician and a philosopher. Who'd have thought it," Blind Watchem said. "Oh, and another thing. Posh people put fences and walls around things because they don't like sharing. Remember that."

Today, as Charlie neared the gatehouse, Blind

Watchem's words seemed to lose a little of their significance. So far, he'd seen no real crime to speak of and the places he'd played, the punters had been more than happy to share their coin with him.

"How do, Charlie?"

"All right, Dave?" Charlie replied as he approached the first pair of King's guards stationed at the entrance to the gatehouse.

"'nother gig, is it?" Dave said.

"Bugger me, sharp as a tack this one," said the other guard. "Your deductive powers constantly amaze me, you know that?"

"Sod off, Frank," said Dave. He turned to Charlie. "How's things?"

"Same old, same old," Charlie replied.

Dave nodded. Then his face tugged into a somewhat mischievous smile.

"Here," he said leaning in, his armour clunking. "You must get a fair bit of it, right?"

"Oh gods, here we go," said Frank, shaking his head.

"No, listen. You being a musician and all that. You must get around a bit. Girls throwing themselves at you and the like?"

"Dave, we've been through this before," said Frank. "Our Charlie here's not going to reveal the lurid details of the spoils of his profession."

"But there are what he said – spoils of your profession. Tell me there are Charlie."

"Good gods man, what is wrong with you, you dirty old pervert!" Frank said.

Charlie left the guards to squabble over his love life, and made his way through the archway and into the gatehouse within the huge wall separating Lower and Middle Calver.

Out the other side, he took out the bit of parchment with the map of how to get to the party on it. He knew roughly where he was headed. The guy who'd asked him to play had approached him after one of his gigs in Middle Calver. More and more of his late night shows were coming to him in this way. And he agreed to play at them all.

For Charlie, it was about playing as much as possible. It was what he loved to do and every time he played he got better.

And got paid.

After following the King's Pass for a short while, Charlie came to a crossroads. This one had an island in the middle which you were supposed to go around. To make the point, there was a large pot in the very centre of the junction with lots of lovely flowers planted in it. When he'd first seen it, Charlie had wondered why someone would leave a tub of flowers in the middle of the road but Blind Watchem explained it was a 'roundabout' and you were supposed to drive your cart or ride your horse around the tub of flowers in a calm and sophisticated manner. Also, you were supposed to let the person to your right go before you did.

To Charlie this made little sense. Blind Watchem explained this was what made the people of Middle Calver different. Enforced civility.

Charlie took the road on the left, Forthright Avenue, smiled, and shook his head. It really was a different world up here. At this time of night, Charlie had most of the streets to himself. The majority of the buildings lining Forthright Avenue were places of business, their wooden signs overhanging the walkway. Most were now shuttered and dark.

After a distance, the shopfronts gave way to houses, and here, the windows were lit, often by a number of candles burning in ornate holders, which afforded Charlie a chance to gaze in as he passed by. This was the part of coming to Middle Calver at night he enjoyed the most. The soft, warm glow of candlelight drew him in, and he always slowed his pace to get a glimpse of what was inside.

Charlie crossed the road and made for a grassy area— called a park, Blind Watchem had told him. He followed the path through the park, past rows of very neat and very precise flowers, around a silent bandstand, and through the iron gate on the other side.

He looked at the paper in his hand. This was the street. The houses here were big and they towered over him. Most had four floors and all overlooked the park. Charlie spotted the one he was looking for, crossed the road and walked up the steps to knock on the door.

Before he could do so however, the door swung open and he was confronted by, what appeared to be at first glance, a skeleton in a suit.

"Good evening, sir," the skeleton said, "won't you come in?" His words came out in a barely audible whisper and sounded like they were being scratched across a very rough piece of parchment.

Charlie stepped cautiously past and inside. Upon close observation, Charlie determined the skeleton was in fact a man who seemed to be older than time itself, rail thin and about one unnecessary scare away from breathing his final breath.

"Good evening," Charlie replied.

"I'm Woodson," said the dusty figure. "I help look after his lordship's residence, if I can be of any service to—"

Woodson stopped, mid-sentence, his eyes dropped shut and he remained motionless, save for the occasional gentle swaying. Charlie, unsure whether the ancient Woodson had breathed his last and died standing up, chose to remain where he was.

"—strange ocular movements after smashing squiffy mushrooms!" Woodson shouted his eyes bursting open and, in the process, nearly causing Charlie to soil his trousers.

"May I take your coat?" Woodson continued, barely missing a beat.

Bewildered, Charlie said nothing, he simply handed over his coat.

"Thank you, sir. Now if you'll be so good as to follow me, his lordship and guests are outside on the veranda."

Woodson draped Charlie's coat over his arm, made an abrupt about face and led Charlie straight back out the way he came, through the front door, shutting it behind him.

He stood silent, taking in the quiet street. Charlie scratched the back of his head and shifted his feat. He wasn't sure how to proceed.

"Ah," Woodson said after a moment, "It would appear his lordship has had some remodelling done and replaced the back of the house with the front. How perplexing."

"Uhh… maybe we should head back inside and see if we

can… work things out?" Charlie suggested, not wanting to confuse the man any further.

"Yes. That might be a good idea, sir," Woodson said.

As they both turned, the front door opened and a young woman stepped out.

"Oh, there you are!" she said as she walked down the steps, and for an instant—a brief and totally irrational instant—Charlie thought she was talking to him. "Come on inside Grandfather, mother's been looking for you."

She took the old man's arm—not before deftly removing Charlie's coat and handing it back to him—and began to lead him back inside.

Charlie followed her into the house and watched as she led the old man into a room and sat him down. She turned to Charlie.

"Sorry about that. Sometimes he gets a bit confused. Who did he say he was this time?"

"Uh, Woodson," Charlie replied.

"Oh, that's a new one," she said. "Normally, he just wanders off and we find him in some room, looking a bit confused like he's just woken up or something." She smiled and rolled her eyes. "Oh, by the way, I'm Millicent, but most people just call me Mills."

"Charlie Lightfoot," Charlie said. He always felt a little awkward in these situations. Was he supposed to bow, take her hand or just wait until spoken to?

"Millicent, you are needed in the drawing room," said another woman as she strode into the hallway. She stopped, looked Charlie up and down, then turned to Millicent.

"Hurry up dear. The Duke is running out of stories; Lady

Margaret is struggling to string two sentences together; and your father is, well, being your father."

She shooed Millicent in the direction from which she'd come.

Millicent paused on her way through the doorway.

"Nice to meet you, Charlie Lightfoot," she said with a smile. Charlie smiled back then stopped as the older woman moved in front of his vision.

"I am Lady Gwendolyn," she said with an air of a slight distain. "You, I assume, are the hired help, is that correct?"

Charlie nodded. "I'm here to play for you."

"Ah yes. The *fiddler*." The way she said the final word made it sound like Charlie played with turds for a living. "You come highly recommended. But while those recommendations may have got through my front door, if you ever look at my daughter like that again, I'll chop your man-bits off and catapult them back down the Kings Pass."

"Suppose it would stop me fiddling with myself," Charlie said.

Lady Gwendolyn gave Charlie the kind of stare which could freeze tar.

Charlie coughed.

"Sorry," he said.

"Better," Lady Gwendolyn said frowning. "Remember your place and all will be well. Now, follow me and I'll show you where you'll be playing."

Charlie picked up his fiddle bag and did his best to keep up with Lady Gwendolyn as she swept through the enormous house. It wasn't easy to keep up, not just because she walked so quickly, but because Charlie couldn't help but be distracted by the sheer opulence of the place. The rooms which led off the hallway seemed to continue on forever, each one draped in the finest materials, with glittering objects placed on shining surfaces, and decorated rugs covering highly polished floors.

Charlie was so engrossed he nearly walked into the back of Lady Gwendolyn as she came to a stop in front of two huge doors. The doors stood open revealing a large lawn the size of Auntie's house and the Burnt Tankard combined.

"You'll play out here in the garden. I've picked you a spot over in the far corner, by the azaleas. I want light background music, nothing too modern. Stick to the classics, thank you. My guests want to be able to hear themselves talk not have to compete with a screeching warbler. Any questions?"

"What's an azalea?" Charlie asked.

Lady Gwendolyn shook her head dismissively, turned on her heels and marched away.

"Marcus, deal with the simpleton!" she shouted back through the double doors.

CHAPTER 9

It's all very nice until it isn't.

MARCUS, IT TURNED out, was Lady Gwendolyn's son, and therefore Millicent's brother. He strode over to Charlie with a long, languid gait, his flop of hair swishing this way and that.

"Hey, my man," he said, flicking his hair. "Name's Marcus. You can call me Marc or even M if the mood takes you." He flashed a smile at Charlie, then winked. "Place is a major bore, is it not? Can't wait to bust out of here. Go find some real action, you get my meaning?"

"Not so sure that I do," Charlie said.

"You know," said Marcus, giving Charlie a nudge. "Blow the joint, head on out and find some crazy party. Get away from all these fuddy-duddy's."

"These fuddy-duddy's are paying me coin to play here," said Charlie, "so I'm afraid this is where I'll have to stay."

"Sure, sure, but you look like the kind of guy who knows how to find a decent scene. Am I wrong? Tell me Mr. Music Man, where are you from?"

"I come from Lower Calver," Charlie said feeling a little embarrassed then hating himself for it.

"Lower Calver!" Marcus gasped, eyes widening. He leant

closer. He smelt of flowers and powder and something else Charlie couldn't quite put his finger on.

Marcus looked around, "Have you ever been to... The Backstreets?" he said, mouthing the last words almost silently as if someone might overhear him.

"Erm," said Charlie, "that's where I'm from."

Marcus slapped his knee and did a little hop. "Whoa," he said, "this is unreal! Tell me all about it. I want to know everything. Is it true they shit in the gutter down there? Do the women screw you for less than a drink? How many people have you seen killed? Have—"

"Marcus!" Lady Gwendolyn shouted as she blasted through the huge doors like an unforgiving wind. "Why isn't the help playing his fiddle yet? The rest of the guests are beginning to arrive!"

She grabbed hold of Charlie by the arm and part marched, part dragged him over to the far corner of the grassy area.

"Right," she said. "You see these plants with the pink flowers on?"

"I'm guessing they're asshailers," Charlie said.

"Azaleas," Lady Gwendolyn corrected. "This is where you play. I'm paying you for an evening's entertainment which means, for this evening only—thank the gods—you're mine. To wit, you will do exactly as I say. Now get your bloody fiddle out, start playing, and don't stop until I tell you to. Do you understand?"

"Happy to oblige, Lady G." said Charlie, with only a hint of irony. "Stay here, play nice twinkly music, keep people happy. Got it. One quick question?"

"What?"

"That thing you said. Just before 'do exactly what I say.'. What was it?"

Lady Gwendolyn blew out air in exasperation. "I wouldn't expect you to understand. I said 'to wit'—"

"To woo!" Charlie said, a huge grin plastered across his face.

Lady Gwendolyn's left eyelid began to twitch.

"Go and see to your guests, my Lady," Charlie reassured, unwrapping his fiddle, "All will be well here."

"It had better be," Lady Gwendolyn said, and turned about face and made her way back inside, but not before a few choice words with her son.

"Must apologise for mother," Marcus said as he sauntered over once she'd left. "The old bird's a little highly strung. Family business and all that—big night tonight. Anywho, we were just getting into the nitty-gritty about life on the Backstreets. Bloody interesting stuff, what? So—"

"Sorry Marcus," Charlie interrupted. "But I don't want to upset moth… Lady Gwendolyn. I need to get paid."

"Absolutely, my man. Absolutely. We'll save the hardcore chat for after, when the fogeys have tottered off to bed. My nights don't usually get started till way after midnight anyway."

Charlie set his fiddle and began to play and said a silent prayer that Marcus would forget all about his promise of a 'hardcore chat' later.

He had a sinking feeling he wouldn't.

THE GIG WENT about as well as Charlie could've expected given he felt like a fish out of water. Actually, he felt more like a fish who'd managed to flop out of its pond and lay floundering on a neatly manicured bit of garden, in the midst of a bank of hungry swans. Occasionally, people would look at him, or rather, they would notice him, but their glances were brief, and their gazes soon moved on.

Towards the end of the night, as the number of highly polished and immaculately presented guests began to dwindle, Millicent made her way over to him. She was accompanied by a man with the most ridiculous moustache Charlie had ever seen. He was reminded of one of Auntie's many sayings.

Never trust a man with a moustache. Either grow a beard like a man or shave like a man. Someone with a moustache looks like they should never be left alone with children.

The man was tall, with so many points and angles about him he looked like he could shave rain.

"Millicent, my fruit, we're missing all the fun!" His voice came out in a nasal whine.

"Don't be such a spoil sport, Roderick," Millicent said. "I want to hear our fiddler play. I've heard he's rather good."

"We can hear him from over there, where the boys are," he muttered through his bushy moustache, a whinge creeping into his voice.

He gestured over to the huge doors which led out into the garden, where a group of four men stood in a tight pack, heads close together. Apparently one of them said something funny because, almost as one, they threw their heads back and guffawed heartily into the night air.

"Millicent!" Roderick said. "The fun's over there! Come onnnnn!"

"You go Roderick. I'll be there in a jiffy."

She blew a soft kiss in Roderick's direction but, having been granted his leave, he was already trotting across the grass towards his friends.

Charlie continued playing.

"My betrothed," Millicent explained. "Soon to be the third richest man in all of Calver. His father owns half of Middle Calver, in one way or another. Lots of property. We're due to be wed next month."

Charlie followed Millicent's gaze towards Roderick who had joined his friends. They looked over at Millicent. One of them gave her a wave which she returned. The friend then dug an elbow into Roderick's ribs, said something, and they all burst into peals of laughter.

"He was hand selected for me by my dear mother and I for him by his. Our union will create one of the wealthiest dynasties in the entire Kingdom."

"I'm very happy for you," said Charlie as he transitioned from one twinkly, light background tune to the next.

"I'm not. He's an absolute cock," Millicent said matter-of-factly, still smiling in the direction of Roderick and his friends.

Charlie squeaked out a missed note.

"Why, Mr. Charlie Lightfoot, I do believe I've caught you off guard."

Charlie quickly corrected and continued the tune.

"Didn't see that one coming to be fair. Also, didn't have you down as a potty mouth."

Millicent folded her arms. "Why because I'm a girl?"

"You've clearly never met some of the girls I have," said Charlie. "Girls from round my way can make your ears blush."

"Why then?"

"Just didn't think... posh girls knew words like that."

"Oh, you'd be very much surprised what 'posh girls' know, Mr Lightfoot."

Charlie chose to say nothing. Instead he switched from one nondescript background tune to another.

"Mr. Charlie Lightfoot the music man, do you ever think about a life beyond all this?" Millicent said sweeping her arms outwards. "A simpler life, more spontaneous, more normal?"

"Oh yeah Lady Millicent," Charlie said, negotiating a slightly tricky key change, "all this wealth and abundance is just so hum-drum for me. In fact, I'm sick to the back teeth of having people wait on me hand and foot, not to mention the whole not having to worry where to get my next meal."

"You know, Charlie, if I didn't know any better, I'd say you were mocking me."

"Not at all my lady," Charlie replied with a wink.

"You know, life isn't always peaches and cream for me," Millicent continued, "I didn't choose any of this. I certainly didn't choose him." She pointed over to where her future husband was trying to snort a vol-au-vent. Even with a nose his size he only managed to get it halfway up before his eyes bulged and he catapulted it out, hitting one of his friends square in the face. As one, they fell about laughing.

"So why don't you say no," Charlie asked.

"I'm sorry, would you like me to introduce you to my mother again?" said Millicent, raising an eyebrow.

"Ah, good point."

Charlie played on, and the crowd thinned as the stars began to glimmer above.

Millicent sighed deeply. "Do you know what I wanted to be when I grew up?" she asked.

"Be a bit weird if I did," Charlie said.

"I wanted to be a nurse. I used to practise on my stuffed animals all the time. It was all I ever wanted. Instead, I get to be a combination of ornament and baby-making machine."

Before Charlie had a chance to reply, Lady Gwendolyn once again swept across the lawn towards them. Charlie wondered if she ever just walked.

"Right, that's enough," she said. "You can stop playing now and go home." She threw a bag of coin at Charlie's feet. "Here's your pay."

"I take it that her ladyship was satisfied with tonight's performance?" Charlie asked, and finished the piece he was playing with a light flourish. Lady Gwendolyn's eyes narrowed.

"Let's get one thing straight, Mr. Lightfoot," she said, looking Charlie dead in the eye. "You were good enough. Nothing more. I'll admit I had my reservations, but you managed not to disgrace yourself in the kind of company one can only assume you're unaccustomed to. But let's not kid ourselves. You are background. You came, you played, and now, you shall leave. If I ever need someone to play at such an event again, I may consider you."

She linked her arm through her daughter's. "I'm sure you

can find your own way out. Come, Millicent" she said, and escorted Millicent away before anymore could be said.

Charlie stooped, scooped up his bag of coin, and placed his fiddle back in its cloth bag.

"Not the most glowing review I've ever heard, old chap."

Charlie stood up to find Millicent's fiancé in front of him.

"I've had worse," Charlie said, with a shrug and a smile.

"Name's Roderick. Roderick von Haugen," Millicent's fiancé said, extending a hand. Charlie took it and introduced himself.

"Thought you played pretty well, to be fair," Roderick continued.

"Thanks," said Charlie. "Not my usual scene but I'm grateful for the work."

"Yes, quite," Roderick said in that way people do when they aren't particularly interested in anything you have to say. "Listen, wanted to grab a quick word before you shot off to… wherever it is you're from."

Charlie bent to collect up his belongings. "Fire away, my good man," he said.

"Yes, rather. You see," said Roderick shaking a finger, "that's very much the gist of what I wanted to converse about."

"Excuse me?" Charlie stopped packing his fiddle away and stood upright.

"Well, here's the ticket. This 'my good man' business. It simply won't do, dear Charlie. I was watching you from over yonder and, I have to say, you seem a tad… over-familiar. A bit too chummy, especially with my betrothed. Sorry to have to bring it up and all that but I think it's always best to nip these things in the bud."

"Erm… okay," Charlie said reticently, more than a little bewildered.

"Oh, don't worry about it old chap. Not in the least offended. Just wanted to give you the heads up. It's best everyone knows their place, what? Keeps to their own station? Probably not used to all of this." Roderick waved his arms in an all-encompassing arc. "Things undoubtedly and understandably got to your head. Tell me, where is it exactly that you're from?" He held Charlie's gaze.

"The… Backstreets," Charlie said, unable to stop the colour from rising in his cheeks.

"Ah, yes. The Backstreets. That explains it. Well, hopefully our little chat has helped. Maybe next time you're up this way, our little tête-à-tête will be of some use and things will go swimmingly for all concerned."

"Absolutely. Th-thank you," Charlie said unsure of exactly what had happened but able to make a good guess.

"My absolute pleasure, old bean. Always happy to help. Oh, and just one more thing. My family practically own Middle Calver, so if I ever catch you speaking to my Milly again, it will be the last time you ever set foot in this part of the city."

Roderick didn't wait for a response. He turned on his heel and strode back across the lawn. Charlie wasn't entirely sure he could've given Roderick a response, mainly because he wasn't entirely sure how he was supposed to feel. Part of him felt anger, part felt a certain type of confusing shame.

Mostly he felt that he just wanted to get back to Auntie's kitchen.

CHAPTER 10

The official greeting of the regular.

I T WAS GETTING late. Charlie hurried through the streets of Middle Calver, determined to focus on the coin in his pocket, rather than the lacklustre gig he'd just played.

He couldn't quite explain the way he felt about it. It hadn't gone badly and he'd certainly had far, far worse gigs— just last week a mass brawl had broken out at the Broken Molar whilst he was playing. Charlie managed to escape unscathed, but for a moment, it looked touch and go. He'd returned the following day to see if the landlord would still pay him but when he got there he soon realised he wouldn't be seeing any coin from this gig.

He'd found the landlord sat on a barrel out on the cobblestones, the burning embers of the Broken Molar still smouldering behind him.

"Just my bloody luck," he'd said, shaking his head and trying to clean the soot off his arms with a damp rag. "Group of assassins in for a leaving do. Once they got involved, it was all she wrote."

The problem with gigs like the one he'd just played was that it left him in a bit of a quandary; on the one hand, the pay was very good, on the other, he had to spend time with the people who paid him.

》》》《《《

ONCE CHARLIE PASSED through the gates and back into Lower Calver, he felt much calmer. So much so that, instead of heading home, he decided to stop off at the Halfway Barrel for a quick chat with Arthur.

Lately, he'd been stopping by the Barrel whenever he got the chance. Charlie enjoyed his time with Arthur. Maybe it was a touch of the publican in Arthur, but Charlie felt like he could tell him just about anything. Arthur was a very good listener. He was also becoming a very good musician in his own right.

Charlie pushed open the door to the Barrel and was greeted by the old familiar smell of ale, wood, and candle wax. It was a smell that, if bottled, you could probably sell to a certain type of individual from Middle Calver for as much coin as you wanted – especially if you called it something as obtuse as 'Authentic Artisan Hostelry Aura'.

The Barrel was full, as it was most nights. Charlie knew a lot of the regulars by now. He'd kept up his regular Sunday evening gig and added a Thursday night into the mix too, but if he was now the reason that many people turned up to the Halfway Barrel every Thursday and Sunday, the regulars of the Barrel certainly didn't show it.

As Charlie made his way towards the bar, the most he got by way of a greeting was a nod of the head or the occasional grunt of acknowledgment.

"Folk who come to the Barrel on the regular are as tight with their praise as they are with their pork scratchings," Arthur once told him. "Trust me, getting a nod from a regular in here is like the King stopping by for afternoon tea. Took most of them a good few years before they'd call me Arthur—most of the time I was either 'lad', or 'young-un' or 'bairn'. It's hard to get carried away with yourself in a place like this."

All of which suited Charlie fine. As he bundled from gig to gig, playing everything from the old classics to background tunes, he found he needed a place like the Barrel and someone like Arthur. He had Auntie's place in the Backstreets and now the Barrel in Lower Calver.

Arthur saw Charlie approach and waved him down to the end of the bar. Charlie managed to squeeze in and plonk himself between two regulars.

"How do, youth," said Reg, not looking up from his pint.

"How's it going, Charlie?" offered Pete, briefly raising his glass by way of a greeting.

'How's it going?' was one of those phrases that, depending on where you were from, could be taken in all manner of ways. Some were genuinely interested in how things were going at that present moment in time and, if you had a minute, they'd be more than happy to have a sit down and a good old natter about those things.

In here, that was not the case.

In the Halfway Barrel, if you chose to answer the greeting of 'how's it going?' with a full and frank assessment of the ins and outs of your day to day occurrences, not only would you be met with a stare with the emotional bearing of a wet brick, but you could also bet your bottom coin that you'd never get greeted in that way ever again.

Instead, Charlie answered both Reg and Pete in the only

way socially acceptable in the Barrel.

"Reg," nod.

"Pete," nod.

With that done, he turned to Arthur.

"Alright there, Charlie," Arthur said. "Give me a minute and I'll pop out and join you. Just got to change a barrel."

"Tell you what, old pal of mine, I'll come down and give you a hand," offered Charlie, rising from his stool.

"Two dashing young chaps, heading off to change a barrel together," said Reg, still with his eyes fixed on his pint, but one brow raising.

"Aye," Pete said, joining in. "People will talk."

"They'll be wondering what you get up to down there, in amongst all the ales and whatnot."

"You're just jealous," Charlie said.

"Too bloody right I am," Reg admitted. "This old sod's about as much fun these days as a soggy fish supper."

"Words like that cut to my very soul, Reginald," Pete said whilst shaking his head.

Charlie made his way down; candle in hand, though he needn't have bothered. Arthur had lit all the candles set into the wall and, as such, the beer cellar was bathed in a soft, flickering orange glow. Arthur and Charlie often came down here for a chat, to play a game of cards, or, as had become the case increasingly often, to practice.

Arthur liked to accompany Charlie on his bodhran and Charlie had to admit, he was starting to get pretty decent. What Charlie liked most about Arthur's playing—and he had no way of making this sound any less pretentious—was that Arthur knew how to keep to the background. He was a generous player who allowed Charlie to do his thing, all the while providing a steady constant beat, keeping everything just where it should be.

On a number of occasions, Charlie asked Arthur to play at gigs alongside him, but Arthur always refused.

"Good grief, no," he'd exclaim. "I'm nowhere near good enough. And besides, my dad needs me here. I'm up to my eyeballs pretty much every night."

This didn't stop him from taking time to play down here with Charlie. In fact, by the time Charlie made it down the rickety wooden steps and over towards where Arthur stood by the old blocked off exit to goodness knew where, Arthur had his drum at the ready.

"If Reg and Pete knew you were stood in a dark corner with your instrument out waiting for me, they'd have a field day," Charlie said.

"Sod off, Lightfoot," said Arthur, "you're not my type. Fancy a crack at Corn Circles tonight?"

"Reckon you're up to it?" Charlie asked. "Only it's quite late and I'm sure you're tired, so I'd understand if you struggle to keep up with me."

"Is that so?" said Arthur, taking up his tipper. "Might be I can outstrip you on this one. Everyone knows Corn Circles is for an earthier style of player; not one for those more accustomed to the tastes of Middle Calver. Could be all the fancy twiddling you do for those fancy folks may have dulled your edges."

"Why don't we find out then?" said Charlie, unwrapping his fiddle and placing it under his chin. "Try to keep up."

The two of them launched into a rousing rendition of

Corn Circles, each one pushing the other to play just that little bit better, just that little bit crisper. When they came to the end, both flopped down on to a couple of barrels, sweat dripping.

"That's the best we've played that, without a doubt," Arthur panted.

"That's the best *anyone's* played that," Charlie laughed.

"I actually lost myself for a moment there," said Arthur, sitting up. "Man, that felt good."

"Blind Watchem calls it 'riding the lightning'." Charlie stared up at the ceiling of the cellar, taking in the moment. "It's a feeling like no other,"

"Amen to that," Arthur said, wiping his forehead on one of the many dishcloths, rags and general bits of material he always seemed to have somewhere about his person. He began to wrap his bodhran.

"Listen, Arthur…" Charlie began as he bent down to pack away his fiddle.

"The answer's going to be 'no'," Arthur said curtly.

"You don't even know what the question was going to be! I could be asking if you'll look after me as I've discovered I've contracted a rare and incurable disease."

"Being an arse isn't all that rare," said Arthur, "and it's nothing a good slap wouldn't cure."

"Seriously, what if I told you I was going to die?"

"I'd say your hair looks fine the colour it is."

"Har-bloody-har," Charlie said, fetching his coat from one of the barrels.

Arthur put a hand on his hip, "Look, we both know you were going to ask me to play with you again."

"I absolutely was not!" said Charlie, feigning astonishment. "The very cheek of it. You've made your position very clear. Under no circumstances would you ever consider playing in public with me. This is naturally on account of the fact I am considerably better looking than you and people may think I'm being inhumane forcing someone with a bum for a face out in public.

Arthur frowned, but a smile tweaked his lips.

"You don't want to do it and that's the end of it," said Charlie, raising his palms.

"Yet…" added Arthur.

"Yet…?" Charlie said.

"Oh, go on and say it. I can see you're desperate to ask."

Charlie was. He was nearly bursting. "Arthur, I really think you should play with me," he said.

"Mate… that's disgusting."

Charlie thumped him gently on the arm. "Get your mind out the gutter. Just one gig. You'd love it, I promise. Imagine it: me and you playing Corn Circles to a packed house. We'd tear the place down, man."

"You finished?"

"I… also think you've got beautiful eyes," Charlie added.

Arthur sighed and shook his head. "I've told you before, I can't. I'm here at the Barrel most nights and, even if I could, well, I'm not sure I could do it. Stand up and play in front of other people? No thanks."

"You play in front of me."

"You don't count," Arthur said. "So, please, just drop it."

"If you say so, but you don't know what you're missing."

"I'll just have to take your word for it. But for now, if you don't mind, please stop asking me. I don't want you questioning me anymore."

"Shame," said the landlord, as he made his way down the first few steps from upstairs, "because I've got a really good question for the both of you. Namely, why is there a posh blond girl sticking out like a sore thumb upstairs in my pub asking for her fiancé, and I quote, 'the musician Charlie Lightfoot'?"

CHAPTER 11

A friendship you can feel in your waters.

IT WAS PAST closing time and everyone had left the Halfway Barrell.

Except, that wasn't strictly true.

It was empty of its usual clientele; the people who, for the most part, lived normal, uneventful lives, and for whom a nice quiet pint at the Halfway Barrel was a perfect way to spend an evening. How Charlie envied those normal people because what it wasn't empty of was a musician, his friend and, as far as Charlie could see, a completely lunatic girl from Middle Calver who appeared to have not only lost her marbles, but to have flicked each one individually off a cliff.

"Let me get this perfectly straight," Charlie said, rubbing his eyes. "You, Millicent Hargreaves—heir to one of the wealthiest dynasties in the Kingdom—have left the warmth, safety and all-round cushy existence you have up there in Middle Calver, and travelled under the cover of night down to Lower Calver and the Halfway Barrel, because you are madly in love with me."

"That is correct," Millicent said, adjusting herself on her stool. "How in the god's names are you supposed to get comfy on one of these?"

"Ah, well," Arthur said, "it does take a bit of practice. Once you've been on one long enough though, it becomes a perfect fit for your ar- sorry. Meant to say derry-air. Begging your pardon, ma'am."

Arthur gave a little nod of the head.

"She's from Middle Calver, not the palace, you daft pillock," Charlie said.

"Sorry, Lady Hargreaves," offered Arthur. "I'm not used to posh girls... I mean proper birds... I mean..."

Arthur let his words trail off, possibly in the hope they'd strangle one another.

Millicent smiled at Arthur and patted him on the hand.

"Well, I appreciate the effort, dear, I really do. And you can call me Millicent, that's quite alright you know."

"Certainly. Would be my pleasure... Millicent," Arthur blushed and his gaze fell to his feet.

"Have you two finished?" Charlie asked, standing.

"Sorry, my love, I was just trying to put your friend at ease. Say, do you think he'll be your best man when we wed?"

"Ooh, I've never been a best man!" Arthur said excitedly, "Or a best anything for that matter..."

"From what I hear, there's nothing much to it," Millicent said. "You just have to take the groom-to-be out the night before, make sure he drinks his bodyweight in cheap ale, tie him to a lamppost, and that's pretty much it, I think."

"I've heard some folk hire those ladies who take their britches off and do a funny dance..." Arthur looked first left and then right, "...in the nuddy and everything."

"Good grief! How very bohemian!" Millicent said, waving away mock embarrassment whilst giving Arthur a playful shove.

Charlie cleared his throat loudly.

"Oh, he's such a grump, this one!" Millicent said.

"He can get a bit that way," Arthur replied.

"No, I bloody don't!" said Charlie. "Not normally anyway. But there are certain occasions where I may start to feel a little bit peeved. This, I very much think, qualifies as one such occasion."

"Whyever's that, my little snookums?" Millicent asked, fluttering her lashes.

"Yeah, whyever is that, her little snookums?" Arthur added with a smirk, leaning forward on the bar.

"Because I am *not* her bleedin' snookums!"

"How about about pooky? Or snugglebear? Or—"

Charlie reached forward and grabbed Arthur by his shirt collars.

"One more word from you and I'll stuff your bodhran so far up your nose, there'll be a drumroll each time you blow it."

Millicent fanned herself with one hand. "Oh, I do love a masculine man. One with passion in his veins!"

"And as for you," Charlie said, whirling round to face her, "I know exactly what you're doing and it's not going to work."

"And what do you suppose it is I'm doing, Mr Charlie Lightfoot?"

"It doesn't take much of a leap to work it out," he began. "Clearly you don't want to marry Roderick von Prickface and that's your business. Why you can't just tell the angular turd yourself is beyond me, but one thing's for sure, you aren't about to drag me into your mess. Things have just started to go well for Mr. Charlie Lightfoot, and the last thing I need is some screwed up toff playing games with my life for fun. How about you take your little rich girl problems and take a hike!"

Millicent looked like she was about to say something. She opened her mouth for a second, and then snapped it shut. Instead, she gathered her coat from the stool next to her, turned to Arthur and said, "Arthur it has been lovely to meet you. Thank you for your hospitality."

Then she turned, slapped Charlie hard across his face, and strode out of the Halfway Barrel.

After a moment, Arthur spoke.

"Angular turd. That'd make your eyes water."

IT DIDN'T TAKE Arthur long to convince Charlie they ought to at least try to find Millicent. To be honest, Charlie felt pretty bad about some of the things he's said—not all of them, but some of them for sure. He wasn't entirely sure why he'd gotten so angry in the Halfway Barrel; he knew full well what Millicent was doing, could see it as clear as day, and yet he'd still taken the bait. And boy had he bitten hard.

He had a feeling his reaction was mostly to do with her sense of entitlement—that she felt she could waltz right on in, announce herself as Charlie's fiancé, and completely mess with his life. Nevertheless, Arthur and Charlie headed out onto the King's Pass, in the hopes of tracking her down and offering an apology.

The sky was clear and the moon full, fully illuminating

the streets when combined with the burning lamplight, and they soon found her, sitting on one of the many benches lining the King's Pass that were set forward from the now shuttered shops and inns.

Arthur nudged Charlie forwards, and he walked over as nonchalantly as he could.

"Evening," he said.

"Evening," she replied, without looking up.

"Thought you might've already headed back up through the gates."

"Yes," she said, her eyes still fixed ahead, "well that's where my little rich girl problems are, so I thought I might stay here."

Charlie rubbed the back of his head. "Ah, yes, about that…" he began.

Millicent turned her face to him. She'd been crying.

"Do you know what, Mr. Charlie Lightfoot?" she said. "The sad truth of it all is what you said—it's true. They are little rich girl problems. In the grand scheme of things, my not wanting to marry into even more wealth isn't exactly a burning issue on the minds of the Kingdom, so you're absolutely right."

"Well, I don't know about that…" Charlie said already starting to feel bad.

"No, you were right. And I shouldn't have just turned up at that Halftime Flannel place like that."

"Halfway Barrel," Arthur corrected from a distance. "Sorry, it's just that the Barrel's a bit of an institution round these parts."

"Halfway Barrel," she repeated, "of course. Sorry Arthur.

It was wrong of me to just show up there. Unannounced. Did you know, I followed you there?"

"You did?" said Charlie.

"Yes, I... I just needed to get out of there. And you seemed a decent sort."

"We barely spoke!" Charlie said in disbelief.

"Although it doesn't normally take folk long to work out he isn't so decent," Arthur chimed in again.

Charlie ignored his friend's remark. "So, after you arrived at the Halfway Barrel and announced we were getting married, what was the next part of your brilliant plan?"

"You'll probably laugh when I tell you..." Millicent said. She looked away.

"No," said Charlie, and he took her hand, "I promise I won't. Tell me."

"Well..." she began, "first of all, of course we weren't *actually* going to get married. I just needed my family to think that was the case. Then, I thought I might leave Calver for a while. Maybe head out beyond the gates and travel around a bit. See what's out there."

To his credit, Charlie didn't laugh.

"I didn't mean, you know, to *elope* with you or anything like that," Millicent said quickly. "I just thought that, oh I don't know, if I could get away from this place then Roderick might move on—probably quite quickly—and all of this would somehow be behind me."

Charlie kicked his feet. "I'm just guessing here, but after having met your mother... if you pulled a stunt like that, I'm pretty sure your family would disown you."

"Oh, absolutely," Millicent confirmed. "Remember when

I said you were right about my problems not being the most important thing in the world?"

"I believe he said, 'you needed to take your Middle Calver little rich girl problems and take a hike,'" Arthur corrected.

"Yes, thank you, Arthur," said Charlie through his teeth, "We are all well aware of what I said." He turned back to Millicent. "Sorry, you were saying?"

"Well, you were right about most things, but in being right about them, you missed the point completely. Hence, why I slapped you."

Charlie ran the words over in his head. "I'm not sure that makes sense…"

"It wouldn't. You're a man," Millicent said matter-of-factly.

"Begging your pardon?" Charlie said, even more confused. Millicent turned to face him and stared into his eyes.

"I'll try to put it in a way you'll understand. Imagine what it's like, Charlie, to practise and practise, beyond the point of sprains and bleeding fingers—right past the point where your hands are almost permanently numb. Now, try imagining someone telling you that you can't go out and play—not anywhere, not ever. No matter how hard you've practised, no matter how much you've worked or how much your fingers have bled. Can you imagine that, Charlie?"

"I can't," Charlie said.

"Imagine having hopes and dreams that will never be achieved. A life never realised. Imagine reaching your teens and, in a wave of growing dread, discovering that you will end up nothing more than a baby making machine for a man who thinks women should look pretty and keep a nice house.

Charlie kept quiet this time.

"Maybe now you'll understand just a little bit better why, at this moment in time, I don't particularly care if I lose everything," she continued. "Maybe you'll see why I ran away from my Middle Calver little rich girl problems without a forethought. Why for just a moment, I wanted to forget about being Millicent Hargreaves—daughter to Lady Gwendolyn, fiancé to Roderick von Haugen, and heir to a vast fortune."

"Blimey. You weren't kidding when you called her a toff!" Arthur exclaimed.

"Once again, thank you very much, Mr. Memory," Charlie said. He looked at Millicent, shook his head, and laughed.

"You know, for someone who probably received a pretty spenny education, following a musician from the Backstreets—one who you'd only just met—to a pub whose name you can't even pronounce, and then pretending you're engaged to him is just about the daftest plan you could've come up with."

"Well," she began, a little flustered, "I'll admit it may have been a tad on the rushed side of things, but I disagree. A much dafter plan would've been to pretend I was actually in love with you. I mean, come on—have you seen yourself?"

"Ooh," said Arthur, sucking back a breath, "the lady from north of the wall scores with an absolute zinger!" He slapped Charlie on the back. "To be fair, old pal of mine, you did deserve that."

Charlie stood and opened his arms wide. "What's wrong with the way I look?"

"How long have you got?" said Millicent.

Charlie bowed low, but threw her a wink. "Harsh words, m'lady,"

"Call me m'lady again and I'll slap the other cheek."

Arthur slapped his hands together and stepped between them, "Right then. That's us all friends again," he said. "Don't like it when people fall out. Affects my waters something rotten."

"I've smelt your waters, Arthur," Charlie said. "They're already rotten."

Millicent stood up and regarded the two friends. "How in the god's names did I end up with the two of you? If my mother could see me now she'd—"

"Millicent!" came the shout from Lady Gwendolyn as she marched towards them down the King's Pass.

CHAPTER 12

The things sea air does to your bits.

"O OER!" SAID ARTHUR summing up the mood quite nicely. He moved behind Charlie.

"Oh, yes, I might have known!" Lady Gwendolyn said as she approached. Behind her, and struggling to keep up, were two members of the King's Guards. When she reached Charlie, she gave him a look which could not only curdle milk but cause it to grow legs and then use those legs to run for cover. "Of course you'd be involved. Roderick warned me about you after the party. 'Far too familiar,' he said. I see exactly what he means. Let me tell you something, you little—"

"Mother!" Millicent said, astonished, but Lady Gwendolyn carried on.

"I knew you were bloody trouble the first time I clapped eyes on you. Walking about with that cocky little swagger of yours—my god's, what's wrong with you people?"

"Mother!" Millicent repeated, and again, Lady Gwendolyn ignored her.

"Well, let me tell you something, Charlie whatever-your-name-is—you'll never play in Middle Calver again! I'll see to that all right! And that's just for starters!"

"Moth—"

"Pipe down, Millie," said Lady Gwendolyn, finally acknowledging her daughter. "Can't you see I'm trying to sort out this god's-forsaken mess you've gotten yourself into?"

Charlie nodded to the two guards. "All right Dave, all right Frank," he said.

They were huffing, red-faced, and adjusted their uniforms as they approached, having finally caught up to their charge. Clearly, they hadn't seen much action in a while. Normally, a night shift in service of the Kings Guard involved steering the odd sozzled, wealthy Middler back through the gatehouse, and then pointing them in the approximate direction of their home. It generally did not involve chasing down the King's Pass after one incredibly irate aristocrat.

"Ah, yes, you two," Lady Gwendolyn said to them. "Arrest this... person."

"Arrest me??" Charlie said incredulously.

"Arrest him?!" said Dave, equally perplexed. Normally, Dave liked the night shift; not much ever happened and, besides, it was better than being at home. Ever since his wife had visited that doctor to get something for her sleeping problems, she'd been snoring like a drunkard.

"Oh, for heaven's sake! Are we in a cave?" said Lady Gwendolyn. "It would certainly account for the moronic echo. I'll try to put it as simply as I can—you two with the pointy weapons and armour, arrest the scruffy looking one stood next to my daughter." She flicked her gaze to Arthur, looking him up and down with distain. "Probably the other scruffy looking one too, just for good measure."

"I'll have you know, this is my good shirt," Arthur said defensively.

"Erm, begging your pardon, m'lady," said Dave, "but on what grounds are you requesting that we arrest said scruffy gentlemen?"

She scowled. "On the grounds that he's coerced my daughter into to abandoning the realm of good sense and reason, and in doing so, has kidnapped her."

"Mother, that's ridiculous," said Millicent. "I came here of my own free will."

"Did you though?" Lady Gwendolyn said, now turning on her daughter. "I mean, you may think you did but, let's face it, you've never been one for good judgement, have you? I seem to be forever bailing you out of one bad decision or another. What is it you don't understand about the way things need to be done?"

"Erm, once again, begging your pardon," said Dave, "but I don't think we can arrest someone for kidnapping if the kidnapee is, in fact, refusing to acknowledge they have, per say, been kidnapped…"

"I don't think that's… quite right." said Frank. Frank also liked the night shift. Unlike Dave, he liked the night shift because it gave him the chance to rough up a few drunks and generally vent some pent-up aggression.

"What's not 'quite right'?" asked Dave.

"I'm not quite sure what you call someone who's been kidnapped, but I'm pretty sure it's not 'kidnapee'. That sounds like something you'd put on a baby's bum."

Dave considered this. "Reckon you might have a point there Frank," he said.

"I think they're called 'a hostage'," Arthur said, leaning in.

"For goodness sake, can everybody please shut up!" Lady Gwendolyn shouted, her words hitting the group with full force.

The street was silent.

"Right," she continued, pointing viciously at the guards. "I'm going to say this very slowly and very clearly so that the two of you can understand me. I happen to be very good friends with the Sergeant at Arms for Middle Calver. He plays seventeen card brag with my husband once a week and owes him a fair few coin as a result. One word from me and he will make sure you two spend the rest of your miserable careers on the south side of the hill. So, I'll tell you one final time – arrest these two. Now!"

Dave and Frank looked at Charlie, then each other, then shrugged.

"Sorry about this Charlie," said Dave, "but I don't think we've got much of a choice. Frank's gammy knee wouldn't survive one winter on the south side, and my gout's already giving me such bother I can barely get out of bed in the morning."

"Mother, this is ridiculous!" Millicent said, stepping forward. "None of this is Charlie's fault. *I* came down here. *I* got him involved. He had no part in what I was doing. You can't have him arrested. And, as for Arthur, he's never even met me before!"

"That's as may be, Millicent," said Lady Gwendolyn, "but if you're foolish enough to come down here in the dead of night for whatever frivolous reason popped into that silly head of yours, it stands to reason that if I remove the purpose for your being here, you'll have no inclination to make such a mistake again, will you?"

Frank stepped forward, taking Charlie by the arm. "Come on lads," he said. "Let's be having you. Tell you what, we'll make sure the cuffs aren't on too tight and Dave here will take charge of your bag of coin, Charlie. Make sure you get it back in the morning. Can't say fairer than that."

"Charlie, are we really going to jail?" Arthur asked, as Dave moved forward, taking the shackles from his belt.

"I think we are," Charlie said. "Don't worry, we'll be out by morning."

"I wouldn't bet on that," Lady Gwendolyn said. She grabbed Millicent by the arm. "Come on Millie, let's get you home."

She shook herself free. "I am not going anywhere with you!" Millicent said, recoiling from her mother's grasp as if burnt.

"Is that so? And just where do you hope to stay for the night? Have you even thought that far ahead? Of course you haven't!" Lady Gwendolyn shook her head and sneered. "You know something, Millicent—you are becoming an ever-increasing burden on this family. When will you stop resisting and just do as you're supposed?"

"How about the first of never!" Millicent shouted as she stepped away from Lady Gwendolyn and towards Charlie and Arthur.

"Millicent," Charlie said, as Frank brought his wrists behind his back. "Listen to me. You should go back with your mother."

"Ah, the simpleton musician actually possesses a grain of common sense!" Lady Gwendolyn said, still sneering.

"Oh put a sock in it, you old hag!" said Arthur.

Charlie and Millicent turned to face him.

"Well, I mean. She does go on a bit, doesn't she? Sorry Lady Gwendolyn—your ladyness—but I think you've said enough horrible things for one night. Just pipe down and give us a minute. Thank you, begging your pardon."

Lady Gwendolyn looked as if about to speak but instead plumped for a shake of her head and folded her arms.

"Millicent, you should—" Charlie began.

"Yes, but—"

"Don't worry about us, we'll be fine. However, if we're in jail, it reduces the people you know in Lower Calver to nil. You can't spend the night down here—you have nowhere to go and, if you're not careful, you'll end up somewhere you shouldn't, and that might be the last anyone saw of you. Tomorrow's another day. Just go home."

Millicent sighed. "You're right, of course," she said. "But I don't think I can bring myself to walk back with mother as if I'm some hound who's gone astray; leading me home, tail between my legs. To be perfectly honest, I don't think I can even look at her right now."

"Then let her follow you. You've probably inherited a decent serving of the ability to stride off. Give her a taste of her own medicine."

"I really am very sorry about all this…" said Millicent.

"I know. And trust me, we'll be fine. To a couple of lads like me and Arthur; a night in the cells is no sweat. Trust me."

Millicent nodded her head and then, without another word, turned on her heel, pushed past her mother and headed up the King's Pass.

"Looks like she's finally seen some sense, no thanks to you!" Lady Gwendolyn said.

Hands now cuffed securely, Charlie took a step out of Dave's grip and closer to Lady Gwendolyn. "Pardon me, Lady Gwendolyn," he said, "but you might be the most overbearing, stuck up, nasty piece of work I've ever met."

Lady Gwendolyn's jaw fell suddenly, but she caught it fast, snapping it closed. Her eyes beaded and looked Charlie dead in his, before slapping him hard across the same cheek Millicent had, and setting off after her daughter.

"Yeah, and you've got more wrinkles than a sailor's nutsack!" Arthur shouted after her.

Dave and Frank both stifled a laugh as they led the two of them away.

"You do have your moments, old pal of mine," said Charlie, shaking his head. "A sailor's nutsack?"

"Ever seen one? All wizened and the like. Must be from all the salt."

Charlie raised an eyebrow. "Frank, can me and him have separate cells please?" he said.

CHAPTER 13

A bit of hob-nobbing and ninnying.

WHEN CHARLIE TOLD Millicent that a night in jail would be no sweat, he wasn't exactly telling the truth. It wasn't a lie; more a statement made from a position just around the corner from the truth. The truth was that although he was pretty sure a night in the cells would be no sweat, having never spent a night in the cells before, he couldn't say for certain.

Frank and Dave led them up towards the gatehouse but, upon reaching the wall, they turned left towards an alley. Partway down was a building with a single door. It was embedded in the stone of the wall, and through the door were ten rooms, each set into the wall itself. Each of the rooms had a single door, and these were wooden and very, very thick.

"Right then chaps," said Dave, leading Charlie and Arthur to a cell. "Welcome to your hotel for the evening. What we have here is your typical first-class level of accommodation. I won't run you through all the features; it'll take me too long. But the main amenities are the door—which is used to go in and out of—the pallet—which is used to sleep on—and the pot in the corner—which is, well let's just say it's not the mini bar!"

He laughed heartily.

"Does this every bloody time, he does," said Frank. "Thinks it's hilarious. You know how many times I've heard this bloody spiel?"

"Well, I quite liked it," Arthur said. "Very funny Dave."

Dave smacked his colleague gently on the arm. "See, now there's someone who appreciates a drop of humour. You've got to try and brighten an otherwise dreary situation."

Charlie took a seat on the pallet. Frank stepped forward.

"Look, Charlie lad. I'm sorry about all this. But if that Lady Gwendolyn got onto the Sarge about us, then… well, you know."

"Frank, it's fine," said Charlie, "Really. I know it's not your fault. And it could've been a lot worse."

"Yeah, good job her Ladyship doesn't know the difference between the drunk tank and proper jail. You can spend the night here and then be on your merry way. We've done our bit, and you haven't had to spend any time in the real lockup."

"Right then, you two," Dave said, unshackling the two of them. "Enjoy the complimentary mints and feel free to take your bathing robes home with you as a token of our appreciation for choosing to stay with us."

"Dave, you really are a numpty sometimes," Frank said, shutting the wooden door and locking it.

"Night-night, lads!" Dave shouted as the two guards made their way back out onto the streets, closing the huge main door behind them.

Charlie took a moment to take in his surroundings. It

didn't take him long.

"Just think," Arthur said, joining him on the pallet in the corner. "Only a few hours ago, you were hob-nobbing with the posh folk up in Middle Calver. And now…" He let his words trail off as he spread his arms to encompass their surroundings.

"I'm not quite sure if that was an attempt to make me feel better, worse or want to slap you," Charlie said. "Whatever it was, it worked."

He sighed and shifted on the hardwood. "Call me cynical but I can't help think we've been stitched up old pal of mine."

Arthur looked around. "Whatever could you mean?" he said.

"Funny how the world works, isn't it?"

Arthur lay back, adjusting himself on the slats of the pallet until he was only moderately uncomfortable and laced his fingers behind his head.

"I know I'm not much in the grand scheme of things," Arthur said, "you, know a Landlord's son and all that, but you do pick up on a few things tending bar."

Charlie lay back next to his friend. He too laced his fingers behind his head. It seemed as if the moment called for it. They both stared up at the ceiling.

"I feel you're about to get all philosophical on me," Charlie said.

"Don't know about that but I do like a good think every now and again. Dad calls me a dolly day-dreamer but, well, sometimes you've got to have a moment to let things settle."

"Like a proper pint?" Charlie said.

"Like a proper pint," Arthur agreed.

For a while neither friend spoke. Charlie watched as a spider moved around its web checking each strand, busying itself in preparation.

Arthur propped himself up on his elbow and turned to face Charlie.

"Don't you think it's a bit funny how the world works?" he said.

Charlie sat up, plucked a piece of straw from the floor around the pallet and tried not to think about why there would need to be straw on the floor around a pallet.

"Where's this going, Arthur?"

"Probably gets thrown out with all the other bits of straw in the morning…"

Charlie shot his friend a tired glance. "I'm not talking about the straw, daft lad, and you know it."

Now, it was Arthur's turn to sit up.

"I guess I'm just feeling… a bit out of place. I've never spent a night in the drunk tank before. Chucked plenty out who probably ended up here, but now the shoe's on the other foot, it's got me thinking."

"About what?" Charlie asked.

"Well…" he began, "and it's probably me being a bit of a ninny…"

"You can be a bit of a ninny."

"That I can—I am well known for my ninnying. I don't know, it's just seems like even when you get your head down, and you graft, and you try to always do the right thing—"

"You still end up in the drunk tank, sitting on a wooden pallet covered in straw that smells like wee?" Charlie suggested.

Arthur laughed. "Yeah, something like that. You've worked hard to get where you are in life and, in my own way, so have I. It's nights like this that remind you that, when it comes to it, none of that matters much."

"Crikey, you are on a bit of a downer," Charlie said. Arthur shrugged.

"I suppose. Ignore me. It'll wear off by the morning, which is more than can be said for the smell of this straw…"

Charlie stood up and walked over to the wooden door. Through the three bars set into it, he could see the brickwork of the wall opposite, but nothing more.

"I know what you mean," he said, still facing away from Arthur. "And you're right. It's like you said—up until a short while ago I was up in Middle Calver hobnobbing with the good and the great. Except, I'm not so sure how good they are, and I'm pretty certain most of them aren't that great." He kicked at the roughshod ground. "I couldn't shake a feeling I had on the way back from the gig earlier, but I think you've hit the nail on the head. No matter what I do, no matter how hard I practice or how good I get, I'll always just be the lad from the Backstreets of Lower Calver. I'll never be one of them… not that I'd ever want to be."

The bricks outside their cell held no secret meaning, but Charlie struggled to tear his gaze away. "What got me was how quickly things can change, you know?" he continued. "That Lady Gwendolyn; she came down into Lower Calver for all of five minutes and here we are"—he opened his arms once more—"spending the night in the drunk tank because… well, I'm not quite sure of the 'because' behind this whole situation."

Arthur got up and walked over to Charlie. They both stood there for a moment, staring out into nothing, lost in their thoughts. The moment was broken by the sound of an enormous belch from the adjacent cell, followed by an apologetic voice.

"Oh, I do beg your pardon!" it said. "How terribly rude! Although 'better out than in,' as the bishop would never say to the actress."

Charlie tilted his head. Didn't he know that voice?

"Drunk Morgan?" he said.

"Oh hello, Vera," came the reply, "is that you calling from the other side?"

"No, you sozzled old git," said Charlie, "it's me—Charlie Lightfoot. I'm in the next cell down."

"Good gravy!" said Drunk Morgan. "What the devil are you doing in this neighbourhood? Admittedly, the rent's exceptionally cheap, but the furnishings are far from luxurious," He moved towards the bars in the door of his cell; Charlie and Arthur knew this from the eyewatering stench of alcohol that tripped over itself as it wafted on its way to theirs.

"It's a long story," Arthur said.

"Blimey, have you got a roommate there, young Master Lightfoot? My cell only came with a piss-stained pallet."

"I'm in here with Arthur," Charlie replied. "The landlord's son from the Halfway Barrel."

"Very wise," Drunk Morgan said in a stage whisper. "Very wise indeed. Getting in with a publican's offspring. Free drinks all round!"

Charlie laughed. "We're not actually drunk."

"Neither am I, my boy!" Drunk Morgan said, followed by

a loud hiccup. "Actually, don't tell anyone, but I may be a wee bit tipsy."

"Really? I never would've known," Arthur said.

"Ah, a gentleman of tact and the ability to lie with a straight face. I like you, Arthur of the Halfway Barrel."

"How come you're spending the night in here?" Charlie asked.

Drunk Morgan, somewhat surprisingly, spent very little time in the drunk tank. Most people who lived on or around the Backstreets knew him and as such accepted him as part of the surroundings. Besides, Drunk Morgan was about as harmful as a wet feather.

"Funny you should ask," he said. "I'd been having a jolly good go at ensuring the blood in my veins was at least twenty percent proof on account of the weather taking a turn for the worse. A bit of warmth from the inside out seemed wise given I'd probably end up sleeping under the stars as is my want of an evening."

He cleared his throat and gobbed something onto the floor that both Charlie and Arthur were glad they couldn't see. "Everything was proceeding nicely right up until the point I settled down, when I realised I simply hadn't consumed enough of the god's liquor. I was freezing my giblets off. So, I made my way out onto the King's Pass, waited until I saw a couple of guardies on patrol, dropped my pantaloons and piddled up against the nearest shop I could find. They tend not to like that sort of behaviour and so, here we are!"

There came a sudden thud from the adjacent cell, followed by a curse, followed by another thud and yet another curse.

"Are… you all right?" Charlie asked in response.

"Never better," came the slurred response. "Just had a moment when something which I thought was there wasn't… namely, the floor. It's appeared to have swapped places with the ceiling."

"Are you hurt?" Arthur said, flashing Charlie a wince.

"Good gods no!" said Drunk Morgan confidently. "I'm a combination of pure grain alcohol, grime, and… whatever this stuff is I'm now lying in. Takes more than someone playing silly buggers with gravity to stop me." He cleared his throat again. "Anyway, enough of this piffle. Why are *you two* in here?"

Charlie sighed. "It's a long story," he repeated.

"Ah yes well, the best ones are," said Drunk Morgan, sounding almost philosophical. "It's just a case of leaving out the boring bits so things move on at a decent pace. Why don't you have a bash at that? Should help pass the time."

So, Charlie told Drunk Morgan. About the gig up in Middle Calver, about Lady Gwendolyn and Millicent, and how both he and Arthur had ended up in shackles. He tried to keep it brief, well aware he was talking to someone who, at any given point, could either fall asleep or over. Or possibly both.

"So, there you have it," he concluded. "I'm pretty sure Dave and Frank will come by first thing in the morning before they finish their shift and let us out. They're a good sort. And they were only doing their job."

For a while there was no sound from Drunk Morgan's cell aside from the heavy breathing of someone who's lost the use of their nostrils. Charlie was about to give it up and go and sit back down on the pallet, when their neighbour finally spoke up.

"What a fascinating tale!" he said. "Full of twists and turns. The daring deeds of the boy from the Backstreets heading up into the land of the toffs, looking to make his fortune, only to be swatted down by the evil Queen."

"Actually, she's a Lady," Arthur corrected.

"Of course she is, but in title only," said Morgan. "And it was only a metaphor. Or a simile... Or maybe just a symbolic representation of the dominant class establishing a semi-resonating semblance of subservience. Or not..."

Arthur looked at Charlie. Charlie shrugged and gave his friend a look which said something along the lines of, 'it's Drunk Morgan, what did you expect'.

"Apologies," offered Morgan, "you do have to remember that most of what I say comes filtered through many years of being thoroughly sozzled. Whichever way, you've both had quite a night of it, haven't you? Might I suggested we all try and get a few hours of shut eye? I often find that many of life's problems can be put into perspective with the rising of the morning sun. And if they're not, well at least you're not tired when dealing with them the next day."

Following this surprisingly sound advice, there was a thud, and then the gentle snoring of a man who, thanks to years of practice, could fall asleep just about anywhere.

"Suppose he's right," said Arthur as he made his way back over to the pallet. "By morning, if all goes well, we should be out of here and then we can get back to a bit of normality. Forget this all happened."

Charlie joined him. "Yeah, I suppose," he said. Then more cheerfully, "yeah, by this time tomorrow, everything'll be back to normal."

CHAPTER 14

A right-hand man, or, an easy way to become a lefty.

CHARLIE AWOKE TO the sound of the main door grinding open on its rusted hinges. The sound echoed along the corridor and seemed to bounce around the cell before settling somewhere just behind his eyes. He hadn't felt this rough in a morning since Blind Watchem took him to the Ruined Stones all those years ago.

By the sounds Arthur was making, his friend felt much the same. "Oh good grief!" he said as he tried to get up. "Everything seems to hurt."

Charlie attempted to sit but had to resort to flopping off the pallet and onto all fours.

How in the god's name was it possible to feel this bad after not touching a drop of alcohol?

"Morning gents!" Dave shouted through the bars to their cell. "Blimey, you two look as rough as a badger's arse!"

He rattled the key in the lock and swung the door open.

"Ah yes," Frank said strolling in. "What we've got here is the absolute worst of both worlds. A night in the drunk tank, sleeping on a knackered old wooden pallet, but without the numbing benefits of copious amounts of alcohol."

Charlie decided the best way to stand was in stages. Very small stages. His back felt as if he'd been hammered to the spokes of a cartwheel all night long. Arthur made the mistake of trying to get it all over and done in one fell swoop; launching himself bolt upright, only to discover just a little too late that one of his lower limbs was completely bereft of feeling. He ended up doing a strange circular walk, all the while trying to shake the feeling back in to his leg.

"What a sorry sight," Dave said, a huge grin plastered across his face. "If me and Frank stumbled across you acting like this last night, we'd probably have thrown you in here anyway."

"The irony is," said Frank, folding his arms across his chest, "is had you indeed been sozzled last night, you'd have woken up in a much better condition than you are right now."

Charlie managed to get himself upright through a series of clicks, cracks and one slightly worrying clunk.

"If you two gentlemen are finally ready, Frank and I will escort you from the premises. It's still early so you should be able to get away without much trouble," said Dave.

"And if you take my advice," added Frank, "you'll both head straight home and maybe lie low for a while. I certainly wouldn't head back up into Middle Calver anytime soon, young Mr. Lightfoot."

In truth, Charlie had absolutely no intention of passing through the city wall for a very long time, if ever. The cushy well-paid gigs could wait. What he wanted to do right now was head back to Auntie's; see if she could rustle up a spot of breakfast, maybe boil some water so he could have a bath by the fire.

That sounded like absolute heaven.

"Right then," Dave said, stepping out the way of the door. "Here's your bag of coin back, Charlie, as promised. Oh, and on the way out, please leave your keys at reception. If you'd be so kind as to fill out the guest book with a comment about the level of service you've received, that would be dandy."

Frank shook his head as Charlie took his coin, and he Arthur hobbled out past him.

"Arse," he said, as Dave doffed an imaginary cap at the two friends.

Charlie made his way into the corridor, slowing as he reached the door to Drunk Morgan's cell. He peered in to find him curled up in a ball on his pallet, looking comfy and content as if he were tucked up in a king-sized bed.

Charlie shook his head and laughed.

DAVE WAS RIGHT; it was still early enough that the sun had only just begun to glance over the horizon. The buildings which lined the side of the King's Pass cast long shadows across the cobbles as Charlie and Arthur made their way out of the alley by the side of the wall. Both stopped, stretched and yawned.

"That was just about the worst night's sleep I've ever had," Arthur said. "Feels like I've been run over by a barrel cart."

"Not something I'm keen to repeat any time soon, that much is true," Charlie said.

For a while neither of them spoke.

"Suppose I better get back. Reckon my dad'll be worried sick," Arthur said, breaking the silence.

"Yeah, me too. Things to do and all that."

In truth, he didn't know what to do about last night. Or what to feel about it.

"You just watch," said Arthur, as if reading his mind, "this whole thing will probably end up being some funny story we tell our grandchildren by the fire one evening."

"Maybe," Charlie said, but he didn't think so.

"You going to be all right?" Arthur asked.

"Me?" said Charlie, and he threw him a smile, "I'm Charlie Lightfoot. Fiddler of the Backstreets. Musician extraordinaire to the proud patrons of Lower Calver. Course I'll be right. Fall in manure, come up smelling of roses, that's me."

Arthur took a moment to look at his friend.

"Course it is," he said, smiling.

Charlie began to make his way towards the Backstreets. "See you Arthur," he said. "I'll pop round in a bit to collect my fiddle."

"Not if I sell it first," Arthur shouted back as he started in the other direction. "The fiddle once owned by Charlie Lightfoot! Fiddler of the Backstreets. Musician extraordinaire to the proud patrons of Lower Calver. Bet there's many a collector who'd pay good coin for such a rare and valuable item."

"Bog off pub-boy. At least it's worth more than one of

your ale-stained dish cloths."

Charlie laughed and waved a salute using only a couple of fingers.

HE MADE HIS way along Drinkle Street, just as the sun was rising high enough to carry itself above the lowest of the rooftops. The cobbled street became bathed in the morning glow, and the Backstreets slowly came to life as people began their day. Things tended to start early on the Backstreets. Or in some cases, carry on from the night before.

As Charlie reached the end of Drinkle Street and came to Gamble Point, he picked Broken Alley, and made his way towards Grinder's Clearing which was, in theory at least, classed as the centre of the Backstreets.

For now at least.

Calling anything the 'centre of the Backstreets' was like trying to put your finger in the middle of a bowl of jelly—sometimes you hit dead centre, but often it moved and squirted out to the side.

As Charlie made his way further into the heart of the Backstreets, and the people who called it home began their days, he felt something akin to nostalgia creeping up on him.

This was his home.

This is where he belonged.

Not up there, beyond the wall with people like Lady Gwendolyn or Roderick von Haugen, but here—amongst the people who'd taken him in; the people he'd grown up with; the people who were about as close to family as he'd ever get.

So why had he been so desperate to leave?

He told himself it was so he could play more gigs, to get his music out there in the wider world and make a bit of coin along the way, but was that entirely true?

Charlie turned left and emerged into Grinder's Clearing.

As far as anything in the Backstreets could be described as such, it was an open space. Not like the grand spaces up in Middle Calver; more of a place where no one could seem to work out how to get the buildings to meet, given all of the streets which fed into it seemed to do so from different angles. It was an open space simply because no one could quite work out how to fill it.

He stopped for a moment to take in his surroundings. Eight different streets fed into Grinder's Clearing, giving it the impression of a spider with very crooked legs.

In the very centre—and if you asked anyone who'd lived in the Backstreets long enough how it had got there, you'd get a different answer from each—was a tree. At least that was the closest definition for the sorry thing which clung to life in the middle of the intersection. It wasn't a big tree, nor was it a particularly pretty tree, but it was a tree; either that, or a rather large weed which occasionally—and begrudging-ly—sprouted the odd leaf, but, for the most part, remained bereft of anything one might consider living.

And yet it had been there for as long as Charlie could remember. Somehow this tree of sorts had pushed its way up through the cobbles and had established its own place in the world.

The symbolism was not lost on him.

As Grinder's Clearing sprung to life, Charlie grabbed one

of the many wooden crates left strewn around the space, turned it over, brushed it down, and sat and watched. People emerged from the houses clustered around the area, while others made their way through from one of the eight side streets as the day began in earnest.

A group of children, maybe eight or nine of them, tumbled out of one of the houses—a ball of arms and legs—and dashed off in different directions.

After a short while, the first of the traders arrived, pushing a barrow full of apples. He pulled up beside Charlie, took one of the fruits from his barrow, gave it a polish on his overcoat, and tossed it over.

"There you go, chum," he said, "You're looking a bit down. Have an apple. Keeps the doctor away."

Thanks," Charlie said and took a bite. It was crisp and delicious.

Yes, this was where he belonged.

In and amongst his people—hardworking, honest people.

"That'll be two bob," said the trader, holding out his hand.

Charlie paused, his mouth already poised and open for the second bite. "Excuse me?" he said.

"Two bob," the seller repeated. "For the apple."

"What? But you gave it to me," Charlie said.

"Indeed I did. That's how the system works. I give you an apple, you give me two bob."

"But… you *gave* it to me," Charlie repeated, standing up. "I'm not paying for it,"

"Oh, deary me," said the trader shaking his head. "Technically—and I hate to bandy this word around, especially at this time of a day—refusing to pay makes you a bit of a *thief*, doesn't it?"

"A thief?!" Charlie was incredulous. "You threw me the apple. You said 'there you go chum, have an apple'. It's not as if I took it from you when you weren't looking!"

"True, very true," said the trader, "and that is something I cannot dispute. However, whilst I did indeed throw you said apple, I did not ask you to take a bite. That, as far as I'm concerned, is where the thievery comes in."

"Then why did you throw it to me in the first place?"

"Why, to look at the quality of my wares. Kind of like taking a horse for a test ride before you buy it."

"That's not the same thing at all!" said Charlie. "You can't take an apple for a test ride. Or a test chew. Or a test anything! Besides, what in the blue hells am I doing standing in Grinder's Clearing arguing with an apple seller? Here's your sodding apple back and if you want the rest, you'll have to wait a day, but I can assure you it won't be in the same state you gave it to me!"

With that, Charlie tossed the half-eaten apple at the trader and stormed off, picking the side street which would, eventually lead him to Auntie's.

Bloody cheek of it, he thought. Bent as a nine-bob note.

But, he reminded himself, not everyone who called the Backstreets home was as crooked as the apple seller. Okay, there were a few... well, bad apples... but on the whole, when it came to the people, he'd take the Backstreets over Middle Calver any day of the week. Besides, it was hard to stay mad when you, hopefully, had a nice, cooked breakfast and a hot bath to look forward to when you got home.

Charlie turned down Innards Lane, holding his breath for the length of it (street names in the Backstreets tended to be somewhat literal), then took a sharp left through a narrow alley known as Funnel Twitchel.

Funnel Twitchel started off wide enough to fit two people side by side but quickly narrowed to the point where one person would have to turn sideways and hope they hadn't had a big lunch.

Once again, Charlie was preoccupied, so once again he walked into a wall… or very nearly did. He managed to pull himself up short just in time so his nose came to rest mere inches from Mr. Lunk's backside.

"Who's back there?" came Dodge's unmistakable voice, along with a yelp from an unidentified owner.

For a brief moment, instinct almost overcame Charlie. He calculated that by the time Mr. Lunk had managed to turn himself around in such a tight space, he could be long gone, but before his legs could carry out his thoughts, Dodge had squirmed around from in between Mr. Lunk's legs.

"Well, well, well," he said, rubbing his dirty hands together.

Charlie congenially, smiled what he hoped was a friendly, isn't-it-nice-to-see-you smile. "How's things, Dodge?"

"Things are just peachy thank you, Mr. Musician Man." He smiled his ratty grin and winked. "If you'll excuse me a moment, I must wrap up something quite pressing. I'll be right with you."

Dodge tucked back around Mr. Lunk's pillar of a leg. Somebody else was definitely back there, and although

Charlie couldn't make out what was said, once Dodge finished speaking, Mr. Lunk bent over, and there was a crack like a snapping branch, followed by a scream which couldn't have been mistaken for anything other than someone experiencing great pain.

Dodge reappeared a few seconds later, wiping his hands on his trousers.

"Don't you just hate it when their bowels go," he said.

Charlie wasn't entirely sure what Dodge meant but he was fairly sure he didn't want an explanation.

There was a creaking, crunching sound as Mr. Lunk began to turn around, and it took Charlie a moment to realise the noise was the giant's shoulders as they scraped along the buildings in the narrow alley. When Mr. Lunk had completed his grinding about-turn, it was impossible not to notice that he was holding a person's arm. Unfortunately for its owner, the arm was no longer attached to what it should've been, namely the rest of the person.

Charlie stared at the arm and tried very hard not to notice the stringy red bits hanging from the end.

Dodge noticed Charlie looking and smiled. It was the standard not-very-nice Dodge smile, and Charlie had seen it many times. It was the kind of smile a person puts on like a garment rather than one used to express emotion. Charlie knew only too well that when people put on such smiles, they were often used to conceal something; in the same way you might wear a long coat in order to hide the lump hammer tucked into the back of your belt.

Mr. Lunk, after a while of both Charlie and Dodge staring wordlessly at the arm in his fist, also looked down. For a moment, his brow creased as he seemed genuinely surprised to find that he had a limb in his hand. He looked first at Charlie, then Dodge, then down at the arm again, and after a moment of thought, shrugged his massive shoulders and threw the arm back behind him where it hit something with a squishing thud. He wiped his hands down the front of his shirt in two very steady and particular movements, and then stood stock still, letting his gaze rest somewhere beyond Charlie. It was as if someone had challenged him to look as much like a building as possible. So far, he was doing a very good job.

Dodge tilted his head on one side and grinned up at Charlie.

"Now then, Mr. Music Man, what brings you here, to this strangest of meeting places?"

Charlie swallowed and tried not to look at the blood and bits of person on the front of Mr. Lunk's shirt. "Just heading back to Auntie's," he said.

"Is that so?" Dodge said.

Charlie wasn't sure why Dodge had to make everything he said sound so accusatory.

"Yes, Dodge, that is so. I've had a bit of a night of it, to be perfectly honest. I just want to get back to a decent bath and a bit of grub."

"Oh, I bet you've had a bit of a night of it, young Mr. Music Man Lightfoot."

Charlie ignored the 'young' part given he was only a couple of years Dodge's junior.

"I bet," Dodge continued, nudging Mr. Lunk in the kneecap, "that our good business partner here had a right proper night of it, if you know what I mean?"

Mr. Lunk looked down at Dodge.

"I do not," he said in his glacial way.

"You know," Dodge said, nudging Mr. Lunk more rigorously, "he's up there, in that Middle Calver with all them toffs, giving it the lar-dee-dah, all the while laughing at us normal folk down here, trying to make an honest living."

Again, Charlie chose not to react, especially to the 'honest living' part. He knew Dodge, and he knew what he was trying to do. Instead he said, "Actually, I spent the night in the drunk tank after a Lady had me arrested."

Dodge's eyes widened.

"Oh, yes!" he said, hopping from foot to foot, clapping his hands. "Oh, yes, oh yes! I knew you'd get above your station. You always did have that look of your turds not stinking. Do tell, young Master Charles, what did you do? Pocket a bit of silverware? No, I know you... I reckon you tried it on with one of them posh bints, didn't you? Go on, admit it, you got caught with your drawers down!"

Charlie let out a long sigh. He wasn't in the mood for this. Before Dodge found Mr. Lunk, he was only an ever-present annoyance with a chip on his shoulder the size of a boulder. Admittedly, he was still all of those things, but with Mr. Lunk now at his side, you didn't really have a choice but to listen. In the past you could've told him to sod off but now...

"Look, Dodge, it was all just a misunderstanding. Someone got the wrong end of the stick, and that was that. Now, if you'll excuse me..." Charlie made to turn and leave the way he'd come.

"Hang on there, lover-boy," Dodge, putting a hand to Charlie's chest. "I get that you don't want to share with us lowly Backstreet folk what you get up to when you're lording it the other side of the wall and all that—but there's still the matter of our business arrangement."

Charlie turned to him. "You're kidding me, right? After the night I've had, you still want to take my coin?"

"Ah, ah, ah," Dodge said, waving a cautionary finger in Charlie's face. "We're not taking, you're *investing*. Partners, remember?"

Charlie dug into his cloak pocket and pulled out the bag of coin Lady Gwendolyn had given him last night, and which Dave had kept safe for him until morning.

"That'll do nicely!" Dodge said, swiping the bag from Charlie's grip.

"Hang on! That's all I've got. You're not supposed to take the lot, remember?"

Dodge, his head almost stuffed inside the bag as his fingers rummaged through the coin said, "Yes, well, I've got investments I need to make. Besides, from what I hear, you seem to be doing well for yourself. Reckon you can spare it."

"That's not the point!" Charlie said. "I worked bloody hard for that. And we had an agreement!"

Dodge stopped counting the coin, stuffed the bag in his pocket and looked up at Charlie. He grinned his rat-grin, his yellow teeth showing from brown gums.

"We *had* an agreement is correct. Emphasis on the *had*. You see, Charlie Lightfoot, *I* decide what kind of an agreement we had, and now have. You don't." Dodge pointed with his thumb over his shoulder. "If you've got a problem with that, then Mr. Lunk can help you become a permanent lefty, just like our associate back there."

Charlie was so close to saying something, so very close he had to clench his teeth to stop the words from coming out. He wanted to scream and shout at Dodge, to punch and kick him, to direct all of his pent-up fury at the injustice of it all.

Charlie knew it wasn't just the taking of his coin which made him want to lash out. It was everything. All of it. Last night, this morning and everything else.

All at once, everything hit him—the frustration, the anger, the otherness, the not ever quite fitting in. With a sense of dawning realisation, it all fell into place. From an early age, he hadn't felt like he'd belonged anywhere, and yet had convinced himself he belonged everywhere. He'd thought learning the fiddle was his ticket out, but now realised he didn't know where his ticket was supposed to get him out of. Or to.

And it had taken this little rat man to bring him to this point.

Charlie smiled. It wasn't his usual smile, but the kind of smile worn by a man not far away from cracking. He leant back on the nearest building, slowly slid down until he sat with his back up against it. Dodge looked confused.

"Yes, well, we'd better get going," he said, stepping over Charlie, all the while keeping a careful eye on him. "Businesses to run. Coin to invest." He shook what was once Charlie's bag of coin. "Come along, Mr. Lunk."

Dodge strode off out of Funnel Twitchel and onto Innards Lane. Mr. Lunk turned sideways and side-stepped down the twitchel until level with Charlie. He stopped and crouched down until he was roughly Charlie's head height, his giant knees springing forward so that they almost came to rest on Charlie's shoulders.

"Are you okay, music man?" he said in his low, slow way.

Mr. Lunk remained motionless, staring into Charlie's eyes, and for the first time, Charlie could see into Mr. Lunk's. He guessed not many people ever got to look Mr. Lunk in the eye, given Mr. Lunk's eyes were in a different time zone. They were of the brightest blue Charlie had ever seen.

Then Mr. Lunk did something very strange. He reached out and, with a hand bigger than Charlie's head, gently stroked Charlie's cheek. Mr. Lunk's fingers felt rough and coarse on his skin, and Charlie was reminded of the sandpaper he'd once used when staying with a carpenter as a boy.

Mr. Lunk looked Charlie in the eyes, held his gaze and then smiled. It was a smile which took its time to form. Each of Mr. Lunk's features needed to receive the message and then gradually move themselves into a position so that they could line up in a smile. But it was a real smile. It wasn't worn, and it wasn't far from anything other than being a smile.

Mr. Lunk said nothing more. Slowly, very slowly he stood up, accompanied by a series of pops, cracks and clicks which seemed to cannon off the nearby walls, as his enormous joints attempted to erect his frame. As he stood, his face slowly settled back to its normal expressionless state. Then, he strode away.

Charlie remained sat on the street for some time after Mr. Lunk had left. He didn't quite know how he felt, what he was going to do or what was next.

Nor did he think anything could get any stranger than Mr. Lunk caressing his face.

CHAPTER 15

You never really get rid of lice.

WHEN CHARLIE FINALLY made his way back to Auntie's, he walked into the kitchen to find Millicent sat at the table.

Of course she bloody is, was Charlie's first thought. Where else would she be?

This all fitted perfectly given the way things are heading. What better way to put a final exclamation point on the whole confusing state of things than to walk into the one place you felt defined you—the one place where you belonged—and to find of course, that too could be invaded.

Maybe that was a tad too dramatic, he thought.

Maybe—and he felt he could go along with this new vein of thought—shit just happened. Maybe.

He wasn't sure about anything anymore. Either that, or he'd just had a bad night followed by a bad morning and was now very, very tired. Right now, he found that actually, it didn't really matter.

What mattered was that Millicent was sat at Auntie's kitchen table with a mug of steaming tea wrapped in her interlaced fingers, whilst Auntie busied herself drying some pots.

"All right, Millicent?" Charlie asked, leaning his fiddle against the big old armchair before he took off his coat then flopped down into it. "All right, Auntie? Got any breakfast going? I'm starving."

Auntie turned from the old tin tub she used to wash pots in, drying her hands on her apron. Millicent looked at Charlie, then Auntie, and appeared about to say something.

Auntie shook her head and Millicent instead took a sip of her tea.

"Of course, love," Auntie said. "Always got plenty of eggs and I reckon I could rustle up some bacon. I've still got a few rashers left from when Jonny Ringworm popped round. Oh, and I've not long made soda bread so you'll have that warmed through, I'd say?"

"Thanks Auntie, you're a saviour," Charlie said. With his fingers laced on his chest, he closed his eyes and seemed about to drift off.

Once again, Millicent looked at Charlie, then Auntie. Once again, Auntie shook her head.

"Right then," Auntie said, busying herself with the necessary pots and pans, "I best get started. Oh, hang on a minute; Lazy Sue's still got my best pan. Better nip round and borrow it back. Won't be long." With that, Auntie scooped up her house coat from the back of one of the mismatched chairs and bustled out of the house.

"I'm pretty sure Lazy Sue hasn't got your Auntie's pan," Millicent said after a moment of quiet. "She doesn't seem the sort to lend out her kitchenware."

"As far as I know, there isn't anyone round here called Lazy Sue either," said Charlie, eyes still closed.

The room descended back to quiet. After a while, Millicent spoke.

"I suppose you're wondering what I'm doing here," she said.

"Drinking tea, by the looks of it," said Charlie without opening his eyes.

"Well, yes, but I meant the bigger picture. How I got here and why. I can imagine it's a bit strange seeing me here."

Charlie opened his eyes and sat forward.

"So far, in the last twenty-four hours, I've been accused of kidnapping the heir to a fortune, spent the night in the drunk tank, been accused of stealing apples, had all my coin taken from me, and had my face stroked by a giant. Seeing you sat at Auntie's table drinking tea probably edges towards one of the more normal things that's happened to me lately."

"Your face stroked by a giant?" she repeated.

"Yeah. He was surprisingly gentle for someone who had forcibly removed someone's arm only moments before."

"The giant who stroked your face is also a surgeon? I would've thought having such large hands would make one unsuitable for such work."

"He's... not really a surgeon. More of a butcher."

"Oh..." Millicent said, and then frowned. "I still don't understand. I've got a feeling I don't really want to either."

"You really don't," Charlie confirmed standing up from the chair. He walked over to the sink, rolled up his sleeves and started to ladle some water from a barrel into the tin tub.

"I suppose I should explain a few things..." Millicent said.

He'd now half-filled the tub, and Charlie bent over and

began to wash his face. The cold water felt good on his skin. Once done, he groped for the dish cloth—Millicent stood up and handed it to him—and he used it to dry his face and hands. Then, he turned to face her.

"So, Millicent Hargreaves of Middle Calver, why don't you and me have a little chat?"

The two of them sat down at Auntie's table; a table, Charlie thought, where many a meal was eaten, many a problem solved, and many a grievance aired.

Millicent explained how she'd gone back home with her mother; how she'd stormed home as Charlie had suggested, leaving Lady Gwendolyn in her wake. She'd locked herself in her room before her Mother had even made it to the front door. She'd ignored her mother's attempts to talk; instead, she'd plotted. She knew she needed to get away; she couldn't be what everyone expected her to be.

"You know," Millicent said, "Roderick actually makes my skin crawl. I look at him and I can feel the bile rising in my stomach. I shudder when he touches me."

"Yeah, and I heard he's got a small willy," Charlie added.

Millicent snorted. It was a good sound to hear.

"It was after meeting you, and later Arthur, and spending even just a small amount of time outside of Middle Calver; it confirmed everything. The way mother came to fetch me like a naughty school girl staying out past her bedtime, the way I had to be brought back so I could be of service to the family—I just had to get out. I needed to get out. And if not now... then when?"

Charlie took in the scene before him—the potential heiress to one of the biggest fortunes in the Kingdom, sat in

Auntie's kitchen, drinking tea.

"You definitely got out all right."

Millicent laughed. She too seemed to fully take in her surroundings for the first time.

"I suppose I did," she said. "I mean, I think this is pretty much the last place mother, or Roderick, or anyone else would look to find me."

Now it was Charlie's turn to laugh.

"You're safer here than if you were in the Palace itself."

"Yes, I suppose I am. I must admit to being a little scared wandering into the Backstreets alone but once I started asking for you and Auntie, people seemed only too happy to help."

The kitchen fell silent. Millicent sipped her tea to the accompaniment of the drip-drip of the water plopping off the ladle Charlie had used to wash with.

"So…" Charlie said, leaving space to be filled.

"What now?" Millicent replied.

Charlie paused "Well I have got one idea," he said.

Millicent sat up straighter.

"At this point," she said, "I'm all ears."

"I don't know," said Charlie with a wink, "they're not *that* big."

"Oh, do bugger off," Millicent said in response, covering her ears.

"I am beginning to discover there are no depths to your foul language, my lady."

"Tip of the iceberg, Backstreets lad. So, what's your idea?"

Charlie told her. It was an idea he hadn't realised was as

fully-formed as it appeared to be; an idea he'd thought of as nothing more than a fleeting notion, one he'd initially dismissed out of hand.

Only now, after the events of last night and this morning, he realised this particular idea had legs.

Real legs that could carry him beyond the Backstreets, beyond even Middle Calver.

→→→‹‹‹‹

CHARLIE LED MILLICENT through the Backstreets towards the King's Pass. With most of their talking done at Auntie's table, left to soak into the thick wood like so many words before it, they'd spoken little on the way.

At some point during their conversation, Auntie had returned. At first, she'd pretended not to listen, busying herself preparing Charlie's breakfast. As Millicent and Charlie continued, Auntie's preparations got louder and generally more *tuttier*. After one particularly loud clang from a cast iron pot and a cast-iron '*ohforgoodnesssake*' from Auntie, Charlie finally put her out of her misery.

"I wonder, Auntie," he said, winking at Millicent, "if we might ask you to share your thoughts on all this, if you're interested that is."

"Mmm?" Auntie mumbled over her shoulder. "What's that, Charlie?"

"Oh, come on," Charlie said. "You heard every word and I'll bet tuppence to a coin that you've got something to say about it."

Auntie turned from the pan she was stirring over the fire

oven. She dried her hands on her apron even though they didn't seem wet.

"Oh, what it must be like to be young and always right," she said as she sat down at the table. "What you might want to consider is plenty of folk have sat at this very table, with bigger problems and deeper thoughts than yours, young Charles Lightfoot. In short, you aren't the first and you won't be the last... nor are your particular troubles all that unique."

Millicent's face fell to one of awe and wonder. Charlie simply smiled and shook his head.

He was going to miss Auntie.

"Remember, Charlie Lightfoot—I took you in when no one else would. You and that screeching fiddle of yours had over-stayed your welcome at so many places, I reckon I could've got folk to pay *me* to take you in. I'd also like to think I played a part in raising you into the young man you've become."

"You have, Auntie," Charlie said, and he meant it. If anything was tying him to the Backstreets, above all else, it was her.

"That's as maybe," she continued, "but right now senti-mentality holds as much weight as spit in your palm."

"I've never heard that phrase before," Millicent said. "What does it mean?"

"Hold out your hand and I'll show you," said Auntie, clearing her throat.

Millicent took her hands from her mug and sat on them.

"Wise choice, girly," Auntie said.

"So you think I should go?" asked Charlie, a little apprehensive of her reply.

"Of course I blooming do!" said Auntie.

"Actually leave Calver?"

"Indeed," she confirmed.

"Through the gatehouse and out into the Kingdom?"

"Why not?"

"You're not going to miss me?" Charlie said.

She turned to him and took his hands, "Of course I'm going to miss you, you daft berk!"

"Really?" said Charlie.

"Oh, yes," said Auntie, "in the same way once you're rid of lice, you can still feel the darn things crawling around in your drawers, even though you know full-well they're not there anymore.

THEY'D TALKED FOR most of the morning—Charlie, Millicent, and Auntie—only pausing for Auntie to finish getting Charlie's breakfast ready, and for the small amount of time it took him to inhale his food.

If Charlie was surprised to learn Auntie was happy with him heading out beyond the walls of Lower Calver, he soon realised his mistake.

Auntie had always wanted Charlie to head out.

After he'd practised with Blind Watchem long enough so his playing had become passable, it was her who encouraged him to get out onto the streets of the King's Pass. Then she'd pestered him to try his luck in the Inns lining the King's Pass. And when he'd told her of his first gig in Middle Calver, her reply had been as expected:

"About bloody time," she'd said over a pot of freshly peeled potatoes.

It shouldn't have been a surprise when he discovered she thought heading out into the unknown was anything other than a good idea.

>>>><<<<

WHEN CHARLIE STEPPED out onto the King's Pass with Millicent, he half expected everyone to stop what they were doing, turn to face them and point and stare. In fact, nobody did anything of the sort. People bustled past, busy in their day. The occasional cart trundled along the cobbles as it made its way up towards Middle Calver, horses straining against the incline.

If the two of them were worried they might be seized the minute they stepped out of the Backstreets, their fears were quickly and abruptly allayed.

"Mind how you go!" shouted a man as he had to swerve around them. "You want to watch yourselves, standing around gawping in the middle of the street like that. Nearly had me over!"

"Sorry, pal," Charlie said, pulling Millicent back. "She's new to town, doesn't know how it works." The man stopped. He was carrying a sack cloth that looked fit to burst with goodness knows what.

"Bloody foreigners," he said with a shake of his head. "Coming here, staring at our buildings. You lot don't offer anything in return—just take bloody take. Some of us have work to do; you know, help keep the Kingdom ticking over.

Certainly haven't got time to stand around staring at buildings. Though if I did, at least I'd be staring at *my* buildings from *my own* city."

"Yeah, sorry about that," Charlie said aiming to keep things as polite—and therefore as unmemorable—as possible. "Off down the square to do a bit of trading are you, mate?"

The man shifted the weight of the sack on his back.

"Too right. Got a load of meat I nicked from the butcher's back there. You want a pig's leg? Could do you a nice little deal."

"Thanks for the offer, but we need to be off," Charlie said.

"Suit yourself," said the trader, "but you're missing out. Reckon I'll shift this lot before lunch. Beats working for a living,"

He shifted the weight of the stolen meat a final time and made his way down the King's Pass and towards the square.

"Pleasant fellow," Millicent said, wrapping her scarf around her head.

"Takes all sorts," Charlie said.

"How long is this going to take?" she asked, glancing left and right. "Every moment we're stood here it feels like Mother, or Roderick, or some person in armour is going to jump out and shout '*Aha, got you!*'"

"Don't worry," Charlie said. "We've got everything we need"—at this Charlie indicated the sack cloth on his own back—"just not everyone we need."

"If everything you've told me is true, then I really don't think he'll come," said Millicent.

"Probably not. But it's worth a try. Besides, if he's not going to come, the least I can do is say goodbye."

Millicent smiled sweetly. "You see," she said. "You really do have a heart. It's just buried underneath all those layers of grime."

CHAPTER 16

A Journey where you don't stop believing.

"**Y**OU'RE BLOODY MAD!"

They'd spent the last fifteen minutes trying to persuade Arthur to join them, and it wasn't going well.

"Absolutely no chance," he insisted, "and for a number of reasons. For one, just... no! Second, you have absolutely no clue what you're doing. Have you ever even left Calver before? Let me answer that one for you—of course you bloody haven't. And third, how do you think you'll survive? Again, I'll answer that one for you, just to save a bit of time— you think you'll toddle along, twiddle your fiddle, and folk'll shower you with coin. That about the short of it?"

"I'd pay good money to see him twiddle his fiddle," Millicent said.

"Take my word for it; it isn't worth entrance fee" Arthur replied. "Tiny todgers aside, what about you, Millicent? Up until a couple of days ago, had you ever even set foot outside of Middle Calver?"

"Well, not exactly..." Millicent said.

"More like, just exactly," said Arthur, now in full flow. "So—and please beg my pardon Millicent, as I do believe this bonehead has well and truly led you right up the garden path—your answer to this whole situation is to run off into the Kingdom, swanning around and... well actually, I don't know what. I mean, as far as rose-coloured, romantic notions of life go, it's bloody perfect. But unfortunately—and I hate to break this to you—but reality doesn't give two turds about rose-coloured, romantic notions of life!"

"Are you finished?" Charlie said.

"Not in the slightest," Arthur said, wiping a spot on the bar of the Halfway Barrel with undue vigour. "Furthermore," he continued, pointing at Charlie with the dishcloth, "you'll both starve within a month. You don't even know where the closest village is, do you? I mean, that is if you don't get robbed first. Or lost. And then what? What's the long-term plan here, Charlie—spend the rest of your days wandering around the Kingdom until you're too old to do so? I don't suppose you've thought that far ahead, have you? Oh no, mister free and easy musician man, who thinks everything will somehow work out fine..."

"Actually, we have planned things out," said Millicent. "And we do know where the nearest village is; Auntie's even drawn us a little map. You'd be surprised what that woman knows. We're going to head out for just long enough for Roderick to lose interest and move on to some other poor unsuspecting fool. Which, by my estimation, should be less than a month, maybe slightly more... I'm not the only valuable trophy in that particular part of the Kingdom, and he'll be keen to move on quick so as not to lose face."

"Okay, fair enough but what about afterwards? Have you thought that far ahead?"

"We have," Millicent confirmed. "Depending on how

things are going, we may stay out in the Kingdom because—and this is something that terrifies and excites me in equal parts—who knows? All my life everything's been mapped out for me. Well—and pardon my language—bugger that. I think I'd like to be in charge for once. If that means leaving things up to chance, not having an exact plan; well, that's fine and dandy with me. At least that way no one has any say in anything. I quite like the sound of that."

Charlie leant forward on his stool and rested his arms on the now sparkling bar. "And you thought I was hard to argue with," he said with a smile.

Arthur shook his head. "I do take your point, Millicent; I really do. It's just that, oh I don't know—it's just so very unknown. And I'd be worried about you both."

"About us both?" Charlie said.

"Did I say you both?" said Arthur, attempting to backtrack, "I meant that I'd be worried about Millicent…. with only you there to look after her. Yes, that's what I meant."

Charlie smiled and leant over the bar to pat his friend on the shoulder.

"Admit it. You care."

Before Arthur could reply, the door to the Halfway Barrel swung open.

"Crikey it's raining cats, dogs, and even the odd splash of water out there!"

The shrunken figure of Blind Watchem shook himself like a wet dog, sending spray up the walls of the Halfway Barrel; a pool forming at his feet.

"Sorry, sir, we're closed," Arthur said.

"No you're not," Blind Watchem said, approaching the

bar, "I just walked in, didn't I?"

"I meant, we're not open," Arthur said, his smile faltering.

"Same difference. And you can't be 'not open'. That's nonsensical. It's either open or closed. You don't say 'hello there, come in we're not closed' do you?"

"Erm…" was the best Arthur could do.

"Blimey, Charles—is this the chap you're taking with you? Are you sure about that? He seems a bit of a boob to me."

Blind Watchem turned back to face Arthur. Or at least look up at him.

"Purveyor of booze," he said, enunciating each word clearly. "I would like a drink of your cheapest rye. In other words, you pour burny-burny juice in cup so I can neck it."

"Erm…" Arthur stammered again, turning his furrowed brow to Charlie.

"Arthur meet Blind Watchem. He's the one who taught me how to play."

Blind Watchem had already turned his attention to Millicent.

"Might I say, my dear, that even though I may appear somewhat advanced in years and have the general appearance of a shrived prune, everything in me nether regions is in tip-top condition."

"Okay!" Charlie said, steering a winking Blind Watchem away from Millicent who had turned a whiter shade of pale. "That's just about enough from you."

"Wait a minute, what did he say about you taking me with you?" Arthur said, making his way around the bar.

Charlie motioned to one of the tables. "Look, why don't we have a seat and sort all of this out,"

"Yes," said Blind Watchem. "The message I got from Auntie wasn't exactly overflowing with details."

Charlie, Millicent and Blind Watchem sat down. Arthur stubbornly remained at the edge of the bar.

"Come on, daft-lad," said his father as he emerged up from the door to the beer cellar. "Get over there and sit down, and then maybe, just maybe, you'll find the stones to make the decision that everyone but you knows you're going to make."

IT WAS TIME for goodbyes.

Arthur hugged his father tightly, both of them a little wet around the eyes. Charlie hugged Auntie, or least was on the receiving end of a bear hug so tight it made his eyes pop.

Blind Watchem tried to hug Millicent but she managed to keep him at arm's length with a pat on the shoulder followed by a neat pivot.

As the three friends moved away, they readjusted various packs, cloaks and, in Charlie and Arthur's case, musical instruments.

The square was deserted. It wasn't market day and, although the rain had stopped, it seemed to have driven everyone away from the wide open space with nothing more than a few trees scattered around it's edges for cover. All that separated them from the rest of the Kingdom was the immense gatehouse.

"Well then…" said Arthur as he stepped away from his father, and added, "You sure you'll be all right without me?"

Arthur's father smiled. "For the hundredth time, yes. I'll up Gloria's shifts and throw a few more hours Florence's way. They're both good workers, as well you know. It'll be fine."

Arthur nodded and shuffled his feet.

"There's not a whole lot of leaving going on here," commented Blind Watchem. "Hurry up and bugger off would you—I'm getting cold."

Charlie laughed, patted the old musician on the arm, said a final goodbye and turned to leave.

"Remember to have fun!" Auntie shouted after them.

"And look after each other!" Arthur's father said.

"And try not to die within the first day!" added Blind Watchem.

Charlie looked back over his shoulder to see Auntie wallop Blind Watchem with her cloth bag.

"Here we go then…" Charlie said apprehensively as the three of them drew closer to the gatehouse looming high before them.

"Yes. I suppose we do," said Arthur. "Think I'm doing the right thing?"

"Of course," Charlie said, clapping him on the back. "Even your dad said so. It'll do you good to see a bit of the world. To have an adventure. The Halfway Barrel will still be there when you get back."

"Yeah, I suppose," Arthur said, sounding far from convinced. "How are you doing, Millicent? You seem a bit quiet."

"I just keep expecting mother or someone to jump out at me."

"Yeah, actually I do too," Charlie said. He couldn't shake the feeling that Dodge and Mr. Lunk would appear at the last minute and haul him back to the Backstreets. There was no way Dodge would want him leaving Calver; partly for fear of losing out on some coin, and also because he knew Dodge could never understand the idea of heading out beyond the wall.

"No turning back now," Arthur said.

All three took a second to take in the city: the vein of the King's Pass running up the middle; the hodge-podge collection of buildings that was the Backstreets; Lower Calver, in stark contrast to the neat precision of Middle Calver; and the Palace on its own beyond the third and final wall.

"Oi! You three! You coming through or what? I haven't got all bleeding day!" shouted a guard by the entrance to the gatehouse.

"Sorry," said Arthur, "just taking one last look. It's our first time out of Calver, you see."

They made their way through the double-wide archway carved into the wall.

"You don't say?" the guard said. "I never would've guessed."

"We're heading out into the Kingdom, the three of us," Arthur continued. "I'm Arthur, this is Charlie, and this is—"

"Barbara," Charlie said before Arthur could finish.

"Yes, that's right," said Millicent, playing along. "My name is most definitely... Barbara. Because that's a perfect name for me, isn't it?"

"Why yes, it is, *Barbara*," said Charlie, stressing the last word. "Barbara Parpington."

The guard looked from Charlie, to Millicent, then back to Charlie.

"You taking the mick, son?" he asked, gripping his pike.

"Not in the slightest, sir," said Charlie, struggling to hide his smirk. "Barbara Parpington. And he's Arthur Grumblechops."

The guard eyed Arthur suspiciously.

"Barbara Parpington… and Arthur Grumblechops?"

"That's right," Charlie said with a wide smile.

"And who, pray tell, might you be?" asked the guard.

"Charlie Fartknocker," offered Millicent.

Arthur stifled a laugh.

"So, I am supposed to believe the three of you stood before me are one Parpington, Grumblechops and Farknocker. Is that correct?"

The three friends snickered through their teeth and nodded.

"You know something?" the guard said, shaking his head. "I'm getting too old for this."

He waved Charlie, Arthur and Millicent through into the gatehouse. Once they'd made their way through the wooden turnstile and out past the guard on the other side, the three erupted into fits of laughter.

"You're an absolute arse, Lightfoot!" Millicent said swatting him on the arm.

"Alright, steady on Barb!" Charlie said still smiling. "Had to give a name, didn't I? Just in case. I'm guessing once you don't return home they'll come looking for you. No harm in trying to put them off the scent now, is there?"

"Well, yes, but… Barbara? Really?"

"I think it's a lovely name," said Arthur. "I once knew a girl called Barbara and she was a great girl. I mean, she had a false leg and the top part of both her ears were missing, but her heart was in the right place."

Charlie and Millicent stopped and looked at Arthur.

"Actually, I'm not sure it was. She used to do this thing where you could feel her pulse on the sole of her left foot…"

"Not the foot of the false leg?!" Charlie asked.

"Yeah, that's right! Did you know her?"

CHAPTER 17

Precision head-lopping.

I T TOOK MOST of the morning for Charlie, Millicent and Arthur to cross the wide expanse outside the gates known as the Bloodwastes.

The Bloodwastes had seen many battles as tribes from across the Kingdom had fought their way towards Calver, eventually killing enough of each other so those who remained could form what would become the great city the three friends had left behind them. Mercenaries still roamed the land; a throwback to a not-too-distant time.

As Charlie, Millicent, and Arthur came to its edge, the road, which had once been barely wide enough for two carts to pass, opened into a crossroads before them. To both the left and the right, mercenary tents lined the edge of the road running parallel to the Bloodwastes. Those who hadn't settled out in the Kingdom had nowhere else to go, so seemed drawn to the one place which still held some form of identity for them.

Also, it was much easier to hire a mercenary if you knew exactly where to find them.

At the moment, on this damp and dreary morning, the roads to the left and right weren't particularly busy.

"Do you think we need to look at the map yet?" Arthur said for the thirteenth time since they'd emerged from the gatehouse.

"No, I don't think so," Charlie said patiently. "Remember what Auntie said: 'Cross the Bloodwastes, turn left, keep going until you get past the last tent, then veer right into the woods'. And besides, there's no way I'm standing here staring at a map. We'd look like tourists—like we don't know what we're doing. Come on."

He led Millicent and Arthur to the left and down the line of mercenary tents.

"Ooh, look at that one!" Arthur said as they passed the first. "What's with the skulls strung up across the entrance? You think they're for decoration or something?"

"I'd probably guess 'or something'," Charlie said.

Millicent hugged her arms around herself as they passed another tent with various bones outside. "I don't think I like it here," she said.

"Oh, I don't know," said Arthur. "I think it's fascinating. We're looking at a piece of our history. People like this lot— these are the people who helped shape our present."

"I think it was people that they shaped. Into little pieces…" Millicent said.

"Hang on a sec," Charlie said, moving closer to Millicent. "Looks like things might get a bit interesting."

Up ahead, three mercenaries were grouped outside a tent. They'd been talking, but as they noticed the three friends approach, they fanned out, blocking the path. Charlie looked for a way around, but they were blanketed by tents on one side and overgrown brambles on the other. Even more worryingly, one of the men appeared to be holding a large jar of something by his side and, as they approached, he took a long swig from it, wiping the amber droplets from his beard with the back of his hand.

"Right then, lads," he said to the two men either side of him, "let's not faff about here. None of the usual *'where do you think you're going?'* malarkey. It's early, my head's still a bit sore, so shall we just cut to the chase?"

The mercenary on the left—a man not particularly intimidating in size, but looked not more than a hair's breadth away from losing it completely—stared manically at Charlie, Millicent and Arthur. One of his eyes was considerably smaller than the other, and this, disturbingly, was the most normal part of him. The rest of him seemed to have been thrown together in the dark to give the general impression of what a person should look like.

The mercenary on the right seemed to be there in body— and it was a lot of body to be there in—but the rest of him— the essence of him—seemed somewhere else entirely.

"Yeah," said the thrown together mercenary. "Let's do it! Doooo it! Hah!" He then preceded to make a series of clicking noises as his body contorted and twitched.

"Huh," said the not-altogether-there mercenary on the right.

The one in the centre paused for a moment, looked at his companions then carried on.

"Yes, there definitely won't be much faffage this morning. So, here we go…" He stepped forward, holding his hand out as the three approached. "By order of me, Hacker Jon, and my two fellow mercenaries, Ticker the Vengeful"—he pointed to the left—"and Steven"—he pointed to the as yet unmoving mercenary on the right—"you three need to pay tax in order to continue on your way."

He held out his hand and waited.

"Yeah," said Ticker the Vengeful, hopping from foot to foot, "tax 'em! Tax 'em real good! Hah!"

"Huh," repeated Steven.

Millicent folded her arms. "I don't believe you," she said.

A flicker of confusion passed over Hacker Jon's face. Ticker turned to look at him, his head bobbing from side to side.

"Huh?" said Steven.

"I beg your pardon?" Hacker Jon said.

"I said, 'I don't believe you'," Millicent repeated, arms still folded. "There's no such thing as a tax people need to pay to walk along any road, let alone this one. I think you're making it up."

Charlie closed his eyes and shook his head. This wasn't going to end well.

Hacker Jon laughed a quick snort. Ticker let out a wild cackle.

"Huh," said Steven.

"Of course I'm making it up," said Hacker Jon. "It's just a different way of saying 'give us your money'. And, for the record, you'd be surprised how gullible folks from Calver can be. I'd say nine out of every ten times, it works."

"Oh," said Millicent a little deflated. "What happens when it doesn't work?"

"We have to go with what we know," said Hacker Jon.

"And what's that?" said Millicent.

Hacker Jon walked over to a tent, carefully put his jar down and picked up the sword resting on a rock next to it.

"Yes!" hissed Ticker and pulled a couple of daggers from their scabbards on his hips. He waved them around in a strange dance-like motion. "Stabby-stabby, leaky-holes time!"

"Huh," said Steven who dragged out a large, uneven club hidden in the brambles by his side.

"Ah…" said Millicent, taking a step backwards.

"Now, hang on a minute," chimed in Arthur. "This isn't right. You can't just go around threatening folk and brandishing your weapons and… and… well, it's just not right! We've barely left Calver and now you want to take all our coin! Charlie, this is exactly what I was worried would happen." He turned to face Charlie. "Didn't I say this would happen? Well, maybe not exactly this but, didn't I say something bad would happen. I did, didn't I?"

"Is he all right?" asked Hacker Jon.

Arthur was bent double, hands on his knees, breathing heavily. Millicent rubbed his back.

"I think it's all just a bit much for him," Charlie said. "First time the other side of the wall and all that. And let's be honest, it's not every day you bump into mercenaries who want to rob you."

"Fair enough," said Hacker Jon. "For the record, whilst we're being up front and honest, it is a bit embarrassing that it's come to this. Honest it is. You know, I actually fought in the Battle of Evensong? Right there." Hacker Jon pointed to the Bloodwastes with his sword. "We all did. That's how Ticker and Steven ended up like… well, like they are. You know, people think being a mercenary is all fighting and ill-gotten gains, but no one ever mentions the consequences of a life like that."

Next to Hacker Jon, Ticker was still swinging his daggers about in a variety of arcs, occasionally pausing to stab an imaginary foe. On his other side, Steven stood motionless staring at his club as if not quite sure how it got there.

"Must be pretty rough now there's no more battles left to fight," Charlie said, hoping to buy some time.

"Oh, that's not the half of it," Hacker Jon continued. "It's all good and well if you've got a solid crew behind you. Plenty of work in and around the rest of the Kingdom; some of the guys who own these tents are hardly ever here. Always heading off on one job or another. But who's going to want to hire us?" He waved his sword in the general direction of first Ticker then Steven.

"I see your point," Charlie said. "But isn't there something else you could do? I mean, no offense, but robbing people like us doesn't exactly tap into your years of experience and, again, pardon me for saying this, but it does seem a bit beneath you."

Hacker Jon let his sword fall. His shoulders sagged.

"It's just hard, you know. When you've spent your whole life living a certain way. Not only that; I was good at my job—really good. People used to say to me, 'Jon, there's no-one can take a head off like you'. It's true. Got to the point where—and I'm not making this up, you ask anyone—I could lop someone's head off, then point to where it would land. Now, I'll admit, as far as life skills go, it's not particular-ly useful in any other line of work, but when being a mercenary is all you've ever known, being the fella who can lop a head off and land it on a sixpence is worth something, you know?"

"Actually, I do," said Charlie, and Hacker Jon gave him a quizzical look. "Not the chopping heads off thing, obviously, but up until not very long ago, I thought I knew where I was headed…. sorry, pardon the pun. Thought I'd got things figured out. Then I realised not only could it all get taken away like that"—he snapped his fingers—"but where I thought I belonged didn't always feel the same way about me. Sorry… I'm waffling."

"No, no. I see your point," said Hacker Jon, fetching his jar and taking a swig. "However, we are in a bit of a predicament. You know, what with the whole robbery thing."

"Reckon I might be able to help with that one," said a voice from behind Hacker Jon, "if, that is, it's help you're after. If not, tell me to sod off and I'll be on my way."

The man who emerged from behind Hacker Jon was not particularly tall, not particularly large, and had slightly greying hair. He was accompanied by a dark-haired girl of about ten who had the hardest stare of any child Charlie had ever seen. She looked like she wanted to fight everyone, including herself.

As innocuous as he looked, the newcomer had the strangest effect on Hacker Jon who stumbled back a step and hid the jar behind his back. Even Ticker slowed down his jittery dagger-dance and came to a twitching stop next to Hacker Jon. Only Steven seemed unmoved.

"Ah… hello there, Wolf," said Hacker Jon timidly. "Didn't see you there…"

"Not many do," the man called Wolf said smiling. "That's how I've managed to reach middle age and remain so dashingly handsome. Now tell me, what's going on here?"

"Well…" said Hacker Jon and then abruptly stopped, clearly unable to think of anything else to say.

"We were just asking these fine gentlemen for directions," Millicent said stepping forward, smiling.

The little girl with Wolf snarled—actually snarled. Wolf laughed. "Steady now, Eve," he said, easing her back. "Not everyone wants to hurt us. You don't want to hurt us, do you?"

Millicent looked at first Arthur and then Charlie.

"I'm not sure that's a possibility. Unless you're allergic to bad jokes and over-worrying, in which case these two are deadly."

Wolf laughed. It was an easy laugh; Charlie got the feeling he'd fit right in on the Backstreets.

"As I was saying," Millicent continued, "we were just asking these gentlemen for directions which they were ever-so kind to give us and, for their trouble…" Millicent dug into her cloth bag and produced two gold coins. She walked over to Hacker Jon and pressed them into his palm.

Jon looked down at the coins, up at Millicent, and over at the man called Wolf.

"Yes, that was very much the agreed fee. Myself and my friends thank you very much for your… donation. If you ever need any more directions, you know where we are."

Hacker Jon walked quickly over to Steven and carefully guided him by the shoulders across the path towards their tent. Steven shuffled across the path, dragging his club in the dirt behind him leaving a trail from one side of the path to the other. Once they reached the tent, Hacker Jon ushered Steven inside then called after Ticker.

Ticker seemed forlorn. He looked at the remaining people.

"No stabby-stabby, leaky-holes time?" he asked.

"Not today, son," Wolf said. "Maybe another time, eh?"

"Okay then. Bye!" he said and ran back into the tent with Steven and Hacker Jon.

"Well now, that seems to have cleared itself up nicely, don't you think?" Wolf said.

"Yes, and we really must be on our way too. Now we've got some new shiny directions to follow," Charlie said moving to leave.

"Of course you do," said Wolf. "Wouldn't want to keep you for a moment longer."

He stepped over to the side of the path to allow the three friends to pass. Eve seemed to think about it for a moment then joined him.

"It was lovely to meet you, Mr. Wolf," said Millicent.

"Yes, thank goodness you came along. Those savages were—" Arthur began.

"I think, if I were you, young man, I might hold my tongue for just a little while longer," Wolf said. "Those three might not be close friends of mine, but let's just say they're finding life a little bumpy at the moment, and it was very nice of you to offer them some coin in return for a little guidance. We'll leave it at that shall we?"

Wolf said this such a conversational way with a pleasant smile on his face that it was almost possible to miss the hardness in his eyes. Almost.

"I think that's very well said and we wish you all the best," said Millicent as she hooked her arm through Arthur's and began to walk him down the path.

"Pleasant travels," Wolf said as Charlie picked up his bag and scurried off after his friends.

CHAPTER 18

Rock of the musical kind.

A FTER CHARLIE, MILLICENT and Arthur reached the final tent—a small brown affair that wasn't much to look at—they did as Auntie said and veered right. The path narrowed up ahead, wound its way up a small hill, and then down into the woods into a valley beyond. Once the three friends reached the top of the hill, they paused to eat and take in the view ahead. They sat on their packs and ate a quick meal of Auntie's homemade bread and a wedge of cheese each.

"I do hope we find somewhere to stay quickly," Millicent said, washing down a bite with water from her skin. "I'm not sure I can stomach bread and cheese for every meal."

Charlie laughed. "Bread and cheese is good enough for most folk. Certainly the type of folk from where I'm from."

"What's that supposed to mean?" Millicent said turning to look at Charlie.

"Do you know what?" Arthur asked then plunged on-wards without waiting for an answer. "I think that there's no finer time to walk through a wood than autumn. And how lucky we are that it's autumn right now!"

"All I meant was that, for some people, bread and cheese

is more than enough, that's all," Charlie said.

"Oh, and I suppose I'm being ungrateful?" Millicent countered, standing up.

"For me, it's the smell of the leaves. I love the smell of leaves. Does anyone else love the smell of leaves?" Arthur continued.

"I never said you were ungrateful. The word ungrateful never left my lips."

"But that's what you meant, isn't it? I'm ungrateful because I'm moaning about bread and cheese."

"Look, I'm sorry if you've chosen to feel guilty," Charlie said, now also standing.

"Who said anything about guilt!" Millicent said, stuffing her things back in to her cloth bag.

"And there just seems to be a lovely light to everything," Arthur said. "A glow of browns and oranges. How about we head into the woods? I'm sure they'll be lovely smells and lovely sights too. Very relaxing it'll be."

"I wondered how long it would take," Millicent said, stepping closer to Charlie, as she adjusted her pack. "You're the boy from the Backstreets who's lived the life, and I'm nothing more than some silly girl from posh old Middle Calver. You know what I think, Charlie Lightfoot? Why you made that little dig about the bread and cheese?"

"And there'd probably be birds singing too," Arthur said, still sitting down.

"I think you made that dig," Millicent continued, "because it was me who smoothed everything over back there with those mercenaries. I was the quick thinker and you weren't, and I don't think you liked it one bit. Little old me from Middle Calver was quicker than the great Charlie Lightfoot. In fact, come to think of it, you were pretty useless back there."

"What a ridiculous thing to say!" said Charlie, also adjusting his pack. "Talk about making stuff up as you go along! The truth of the matter is whilst you may have had it hard, you've never had it Backstreets hard. Your life's been surrounded by puffy cushions and big dinners."

"How in the god's names did you just leap from me not liking bread and cheese for every meal, to the whole 'my life's been harder than yours' shtick.?"

"There might even be—"

"Shut up, Arthur!" Millicent and Charlie said in unison. They both stormed off, jostling for position as the path wasn't very wide and they were heading in the same direction. Arthur brushed the crumbs he'd dropped down his shirt, clambered to his feet, and shouldered his pack.

"I think what we've got here," he said to himself as he adjusted his straps and checked they'd not left anything behind, "is two very different people, very much out of their depth, who have just been made very aware their rose-tinted vision of this excursion might not be all sunshine and rainbows. They're probably just as worried as I am but heavens forbid they should ever admit it."

He looked over at the woods ahead of them. Over to the right, far from the path a family of fallow deer were grazing peacefully right on the edge.

"Oh look, some deer," he said to no one in particular then trudged off after Charlie and Millicent.

》》》《《《

BY THE TIME Arthur caught up with Charlie and Millicent, they were both well into the wood. Under the cover of row after row of huge pine trees, the path widened so the three of them could walk side by side. Although they didn't walk side by side; they walked side by as far away from the other side as humanly possible whilst still keeping to the path.

Arthur took up the middle position and, after a few minutes of silence, could stand it no longer. "So, here's what we're going to do—" he began.

"Not in the mood, Arthur, so don't even bother..." Charlie said.

"Yes, for once I actually agree with your bone-headed friend," said Millicent. "I don't want to talk."

"Yes, well, I do, and it's my journey as much as anyone else's. Besides, you two are beginning to get on my nerves. Sorry, but you're being a pair of numpties, and it needs to stop right now."

Charlie and Millicent stopped and turned to face Arthur, both slightly dumfounded.

"Sorry, but it needed saying. So, how about you listen to the bartender's son who—for those asking, which is no one in particular—has heard his fair share of troubles in his day? Here's my twopenneth's worth of wisdom."

"Really? You're actually going to do this?" Charlie said.

"Shut up, Charlie—why do you have to be so bloody condescending?" Millicent said. "Let Arthur speak."

Arthur turned to face Charlie and continued.

"That bread was about as lovely as you could get given

the circumstances; your Auntie makes a cracking loaf, and I'm glad she sent us on our way with some. When we return, I'm going to remember to say thank you to her. It must be really nice to have someone who cares about you enough they bake bread for you. I bet, and I'm going out on a limb here, that eating that bread back there was a nice little reminder of her."

"Oh, Charlie, I never even thought…" Millicent said looking crestfallen.

"And, Millicent," Arthur said. "That bread was lovely, but bread and cheese for every meal is going to get very boring very fast, isn't it? I'll let you in on a little secret—I don't even like cheese that much. I mean, how can anyone get too excited about out-of-date cow juice left to go hard? But I suppose we might have to get used to not having the type of food we want, and that's not something we even considered when we dashed out here to run away from our problems, is it?" He kicked a stone loose from the road. "Right now, I don't know about you, but everything is just a little bit unknown and a little bit scary."

Both Millicent and Charlie stood and stared at Arthur for a moment. In the near distance a bird called out a tune. It wasn't particularly melodic but it certainly wasn't lacking in effort.

"Right, now that we're done with all this nonsense," Arthur said, "can we carry on as before? I'm aware we've been out of Calver for no more than half a day and you two have already had a blazing row. If you're going to carry on like this, it's going to get very tiresome, so you might want to consider not doing it so often. Y'know, try spacing out your spats a little. Also, I'd quite like to reach somewhere we might find a bed for the night before night's actually here."

Charlie broke out in a smile and slung his arm around Arthur's shoulders and, on the other side, Millicent hooked her arm through his.

"Come on then," Millicent said. "Let's see what we can find."

"Yeah," Charlie said. "By the way, have you noticed, there's a lovely light to everything in these woods today? Gives everything a glow of browns and oranges. Lovely smells and sights too. Very relaxing, isn't it?"

⫸⫸⫸⫷⫷⫷

BY THE TIME they'd reached the other side of the wood, it was the middle of the afternoon. What had once been a sheet grey sky speckled with dark clouds had now cracked in places, allowing brief glimpses of sunshine to filter through.

Beyond the edge of the wood, the path meandered downwards into a small valley peppered with a few buildings. Most were thatched, with only the occasional tiled roof to be seen, and were clustered around a central dais as if trying to huddle together to ward off the cold. Charlie, Millicent, and Arthur reached the edge of the town as the sun began to slip downwards on its way towards dusk.

"Well, here it is," Charlie said, "just like Auntie said it would be."

Arthur looked over at the wooden sign staked in the ground.

"Heverton. Population one hundred and forty-three," he

read, although the original number had been painted over with numerous additions and deductions as the town's residency had fluctuated.

"Auntie said to head straight for the centre and that's where we'll find the Inn," continued Charlie, "but she also said it had been half a lifetime ago when she'd last been out this way. Thing might've changed."

"Nothing ventured, nothing gained," Millicent said and strode off down the path.

No sooner had they passed the first house – a small homestead on the outskirts – than a small child came hurtling past them and off around the bend ahead.

"Crikey, she's in a hurry!" Arthur said. "Wonder what that was all about?"

As they rounded the corner, a young man hustled over to greet them. He was not much older than Charlie and bobbed around in front of them from foot to foot as if the path was too hot.

"How do, folks? On your way from the city? Cor, I bet it's nice up that way. Anyway, wonder if I could interest you in a bit of a bargain? Got a nice set of daggers here you might be interested in. Very useful for the general stabbing of things. You know—people, food, and, erm…"—the man looked around—"and rocks."

Arthur frowned. "Why would you need to stab a rock?"

"What goes on between you and your rock is absolutely your business, my city friend. But should the need ever arise to put something like a rock in its place—show it who's boss—then I have the very implement."

"That's the most ridiculous thing I've ever heard," said Arthur.

"But… is it though?" said the man with a wink.

"Yes, it actually is," Arthur insisted.

"But… is it though?" said the man.

"Yes. It is," repeated Arthur, beginning to get cross.

"Yeah, but—"

"Listen," Charlie said, cutting his sentiment short for Arthur's sake. "We appreciate the offer of daggers for the stabbing of living… and not so living things, but we're musicians, we don't really need daggers."

"Fair enough, fair enough. Say no more, my friend" the young man said and scurried off without another word.

"What a bizarre situation! I wonder how much he paid that little girl to be his lookout?" Millicent said.

"Probably not a whole lot… and not nearly enough, I'd warrant" Arthur suggested.

The three of them continued on a little further and the closer they got to the centre of Heverton, the more the buildings seemed herded together.

As they passed a row of five small houses, some little more than huts, and could now see the town centre in the distance, someone else stepped out in front of them. It was the same young man from earlier, only this time he was wearing what appeared to be a fake moustache made from something which looked like it had once been attached to something alive.

"How do there, my loves," he said through an accent hammered together and kept in place with little more than persistence. "I was wondering if you might be the kind of fellows who would be interested in buying some musical instruments?"

"Erm, we know it's you…" Charlie said.

"Know it's who, friend?" the young man said doing the best his questionable acting skills would allow.

"The person from back there who tried to sell us some daggers," said Millicent.

"Oh, I reckon you must be thinking of my brother. He lives up yonder. Bit of a bugger, should you ask me. Always trying to flog some weapon or another."

"No, it was definitely you," Arthur said. "You did a whole thing about stabbing rocks. And what did that thing under your lip used to be? It looks like a sheep's tail or something."

The young man fingered his moustache which wobbled but managed to stay in place when the young man pursed his lips.

"Well," he said through a pout, "I don't know about where you come from, but around here, it's very bad manners to insult the facial hair of someone you've just met."

Charlie looked at Arthur and sighed.

"Arthur, say you're sorry," he said.

"I jolly well will not! He's trying to swindle us and doing a very bad job of it, too!"

"Yes but we're new in town and we need to make friends, okay?"

"Fine," Arthur said begrudgingly. "I'm sorry for insulting your sheep's tail moustache."

The man brightened and began bouncing from foot to foot again.

"Not a problem. Not a problem at all. Bit of a clash of different folks from different places, that's all. By way of an apology, how about buying one of my world-famous musical rocks?"

"Oh, this is just bloody daft!" Arthur cursed, storming off toward the centre of town.

Charlie shrugged and hurried after him. Millicent smiled to herself, nodded to the young man, then she too ran to catch up.

"But… is it though?" he shouted after them.

CHAPTER 19

From The Cavern to The Lost Plum.

O NCE IN THE centre of Heverton, Charlie, Millicent, and Arthur soon realised that when it came to places to stay for the night, their choices were limited to one. Across the bustling open square in front of them stood a row of shops with the town's one and only Inn wedged in between a baker and a grocer.

The Lost Plum stood head and shoulders above the buildings around it simply due to it having an upstairs. In fact, it had two upstairs. While the first appeared to have come with the building when it was originally built, the second had been added on, with new rooms sprouting haphazardly through the roof like the teeth of a drunk who regularly used his face to break his fall.

"Looks like we've found our digs for the night," Charlie said beckoning Arthur and Millicent across the square. The people of Heverton paid no mind to the three friends as they made their way into The Lost Plum.

"I thought we'd draw a bit more attention than this," said Millicent. "Not that I'm complaining, it's just, I don't know… I wondered if we mightn't stand out being from the city and all that."

"I guess, being this close to Calver, people round here get used to seeing people passing through on their way in and out of town. It's not the most direct route but, still," said Charlie.

Inside, the central room filled most of the downstairs space. Over to the left-hand side was a fireplace so huge it took up most of the entire wall. To the right-hand side, a wide and well used wooden staircase led upstairs. Directly in front of them, a bar spanned the entire rear of the building.

As it was early evening, there wasn't too many people taking up spaces at the tables dotted around the floor. Charlie, Millicent, and Arthur weaved their way around to the back of the room. Upon closer inspection, the bar appeared to be one, long slab of wood, and Charlie had no trouble at all imagining someone splitting a great oak from top to tail and laying it down to form it.

Before any of them could say anything, a man bustled out of the kitchen carrying five steaming bowls of what looked like stew. To Charlie it smelt divine… or maybe he was just so hungry, that anything warm and vaguely appealing would've smelt good.

As the man whisked past them, he called out, "Be with you shortly," then hustled over to a table in the far corner where he placed the bowls down with practised ease. He slalomed back to the bar, grabbed a cloth, and as he wiped the bar in front of them, said, "Sorry about that, folks. What'll it be?"

"We'd like a couple of rooms for the night, if you can?" Charlie said.

"I'm sure we can squeeze you in," the man said looking

around the near-deserted room.

"I'll be thankful to be able to have a wash," said Millicent. "It feels like my road dust is covered in road dust."

"How much will it cost to hire two rooms, have some water heated for a couple of baths, and for a decent meal?" Charlie asked.

The barkeep stoked his chin. He looked the three friends up and down, did some quick maths and said, "Fourteen crowns. And that's me knocking some off for you as you look like a decent sort."

"We'll take it!" Millicent said, clearly eager to take a bathe and eat something other than bread and cheese for the second time that day.

"Excellent," said the barkeep and reached for the ring of keys on his belt. It jingled tunefully as he leafed through, and this gave Charlie an idea.

"Hang on a minute," he said. "What if we play for you tonight? How much then?"

"I'm sorry... what?" said Arthur.

The barkeep ignored him. "What do you mean play for me?" he said.

"We're a travelling band, the three of us," said Charlie. "We could play for you, in here, maybe over by the fire-place?"

"The *three* of us...?" Millicent said. "Are a travelling band...?"

Charlie seemed to have peeked the barkeep's interest. "What sort of stuff do you play?" he said, folding his arms.

"Pretty much anything, really. I play the fiddle, Arthur there the bodhran, and Millicent... sings."

"Wait, what?" said Arthur.

"I sing?" repeated Millicent.

"You sure about this?" said the barkeep. "The other two don't seem so sure."

"Oh, they just get a bit nervous sometimes," assured Charlie. "And they're incredibly humble. We're actually quite good. So, how about it?"

"*Charlie!*" said both Millicent and Arthur in unison, but Charlie waved them away with a shush.

"Tell you what," said the barkeep. "Given there's hardly going to be any bugger in here tonight, sure, you can have a play. If you're rubbish, I'll put the brakes on before you get to the end of the first song. And you'll pay the full fourteen crowns. If you're any good, you can give me ten and call it fair. Deal?"

He held out his hand and before either Millicent or Arthur could 0bject, Charlie grasped it and pumped hard.

"Right you are," said the barkeep. "Well, if you're playing in my inn, then you'll need to know my name's Ernie. The wife's in the kitchen—her name's Gerty and, once you're settled, it's her you'll need to see about getting some grub. I'll tell her to expect you. Rooms are up yonder stairs; take the first flight up, turn left, and take the first two you come to. They aren't locked; I'll get you your keys later. Will you be wanting food or hot water first because if it's water, I'll need to get the fire going."

"Bath first," said Millicent. "Then food."

"Right you are again," said Ernie. "You go get rid of your things then come back down. No rush."

"Don't worry," Arthur said through gritted teeth, gripping Charlie tightly by the arm. "We need to have a little chat anyway."

The three of them headed for the stairs and climbed up to the first floor; all smiles and silence as Ernie watched them go. The walls were empty; same as the floor, save for the occasional threadbare rug. The floor also tilted disconcertingly as if the building was slowly lurching to one side.

They found their rooms easily enough; Arthur and Charlie in one with Millicent next door. Charlie and Arthur's room was basic but clean: there were two beds complete with a hard mattress on each and a woollen throw, a very battered and well used chest for personal belongings, a window which looked out onto a courtyard at the back of the Inn, and nothing more.

No sooner had Charlie and Arthur dropped their bags on their respective beds than Millicent burst in. She said nothing, just stood glaring at Charlie, arms folded. Arthur looked at Millicent, then Charlie, then took up the same pose.

"In my defence," Charlie began, "it was going to happen sooner or later."

"I would've preferred later, along with the option of an actual discussion happening between the sooner and the later," Millicent said incensed.

"Me too," Arthur said with a similar sentiment.

"Arthur, you've brought your bodhran with you; I can see it tied to your pack on the bed over there. What did you think you'd be using it for—sheltering from the rain?"

"Of course not!" Arthur said. "But I didn't expect to be playing at the first inn we came to, and without a jot of discussion beforehand!"

"Look, the way I see it," Charlie said moving over to the edge of the bed and sitting down, "this is the perfect place to see what we're made of. You heard Ernie; the amount of people in tonight will make this more of a rehearsal, or even a practice session. And if we're rubbish, it's cost us four crowns and nothing more."

"Good points, all well made," said Millicent, walking over to the window. She stared out, and without turning to face the others said, "but you've missed one crucial point. Namely, that you two have played together; quite a lot from what I've been led to believe. And you're probably pretty good. I, on the other hand, have never done more than hum to myself in the bath."

Charlie got up and walked over to Millicent. He gently took her by the shoulders and turned her around to face him.

"You'll be fine," he said reassuringly. "Just join in when you can, with the songs you know. Other than that, try to hum along, move around a bit, and generally give off singer vibes. And unlike in the bath, the benefit of humming along this time is you won't have to be naked. Although if you want us to attract a bigger audience…"

"Sod off, Charlie," Millicent said. "Besides, you'd never be able to get a tune out with your mouth hanging open." With that, she walked out of the room, leaving Arthur and Charlie to work out which songs they'd play that night.

They sat down on their beds and worked through a group of five: a much shorter list than Charlie would normally play, but they decided it best to keep it short and sweet. Get on, bang out a few songs, then get off—hopefully without being thrown off. The hard part was choosing songs that Millicent could sing along to. At one point Arthur went to ask her what she knew, but she wasn't in her room, so assuming she must be downstairs making the most of a hot bath, they carried on.

Finally, and after much discussion—mainly revolving around Arthur saying he couldn't possibly play this song and definitely not that one, then Charlie reassuring him that he could—they'd whittled it down to a definitive five. They'd chosen songs which were lively, thinking they could rattle through them in a happy flurry with an aim to entertain.

"Well," said Arthur, with a little bit of disbelief. "The song list for my first ever gig. Feels a bit strange, Charlie."

"Don't worry," said Charlie. "Trust me, once you get up there and start playing, everything just washes away. We just need to make sure Millicent is confident enough to get up and sing with us."

They put their instruments away and made their way downstairs in search of the stew they'd seen Ernie serving earlier. Not much had changed in terms of footfall during their time preparing; the bar was as deserted as before.

"Hope it fills up a bit before tonight," Charlie said as they headed for the kitchen.

"I don't," Arthur replied with a gulp.

They walked around the bar and towards the door leading to the kitchen.

"Hello," Charlie said peering in. "Anyone around? Ernie said we should come back here for a spot of food."

"Now then," came a woman's voice from somewhere, "you must be Charles and Arthur. Come on in here boys, I'm just serving up."

The kitchen wasn't particularly big but was crammed to the ceiling with just about every item a kitchen could need and more besides. There were pots and pans hanging from hooks attached to a wooden rail running around the edge of the wall, and every surface had something on it; chopping boards, utensils, bowls... if it counted in a game of kitchen bingo, it was there.

Over by one wall, a huge fire roared and crackled away while the iron stoves in the middle of the room were laden with bubbling pots and pans of every mismatched variety.

As Arthur and Charlie stared at the sheer mass of objects, a round face poked out from around the side of one of the many hanging pans.

"Ah, you pair must be our esteemed guests—the famous musicians. Now, hang on a minute, let me get a look at you." The owner of the face moved out and around the side of the ovens. She was about as wide as she was tall with a ruddy complexion and thick forearms.

"You'll be Arthur," she said, pointing at Arthur, "and you'll most definitely be the one and only Charlie Lightfoot."

Arthur and Charlie looked at each other.

"That's right," Charlie said, smiling widely. "We're the famous musicians, and might I say what an honour it is to play a gig in the...?"

"The Lost Plum," Arthur finished for him.

"Yes, well, it certainly is a pleasure to meet you, Gerty, I believe? How did you hear about us?" Charlie asked.

"Young Millicent came down about an hour ago," Gerty said with a stern look. "And she told me everything.

Everything. And that's how I knew that the nice, quiet boy would be Arthur and the jumped-up cocky one would be Charlie."

"Ah…" Charlie said.

"'Ah' is about the length and breadth of it," she said scowling. "Famous musicians indeed! Millicent said if I called you that, you'd go along with it, believing your own muck don't even stink!"

Gerty shook her head and looked at Charlie who said nothing.

"Here's what I'll do for you," she said. "You'll get a serving of my rabbit stew, the both of you. Let no one say that Gerty Dowry isn't a good host. But after that's done, you'll head out back and talk to that Millicent friend of yours; she's having a long soak right now. And you'll apologise for dropping her in the deep end without talking to her first." She punctuated each point with a wave of her wooden spoon. "Now, if I were her, I'd give you a piece of my mind and tell you to sod off. And you'd stand there and take it too. Then, I'd stand back and let you die on your arse tonight. But, lucky for you, I'm not her."

With one final wave of her wooden spoon, Gerty stomped off to where a huge pot of stew was bubbling away on top of the section of the oven with a fire lit beneath it.

"Famous musicians?" Arthur said. "We only formed the band a couple of hours ago, you tit. How would anyone have heard of us?"

CHAPTER 20

If in doubt, go hell for leather.

AFTER WOLFING DOWN their stew, Arthur and Charlie found Millicent out the back in a separate outhouse building. The door was closed but they could tell she was in there; she was singing.

How amazing it would be, Charlie thought as they headed over, *if Millicent had the voice of an angel.* Imagine if they got her up on stage and she opened her mouth and glorious notes danced from her very soul to kiss the ears of anyone fortunate to listen.

Unfortunately, as Charlie and Arthur drew closer, it became clear there wouldn't be any soul kissing anytime soon. Instead, it sounded as if someone was committing a depraved act of wanton cruelty with what was supposed to be the tune.

Arthur stopped and gripped Charlie by the sleeve. He turned to his friend with a look that was one-part horror, one-part shock, with a dash of disbelief thrown in for good measure.

"Surely that's not physically possible…" Arthur said.

"How in the blue hells is a noise like *that* coming out of a girl like *Millicent*?" Charlie asked, covering his ears.

The singing, which was to describe it in very generous and flexible terms, stopped.

"Is that you Charlie? Arthur?" Millicent said.

"We're here," Charlie confirmed.

"Just came to check on you and say we're, well… Charlie's sorry for springing the whole band thing on you."

"Yeah," Charlie added in a hurry, "and we'd totally understand if you wanted to back out. Support you completely. It was a rotten thing for me to do."

"Actually, I've had time to calm down and think it over," Millicent said from inside. "It's amazing what a good meal, a nice hot bath, and a long chat with someone like Gerty will do. I think I might like to give singing a try. I need to let go of who I was back in Middle Calver and forge ahead with the new me. Who knows, maybe singing is my calling!"

Charlie and Arthur grimaced at one another.

"What are we going to do?" Arthur whispered. "If she starts up like that tonight, the only calling will be for our heads on spikes!"

"I don't know!" Charlie whispered back. "Erm…"

"Did you hear me practising?" Millicent asked. "I think I'm starting to find the tune!"

"Yeah, and then kick it to death," Arthur hissed.

"What's that?" Millicent called.

"We were… just agreeing with you," Arthur said.

Charlie spun him around by the sleeve to face him.

"Don't flipping agree with her!" he said through the side of his mouth. "We were most definitely not agreeing with her! Why in god's name would you encourage her?"

"Well, I'm hardly going to say, 'Actually we did hear you

and now we think we should send you for a very long walk whilst we perform because the alternative of you strangling a tune to death on stage might not be that appealing to any paying customers'!"

Just then, the door to the outhouse opened and out came Millicent. She was back in her travel clothes, which somehow looked almost as good as new again. Her hair was still wet and hung down over her shoulders, as she dried it with a wool blanket.

"You know, boys, I'm rather looking forward to tonight," she said as she strode off towards the kitchen.

Charlie and Arthur hurtled after her but, by the time they caught up, Millicent was already deep in conversation with Gerty. The two ladies looked up briefly, gave a quick laugh, then turned back to each other and, within moments, were back in deep conversation. Arthur smiled, nodded, and steered Charlie through the kitchen, around the bar, then frog-marched him to a stool.

"How do, lads?" Ernie asked. "All set for tonight?"

"In a manner of speaking," Arthur said. "Two jars of… whatever you'd normally drink, please?"

"Absolutely," said Ernie and scurried off to pull the ale.

"The way I see it," Arthur said, "either we tell Millicent she can't hold a tune because she's likely to choke it to death and deal with the consequences of that…"

Arthur let his words trail off as both he and Charlie contemplated how that might go.

"Or," Charlie said eventually, "we just go for it and hope not to get thrown out on our ear."

Ernie arrived with their beers. He placed the two tankards down in front of Charlie and Arthur.

"Want me to add those to your tab?" he said.

"Might as well," said Charlie. Maybe when they got thrown out they wouldn't have to pay for anything.

"And what will the lady be having? I'm guessing she'll be joining you?"

"No, I don't think she—" started Arthur.

"Actually," Charlie interrupted, "she's just in the kitchen with Gerty, but she'll be with us shortly."

Arthur shot Charlie a quizzical expression.

"What's the strongest spirit you've got?" Charlie asked.

Charlie saw the look of realisation dawn across Arthur's face like the sun breaking through the trees on an otherwise cloudy day. He could tell an internal war was waging inside him; good, honest, amiable Arthur was fighting a valiant battle against the side of Arthur who just wanted to make it through the rest of the night without anyone throwing something at him.

Millicent arrived at the bar.

"You're not drinking before the gig are you? Surely that's not a good idea?"

Charlie pounced.

"It's virtually an unwritten law. If you're a proper musician, you have to have a quick snifter before a gig. It loosens everything up. Helps you relax."

"Here you go," said Ernie, placing a small cup in front of Millicent. "Although, you don't want too many of—"

Charlie cleared his throat loudly. He looked wide-eyed at Arthur and Arthur looked wide-eyed back at him.

"Well, I suppose one won't hurt," Millicent said. "I am a little nervous."

She picked up the cup, gave it a sniff, wrinkled her nose, then downed the drink in one.

She gave a shudder, a cough and then, through a coarse voice said, "Wow! That does the job! I can feel it hitting my boots!"

Sometimes, when you look back on certain events in your life, you relish the chance to relive moments as they bring memories of joy, sound judgement, or simply pure, unfiltered happiness.

This was not one of those times. Arthur and Charlie didn't ply Millicent with booze.

They didn't encourage her one tiny bit.

They certainly didn't pressure her into knocking back a total of five cups of sixty percent proof gin.

But – and this is why they could never look back on that hour with anything other than shame—they also did nothing to stop her.

They didn't listen to Ernie who tutted and fretted every time Millicent ordered yet another round. They simply sat by and let the situation unfold before their very eyes.

Free from the constraints of her previous life, Millicent well and truly let her hair down. All the while unspoken words hung between Charlie and Arthur, neither able to say out loud why they let Millicent drink herself into a stupor and then, thankfully and mercifully, pass out.

"That was not a very nice thing to do," Arthur said, standing and hooking one of her arms over his shoulder. "And I for one think that we're both going to the first level of hell. For a very long time…"

Charlie stood and hooked the other of Millicent's arms

around his shoulder.

"It's not something I'm proud of and I certainly think we could've put a stop to it if we'd tried but, in the long run, maybe she'll thank us."

"Not tomorrow morning when she wakes up with the mother of all hangovers, that's for sure" Arthur said.

Between them, they lifted Millicent from the bar and half-carried, half-dragged her up the stairs and into her room. They lay her on the bed as carefully as they could, unbuckled her boots, placed a bucket by the bed, and made their way quietly back to their own room.

Charlie and Arthur didn't speak much as they readied themselves for the gig. They quietly went over the list of songs, made sure they looked as presentable as possible, picked up their instruments, and made their way back into the hall. After quickly checking on Millicent, who was softly snoring, half on, half off the bed, they looked at each other a final time, then headed off downstairs for their first ever gig as a duo.

THE FIRST THING they noticed when they arrived downstairs was the bar had begun to fill up. Not so much that the phrase 'bursting at the seams' could be used, but nonetheless, there were definitely more people than earlier in the day.

"Word's spread that there's a turn on," Ernie said as he hustled past them with a couple of tankards. "Folks round here like their music, so it looks like things might perk up."

"That's good news," Charlie said.

"I'm guessing young Millicent won't be joining you, state she was in. Shame you let her get that way," he said, and fixed Arthur and Charlie with a hard stare.

Arthur and Charlie found this a good moment to inspect the stitching of their boots.

"Right, on you go then," Ernie said. "And remember, be good."

Charlie and Arthur made their way to the area Ernie had cleared in the far corner of the room. There were people gathered around quite a few of the tables; people clearly ready for a good night out.

For Charlie, as he unpacked his fiddle and began to wax his bow, it felt like just another gig, and he smiled at the thought of how far he'd come. Not too long ago, a gig like this would've sent butterflies tumbling around his stomach; now, it was simply a gig, and not a particularly big one either.

The same could not be said for Arthur. He fumbled his bohdran out of its sacking and proceeded to drop it on the floor with a clang which echoed around the room.

Most of the people waiting for the gig cheered and laughed. Arthur blushed a brilliant shade of crimson.

"I don't know if I can do this," he said, picking up his drum.

"It'll be fine once we get going, I promise," Charlie said.

"I feel sick," Arthur said, trying to breathe evenly.

"That's normal," Charlie said, still working his bow. "It's just the nerves. Blind Watchem said to me that if you weren't a bit nervous before a gig, you weren't open to the possibility of the unknown happening. Only musicians who play the same songs in the same way night after night don't get nervous, and that's because they aren't performing—they're going through the motions. Don't worry—once we get a few songs in, you'll feel like it's just me and you, having fun. I promise."

Arthur didn't look convinced but at least now he was holding his bodhran the right way around. "Erm, how do we start?" he said. "Do we need to make an announcement or something? Ask everyone to quieten down?"

Charlie laughed. "Maybe if we were a string quartet up at the palace," he said. "We're most definitely not that. You know we decided to start with 'Johan's Battle Axe'?"

"I do," Arthur said.

"Right then. I need you to beat the living daylights out of that opening rhythm. Hit as if your bohdran owed you money. Keep going hell for leather until I join in."

"Will that work?" Arthur asked.

"It'll certainly get their attention," said Charlie. Arthur, with nothing to lose and no thoughts otherwise, hit his bohdran so hard he nearly put a hole through it.

As the opening beat of 'Johan's Battle Axe' thundered around the walls of the inn, people stopped talking. Arthur beat the rhythm so fiercely that the tankards and cups on the tables closest to him began to rattle.

Charlie had chosen this song for this very reason.

It began with an almost war-like, emphatic call to arms which gradually got faster and faster until, at the right moment, the drumming paused. Then he and Arthur would launch into one of the fastest and most challenging pieces they knew. It grabbed the room by the scruff of the neck and shook it hard.

This is exactly what Charlie wanted.

Gone was the polite background music of the parties at fancy houses in Middle Calver; gone were the tried and tested, middle-of-the-road tunes played to keep the drinkers happy at the many Inns lining the King's Pass; gone, even, were the beautiful melodies of old played in The Halfway Barrel.

This was different. It *had* to be different. Charlie had chosen songs he'd only ever heard one person play—Blind Watchem.

During their countless hours of practice, Blind Watchem often played Charlie some of the lesser-known songs he'd picked up as he travelled the Kingdom. Songs he'd never been able to play in Calver. Songs that came from the Kingdom and belonged to the Kingdom.

Charlie had taken these songs, played around with them, got them in the kind of shape he could use, then insisted these were the songs he practised with Arthur in the cellar of The Halfway Barrel.

Listening to Arthur beat the holy hell out of his drum, he knew this was how it should be.

This was music.

This was riding the lightning.

CHAPTER 21

Ain't it the life.

THE GIG WAS going well; really well.

Arthur and Charlie had taken almost total control of the room and the people in there with them were along for the ride. Most were now on their feet, bouncing along, tankards in hand and stomping away. In fact, other people had started to make their way into the Lonely Plum, drawn by the music, and the shouts, and a sense of not wanting to miss out on whatever wonderful thing was happening in there.

Sweat dripped from Charlie and Arthur as they attacked song after song; following 'Johan's Blood Axe' by launching into 'When the Winter Ends' with no discernible pause whatsoever. Occasionally, Arthur would look up from the blur that was his beater and grin wildly at Charlie, once even screaming something unintelligible in his direction. Charlie had laughed and doubled down, playing harder and faster.

As they came to the close of their final song – 'Sleeping in the Furrows of my Enemy' – they hit the final note and stood, breathing in ragged bursts as the sweat dripped, forming pools beneath them on the floor.

There was a moment of silence, then the place erupted in

a cacophony of shouts, cheers, whoops, and hollers. Tankards were clashed, people fell into one another and, in one rather misguided moment, two farmers a little the worse for drink misjudged a hug and head-butted.

Right on cue, Arthur beat a heavy drum roll. The room quietened.

"Ladies, Gentlemen, and those happy souls who came to have a good time—thank you for coming. It wouldn't be a party without you!" Charlie shouted.

There were general cheers and shouts in return, none of which was particularly intelligible, aside from someone at the front who shouted, "Let's hear it for…"

And that was when Charlie and Arthur realised they didn't have a name. They'd spent so long working on the music that they'd completely forgotten to think of what to call their outfit.

"We are…" Charlie began, thinking as quickly as he could.

"We are…" tried Arthur, hoping that between them, they could come up with something. Anything.

"A pair of scumbags!" came a slurred voice, somewhere in the crowd.

The crowd roared with laughter and parted as Millicent strode forwards from the back of the room. Actually, she stumbled forwards, bashed into a table, sent the drinks flying, and ended up sitting in the lap of a rather surprised—but not unhappy—patron.

"S'cuse me, sir," Millicent said, standing up. "I do apologise for any inconvenience… but you see, those two turds over there got me rip-roaring drunk then left me to sleep it off whilst they came down and had all the fun." She hiccupped at the end of the sentence and covered her mouth. "Ooh, that was a close call," she said, swallowing hard.

Millicent continued her way up to a stunned Charlie and Arthur.

"Right then," Millicent said. "I might have missed most of the show, but we'll have one more song, thank you very much. An"—she belched into her hand—"encore. Yes, you there—pub-boy—hit that drum thing. And you—arse-face—screech your bloody fiddle. Let's go out with a bang!"

Arthur glanced at Charlie and Charlie glanced at Arthur, but there was nothing they could do. Someone at the side of the room started to stamp their feet and before long, the rest of the room joined in. Millicent clapped along, hands high above her head and soon began stamping her feet too.

"Sod it," Charlie said and shouted over to Arthur, "maybe if we play loud enough, they won't hear her singing. Let's get this over with."

Arthur could see no other option. He put his head down and began to beat a tune. Charlie joined in and soon they were once again rattling through another song. This one, 'The Land of Those Who Are Free', was about as rousing as you could get and, as far as encore's go, it was perfect.

Millicent clearly didn't know the song—there was no way she would've encountered it before—but she didn't let that stop her. Given it had no words, she simply decided to make them up. She stomped around in front of Charlie and Arthur, clapping her hands and wailing along to the tune. Or at least a somewhat reasonable approximation to it.

What Millicent lacked in any form of musical ability, or

timing, or even understanding of how a melody works, she more than made up for with pure enthusiasm. She moved around the room in a blur of manic energy, crashing into people, grabbing some for a whirling dance before careening off into—or onto—others still; all the while the music thundered on. Occasionally, she'd let out a wail or a guttural yelp and, to Charlie's surprise, the crowd seemed to respond in kind.

Once Millicent had bounced and bashed her way around the room, she marched back to Charlie and Arthur, and led the crowd in a call and response the likes of which Charlie had never seen before. Sensing the mood in the room, Charlie quietened his playing, and Arthur followed suit, reducing his beat to a low rumble.

Millicent part vaulted, part launched herself up on to the nearest table, and scowled over the room, pointing out at the people before her. Then she let out a series of shouts, cupped her ear, and waited for the crowd to respond. And respond they did. Once again, Millicent called out and the crowd replied. Charlie could do little more than laugh and shake his head.

He'd never played a gig quite like this before.

He nodded to Arthur who picked up the beat and began to play faster and faster. Millicent, still atop the table, began to spin faster and faster. Arthur's beater became a blur. So did Charlie's bow. Just when they felt they could go no faster, Millicent came crashing down from the table and crumpled into Charlie. The room erupted. Ale flew, cheers reigned down and everyone toasted the band from Calver.

"I've got a bruised arse," Millicent said, still on top of

Charlie, "my head's already pounding and I know I'm going to pay for this dearly tomorrow. But that is the most fun I've ever had. Now if you'll excuse me, I think I'm going to pass out. Goodnight."

>>>«««

ARTHUR AND CHARLIE stayed awake for hours after the gig talking, laughing—too wired to even contemplate sleep. As they discussed the evening Millicent snored softly beside them. They carried her upstairs and put her on Charlie's bed then flopped onto the floor with their backs resting up against the bed.

And so, they spent the remainder of the night basking in that precious post-show moment—the afterglow of a night of performing and losing themselves in the music, being in front of a crowd and completely owning it.

Arthur was beside himself. He kept standing up and pacing the room, talking too fast for his mouth to manage; driven by adrenaline and exhaustion. Charlie too, had allowed himself to get caught up in the moment.

Granted it hadn't been his first gig and it wasn't the best paying one either, but this one was so very different. He'd played the music he wanted to play and truly connected with a crowd.

Songs they'd chosen. Uniting the crowd as they shared something special.

For a brief crinkle in time, the music had joined the people in that room in one happy, messy, thunderous experience.

Of course Charlie knew how ridiculous this sounded. He knew most people would laugh at him for saying such things. He imagined saying something similar to Dodge or just about anyone from back home…

Auntie would probably tell him that the gig went well, and it was great fun, but it was no use to anyone getting too big for your britches, as doing so inevitably led to them splitting and revealing your arse.

Even Blind Watchem would tell him to enjoy the moment but keep in mind that one gig does not a band make.

Or maybe he was just putting words into their mouths. Maybe he wanted them to say those things and feel those things because then he, Charlie Lightfoot, could prove them wrong.

Would prove them wrong.

Is that what he wanted? Is that what this was all about? Proving something?

How in the blue hells had he gone from basking in the iridescent shifting remnants of a gig well-played to struggling with the question of his self-worth?

Bugger that, Charlie thought. Too much thinking. Instead he removed himself from his own head and joined Arthur in the simple pleasure of reliving that night's gig – song by song – then getting completely and irrationally carried away about their possible future.

THE SUN HADN'T been up for long, it's early morning glow barely creeping from beneath the horizon, but both Arthur and Charlie decided to make an early start. They wanted to get to the next town in plenty of time to find a room, and possibly see if they could get another gig.

"Two gigs in two nights," Arthur considered, a wistful look on his face. "If we keep this up, we'll be like those touring bands you hear about. Roaming the land, plying our wares from town to town."

"Not sure anyone would want you plying your wares anywhere near them," said Charlie, "not after they've seen the state of your undergarments."

"Sod off," Arthur said, cramming his belongings into his travel sack. "I'll have you know I wash my wares every single day. They practically sparkle, thank you very much."

"Fair enough, twinkle krackers. Now help me wake up sleeping beauty."

Between them they got Millicent upright and somewhat awake. She didn't speak much, just grunted and kept attempting to flop back down on the bed and back to sleep, but, after much cajoling, Arthur and Charlie managed to help her down the corridor, then down the stairs and across the main room of the inn, before propping her in a chair near the bar.

No sooner had they sat her down, Gerty bustled through from the kitchen. She took one look at Millicent, accompanied that look with a great many tuts, and shot Arthur and Charlie a look that could've split wood. She bent down, threw Millicent over her shoulder as if she were a summer jacket, and carried her off into the kitchen.

As she went in, out came Ernie.

"Well now, boys," he said, with a wide grin. "What a jolly

good shindig last night was, eh? We've not had a knees up like that since… well, I don't know when!"

Charlie took in the now empty room. The smell of ale, sweat and tobacco still clung in the air but, for now, the magic was gone. The room had gone back to being nothing more than an empty room in a tavern.

"So, what I'm going to do," Ernie carried on, coming around the bar to face Arthur and Charlie, "is not charge you a round penny. As far as I'm concerned, last night you earned your room and board. How does that sound?"

"That sounds fantastic!" said Arthur, smiling.

"It's the least I could do," said Ernie. "Not only did we go through three barrels of ale, but for the first time in a long time, this place felt alive!"

"That's very kind of you to say," Charlie said, beaming himself. "We had a great time." He glanced around the room again; nope, the magic was definitely gone. It was just a room again.

"And one more thing," Ernie said, rummaging through the pocket on the front of his thick apron. He pulled out a chunk of parchment, tore off the corner, scribbled on it with a thin stick of charcoal, and handed it over to Charlie.

"If your legs take you over to the west from here, you'll find a village about a day's walk. Gunnerton's the name. There's only one inn—the Traveller's Rest, and it's run by an old friend of mine by the name of Long Tommy. Give him this chit, and he'll give you room and board on my say so. Likes his music too, so he may even let you play a bit. Can't guarantee anything, but it's better than a kick in the lonely plum."

"Oh wow, thanks," Arthur said taking the bit of parchment from Charlie and gawping at it like a holy relic.

"Now then, I expect you'll be wanting to get off. Hang on, I'll see if young Millicent's ready," Ernie said, and then disappeared back into the kitchen.

Arthur turned to Charlie. "You know, this went a lot better than I first thought," he said. "Back when you were calling us famous musicians yesterday, I had visions of us getting thrown out on our ear."

"Oh ye of little faith," Charlie said shaking his head at Arthur. "Sometimes you just need a little self-belief. That, and stones the size of boulders."

Before Arthur could reply, Millicent emerged from the Kitchen. Whilst it would be a bit of a stretch to say she was completely transformed, she was standing upright and was walking unaided. She strode over to Charlie and Arthur who naturally took a step back.

"Right, you two," she said, her eyes bloodshot and little more than slits. "Let's get this out in the open. I believe a person makes their own decisions and, once those decisions are made, the responsibility lies squarely on the shoulders of said person. With that in mind, I did indeed decide to drink a lot of very strong gin yesterday of my own accord. I did it because I wanted to and because I could and, therefore, I will take sole responsibility for that decision." She rubbed her eyes. "And I am currently being punished for said decision with the mother of all hangovers. In fact, if my mother *were* a hangover, I expect this is exactly what she'd feel like."

"You did drink a lot of gin," Charlie said.

"Shut it, Lightfoot!" Millicent snapped. "I've had a very

nice conversation with Gerty back there in the kitchen. She assures me that, first of all, I can't sing for toffee, which is news to me, but I'll take her word for it—she's an honest sort. Says she heard me in the bath yesterday and, in her words, thought 'I'd got some skin trapped'."

Arthur managed to stifle his giggle. Charlie not so much.

"You two also heard me singing," she continued, "and it was you who persuaded me to take that first drink. So, here's what I think—I think whilst you didn't exactly ply me full of drink, you did absolutely nothing to stop me. And I think you did that knowing I'd be unable to sing last night. Is this true?"

"Absolutely not!" Charlie said incensed.

"Yes it is," Arthur admitted.

"You wet lettuce," Charlie hissed at Arthur. "Spine made of pond weed!"

"Just as I thought," Millicent said. She shook her head and looked at Arthur. "Arthur, I'm not cross, I'm just disappointed. Shame on you. Whatever would your father think?" Now she looked at Charlie. "And you, you're just a turd—plain and simple. But at least you've never pretended to be anything different."

She sighed and clasped her hands. "So, here's the new arrangement. If we ever play together again, I *will* join you on stage whether you like it or not. It might be for the first song, it might be for the last, it might be for all in between, but join you I will. There isn't much I can remember about last night, apart from the bit when we performed together; for some reason, that part is crystal clear. And here's the thing—I don't think I've ever had as much fun or felt as free as I did for that one song last night. It was brief and it was fleeting but it was... glorious."

She looked down at her hands and a sudden sadness seemed to pass over her. Then she looked up, defiantly.

"Trust me, for someone who's spent most of her life caged up like a pretty little bird, I'll be buggered if you think I'm passing up the chance to let loose like that again. Are we Understood?"

"Yes, Millicent," Arthur said, head bowed low.

"Charlie?" Millicent asked, turning to him.

"You're right: I am a turd," he admitted, "and I should've stopped you getting drunk. It was wrong, and no matter what the reasons behind it were, I should've been up front and worried about hurting your feelings less. Also, can I just add, that comparing yourself to a caged bird doesn't really work on account of the fact that most birds can hold a tune."

Charlie tried to duck the smack on the head but, despite the hangover, Millicent was just that little bit quicker. Besides, he knew he deserved it.

"Right then," Charlie said, rubbing his sore ear, "now that we're sorted, let's get this band back on the road."

CHAPTER 22

So good, they named him twice.

I T DIDN'T TAKE them long to reach Gunnerton. In fact, it only took a morning's walk. It was a straight forward journey; no mercenaries, no fall outs—mainly due to the silence of Millicent's hangover, and the thoughtful plodding of both Charlie and Arthur. In fact, the only moment of any note was when a young man, no longer wearing a what looked like a sheep's tail on his upper lip, stepped out in front of them as they left.

"Where's the moustache gone, mate?" Arthur asked. "And where the heck do you keep coming from? Do you just lie in wait for people?"

"So, I suppose you're leaving" he said, ignoring Arthur's questions.

"That we are…" Charlie said apprehensively.

"It's just I was wondering if—" the man began.

"Look," said Arthur, cutting him off abruptly, "we still don't want to buy any daggers. Or, to that end, any musical instruments either."

"Ah, no, it wasn't that," said the man, kicking at the dirt in front of him. "I just wondered if… I might get your scrawl? On this here piece of leather." The man produced a thin piece of leather and a stick which he'd whittled to a point.

Charlie, Arthur and Millicent looked at one another.

"Course, if you'd rather not, I'd understand. It's just…" He began to stumble on his words, "My brother… well, both of us actually, we were in The Lost Plum last night and we heard you play. I… me…I mean my brother, said it's the best night of music he's ever heard, and I tend to agree with him."

"So, let me get this straight," Arthur said, stepping over to the man. "You want us to write our names on that piece of leather there?"

"Only if… you want to," the man said.

"For you and your… brother. Because you enjoyed the music we played?"

"That's about the long and short of it."

"And what do you… and your brother plan to do with the bit of leather with our names on it once we're gone?"

"I… don't rightly know," the man said. "Hadn't really thought that far ahead. Probably just keep it, I suppose, as a memory of last night."

"Really?" asked Charlie.

"Well, either that or sell it," the man said. "My brother, he's the business minded one. Reckon he might want to sell it on, you know? Make a cheeky bit o' profit?"

"Huh," Charlie said. "Well, I'm game if you two are."

The three friends took it in turns etching their names onto the piece of leather. When it was Charlie's turn, his was little more than a scribble, given he'd never really seen the point in learning to write.

The man thanked them and strode off with a big smile

on his face, promising to show his 'brother' right away.

"Yeah, as soon as he can get home and slap on that daft moustache," Arthur said.

"I'm still a bit confused by the whole collecting our names thing, to be honest," Millicent said.

"Takes all types," Charlie said, shaking his head.

They walked on for the rest of the morning until they arrived in Gunnerton. It wasn't all that different to Heverton but then, they'd not exactly travelled a great distance, so it was hardly surprising.

Once again, this town started slowly—the odd farmstead here, a lonely building there—but as they followed the main track into the town proper, the number of buildings grew as the space between them shrank.

A large, open, grass-covered space with a large open-sided hut in the middle dominated the centre of Gunnerton. Edging the grass was a double wide cart track and on the other side of that were a great many buildings; each one made from timber, with a traditional thatched roof. Some were houses but most were places of business—a greengrocer, a butcher shop, a cobbler, and a blacksmith all ringed the grassy centre.

Over in the corner stood the Traveller's Rest. It looked smaller than The Lost Plum by about half and, as a sign of how quickly certain ideas had taken hold in Charlie's mind, he was surprised to find himself a little disappointed.

"If we do end up playing there tonight," Charlie said as they walked over, "it'll be a much quieter gig than last night."

"I'm just happy we've got somewhere to stay," Arthur said. "Besides, it's not like we'll get a gig every night."

The three friends entered the Traveller's Rest to find that, indeed it was a lot smaller than The Lost Plum. Not only that, but where The Lost Plum centred around one large central space, the Traveller's Rest was split into a series of smaller rooms. One thing it did share with the Plum was that, at present, the bar was empty. In fact, there didn't seem to be anyone around.

"Hello?" Charlie called out.

"Be with you shortly," a voice called out from somewhere in the back. It was followed by a scraping sound, a thud, then the sound of someone walking up two steps.

The top of a man's bald head popped up from behind the bar, just high enough to see his thick bushy eyebrows and dark, deep-set eyes.

"What'll you be having, folks?" the man said in a voice quite a few octaves lower than any of them expected.

Arthur took out the piece of parchment Ernie had given them and slid it across the bar towards the eyebrows.

"Erm... Ernie from The Lost Plum gave us this," he said. "Told us to ask for Long Tommy. We're musicians. We played at his place last night and we're looking for a couple of rooms."

"We went down a storm at The Lost Plum," Charlie said, stepping forwards. "Do you know if Long Tommy might want us to play here tonight?"

"Hang on," the tiny man behind the bar said. He picked up the piece of parchment off the top of bar and inspected it.

"Is Long Tommy around?" Charlie said, looking up and down the bar.

The man raised one of his caterpillar brows. "You taking

the mick, lad?"

Charlie grimaced. "You're Long Tommy, aren't you?" he said.

"Course I am, you daft wazzock!" the man spat. "And let me tell you, I got this name on account of how far I can throw an axe, not for any other reason, thank you very much."

A hand pointed over the bar, "See those marks over by the door?"

Arthur, Charlie and Millicent looked to the entrance they had not long walked through. It was covered in scratches, scuffs and, in more than one place, the wood had been gouged out in wide splintering chunks.

"One comment about my height and you'd better be able to get through those doors before my hatchet. Believe me, I've heard 'em all. In fact, I've had it up to here." Long Tommy raised a hand to over his own head which was waist height to Charlie.

"So, who's got something to say?"

Millicent and Arthur both turned to Charlie and shot him similar looks which didn't need all that much interpreting.

"Nope. No one. Nothing whatsoever, sir," Charlie sputtered.

Long Tommy burst into a deep, rich barrel laugh as he stepped down from his stool and walked around the bar.

"Only messing with you, folks!" he said, laughing through his thick moustache as he approached them. "When you're this size, you better have a decent sense of humour! Ernie said in his note to give you room and board, and to have a bit of fun with you. He knows I like to have a bit of fun. Should've seen your faces!"

Charlie, Millicent and Arthur let out a collective sigh.

"That being said, if you do make fun of my height, I'll cut your innards out and staple them to my bar."

Charlie, who had started to laugh along with Long Tommy, abruptly snapped his mouth shut.

"Only joking!" Long Tommy said heartily as he gently punched Charlie in the gut. At least, Charlie supposed it was meant to be gentle but Long Tommy was built like a whiskey barrel and, as his ham-size fist connected with Charlie's midriff, he doubled over, the wind completely knocked out of him.

"Blimey, bit soft aren't you, lad?" Long Tommy said, slapping a doubled-over Charlie on the back. "You musicians are all the same! All mouth and no britches. Right then, let's get you sorted!"

Long Tommy turned and shuffled off behind the bar.

"You coming," he shouted back, "or are you waiting for the servants to come and carry your personables? Cos' you'll be waiting for a blooming long time!"

Arthur, Millicent and Charlie grabbed their belongings and followed Long Tommy around the bar and out the back of the Traveller's Rest. They walked out into a small courtyard. Across two sides and the top end ran a single storey, horse shoe-shaped wooden building, with a door set into it every so often. On each door a number had been carved in the wood.

"Right then," Long Tommy said, standing scratching his bushy moustache. "Let me remember." He pointed to each of the doors in turn, counting off on his thick fingers as he did so.

"Yep, here's the thing: by my reckoning, I've only got one room left. The first two got holes in the thatching, and I'm buggered if I'm killing myself clambering up a ladder to fix them; got to wait 'til the thatcher's back out this way. The third room's got nothing but empty barrels in it, and the fourth's where I've been going to pee. So that just leaves the room on the end—number five. You three alright sharing?"

The three friends looked to one another, and then Millicent said, "How many beds?"

"Beds?!" Long Tommy said, starting to laugh. "Not quite sure where you think you are, young lady, but this is Gunnerton—not Upper Calver in the fancy-pants palace. Beds indeed!"

With that, Long Tommy shook his bald head and wandered back into the bar. "Make yourselves at home!" he shouted back over his shoulder, still chuckling to himself.

"I don't have a very good feeling about this," Arthur said as the three of them made their way over to door number five.

"I'm sure it won't be that bad," Charlie said, walking up to the door. "You saw what he was like in the bar; bit of joker. Here, let's a have look."

Charlie pushed the door open... or at least tried to. It wouldn't budge. He pushed it harder but it still refused to move.

"Maybe it's locked?" Arthur said.

Charlie gave the door a hard shove with his shoulder, it scraped open just enough for them to squeeze through, and the three friends made their way inside their room for the night.

Over in one corner, pushed up to the far wall, was a huge kitchen table. It made the one in Auntie's kitchen look like something from a child's play set. Piled on top of it was a heap of curtains that looked like they hadn't been washed since before any of the three of them had been born. The floor was bare, save for a pile of hay, and on the back wall was a dusty window which looked out onto the fields beyond.

Suddenly a ruddy face appeared at the window; or through the window to be more accurate because, to their horror, they realised it wasn't a window but a hole.

"How do?" said the red-cheeked man. He had a pipe in his mouth, and as he leant through the window, he blew a cloud of blue-grey smoke into the room. "You lot staying here tonight?"

"That's yet to be decided," Millicent said, stifling a cough.

"Not much of a lodging, if you ask me," the pipe smoker said. "But suppose it'll keep you dry. Not that there's the look of any rain in the air."

"Useful, thanks," Charlie said nodding.

"Not from round here, are you?"

"I mean, if we were, we probably wouldn't be staying in an inn now, would we?" Charlie said.

"Don't know much about that," the man replied and took a drag on his pipe as if that was all that needed saying. "So how come you're here then?"

Charlie was about broach the subject of privacy and personal distance when Arthur cut in.

"We're musicians, actually," he said enthusiastically.

"Musicians, you say?" The pipe smoker leant an elbow on the window ledge and grinned in at them. "We haven't had many of them come through here for a while."

"Probably on account of the state of the accommodation," Millicent muttered to herself.

The pipe smoker took in their surroundings, tapped his pipe on the window ledge, and stuck his hand through the gap and into the room.

"Name's Jonathan. Jonathan Jonathan. Pleasure to have made your company."

"Wait, what?" Arthur said, shaking the man's hand. "Your name is Jonathan… *Jonathan*?"

"That's right," said Jonathan Jonathan. "Named after of my dad's dad and me mum's dad, who both happened to be called the same. So, Jonathan Jonathan."

"Well that is just brilliant!" Charlie said grinning. He walked over and shook Jonathan Jonathan's hand enthusiastically. "Tell me, Jonny Jon Jon, do you know of anywhere around here that might be able to accommodate the three of us in playing a little gig tonight? I get the feeling there's not going to be enough room in the Traveller's to swing a cat, let alone play a fiddle."

Jonathan Jonathan's face lit up.

"Reckon you could use the shelter in the middle of the green. It's set to be a decent night, like I mentioned, and an open-air knees up would really get people going. Out there in the open, you wouldn't need to be swinging cats around, which is probably for the best. Some folk get a bit particular about their pets."

"Do you think we'd be allowed to play there?" Arthur asked.

"Oh, I should think so. Belongs to my dad's dad does that piece of land!"

"Jonathan, you mean?" Charlie said.

"That's the fella! Do you know him?" Jonathan Jonathan said.

"Lucky guess, Charlie said, and turned to his bandmates. "Well then, my merry minstrels" he said, "looks like we've got ourselves a gig."

CHAPTER 23

Like a bad penny.

A S NIGHT FELL and the stars began to emerge, Millicent, Charlie, and Arthur prepared for their second gig as a band by having a drink at the bar of the Traveller's Rest. They'd since put thoughts of exactly how their sleeping arrangement would work to the back of their minds, deciding instead to focus on the upcoming gig above all else.

They sat at the end of the bar, each with a cup in hand—Millicent slowly sipping at hers, making it last as long as possible—as they talked over the songs they'd play and how they might incorporate a now sober Millicent into the evening. They also had the novelty of playing outdoors; Jonathan Jonathan had left them with a promise to secure the shelter for the evening, and to round up as many people as possible to come and listen.

Arthur and Charlie agreed it would be best to play a similar set to the previous night based on the notion that what isn't broken doesn't need fixing. Millicent, for her part, seemed very relaxed about her part in things.

"So, what exactly are you planning to do?" Arthur asked her.

"Don't worry, I'm not going to try singing this time.

Well, not to begin with at least. I think I'll just see where the mood takes me with the main focus on enjoying myself. Someone's got to collect the money."

"The money?" Charlie said.

"Yes, Captain Echo—the money," she said. "You see, I've been thinking. All those people standing around, listening to you two play, hopefully enjoying themselves; well, wouldn't it be good if someone wandered around collecting a few coin off them in the meantime? I mean, it's not dissimilar to when you play on The King's Pass, except instead of people dropping coin in your coat, I'll go around and they can give it to me."

"That's one smart girl, right there!" Charlie said.

"Of course," Millicent said. "And if you call me 'girl' in that condescending way again, I'll kick you square in the dangleberries. Right, let's get this show on the road."

Ready as they'd ever be, the three of them gathered up their things and made their way outside. As they stepped out of The Traveller's Rest, they were met by a large crowd, all gathered around the shelter in the centre of the green. Dotted around the green itself was a ring of lanterns; each one staked into the ground. As the three friends made their way towards the shelter, the crowd parted in front of them.

"There must be at least a hundred people here!" Arthur hissed to Charlie.

"At least," Charlie whispered back. It was, without a doubt the most people he had ever played to.

As they reached the shelter, also adorned with lanterns hanging from its eaves, Jonathan Jonathan moved through the crowd and made his way over to them, beaming a huge smile.

"Well, what do you think?" he said, gesturing at the crowd.

"How did you round up all these people?!" Charlie asked.

"Just put the word out," he replied, looking just a little smug. "A few friends told a few friends, and here we are. Also, it helped that SimonPeter—my mate from Heverton—came over and volunteered to come around and tell everyone how great you are."

Charlie looked over to where Jonathan Jonathan was gesturing. Stood on the edge of the crowd, waving back frantically and still clutching the piece of leather, complete with sheep-tail moustache, was the young man who'd tried to sell them daggers.

"Well I'll be…" said Arthur.

"Oh yes, been friends with SimonPeter since we were kids. Our dads worked the fields in between here and Heverton together. Gotta watch out for him though – he'll try and sell you anything. Did you know, he's got a brother? Goes by the name of PeterSimon. I've seen them separately; you can tell them apart on account of the moustache. Never seen them together though, crafty buggers that they are. One day I might."

Arthur took one last look over at SimonPeter, then Jonathan Jonathan, shook his head, and followed Charlie and Millicent up the set of steps and into the shelter. As they did so, the crowd began to quiet.

Inside the shelter, lit up by the glow of the lanterns, were three wooden chairs.

"We'll not be needing these," Charlie said. He strode forward, picked the middle chair up, and turned to face the crowd.

"Ladies, Gentlemen, and those happy souls who came for a good time," he said, raising his voice. "If you think this'll be a good chance for a nice sit down, then you're at the wrong gig!"

He threw the chair out of the shelter where it bounced along the grass out of the way of the crowd. Arthur and Millicent followed suit and threw the remaining chairs from the shelter, and as each chair landed, the crowd cheered louder.

"So, without further ado," Charlie shouted. "Get your dancing shoes on and prepare to have more fun than a monk at Maude's House of Dubious Repute!"

As per the night before, Arthur hit his drum so hard, Charlie felt it in his chest. Silence immediately fell across the crowd—not in a wave, but an instant. Arthur held his beater over his head as if it were a hard-won trophy, and the crowd cheered. He brought it down and smashed it on his bodhran, and the boom echoed across the green and bounced back from the buildings around its edges. Once more he held his beater aloft, and once more the crowd roared.

Charlie savoured the moment– how proud he was of his friend who, in the space of one performance, had changed from the landlord's son who would only practice in a beer cellar, to a showman holding the crowd in the palm of his hand—before Millicent belted out what could only be described as a shrieking war-cry.

There was a moment of stunned silence before Arthur launched into the opening rhythm of 'Johan's Battle Axe' and the crowd erupted in exhilaration. The cheers went up and people rushed to grab one another as impromptu dances broke out across the grass.

Charlie dove in and joined Arthur's furious beat along-side Millicent's occasional yelps and hoots of joy. Before they'd gotten halfway through, she was off into the crowd, swinging anyone she could get a hold of around in a whirling mass of energy.

Arthur and Charlie launched into song after song with barely a pause for breath in between. Millicent would occasionally join them on the raised stage where she would dance around, stamping, clapping and generally having the best time she possibly could. Then, she'd dash off the stage and out into the crowd. At some point she'd managed to get hold of a bucket, and would dance past people, shaking it every now and then until they threw a few coins in before continuing with the rhythm.

As Charlie looked out over the crowd, he could see that whilst most were dancing, some, in fact, were not. He couldn't make out all their faces, even with the lanterns dotted around the green, but one group in particular caught his eye. Over by the far edge of the green, nearest to The Traveller's Rest, a group of what looked to be six, maybe seven stood motionless. They were arranged in a strangely stiff formation, almost in a straight line. Charlie couldn't put his finger on what it was that bothered him about the group, anything more than it just seemed odd, that, with all the frivolity surrounding them, they should be behaving in such a manner.

Quickly, he moved his attention on as they neared the end of their final song. As 'Sleeping in the Furrows of My Enemy' drew to its triumphant climax, Millicent joined them under the shelter and the three friends stood together as the crowd clapped, shouted and cheered.

Shouts of 'more!' echoed across the green and before the applause had died down, Millicent began stomping out the opening rhythm to 'The Land of Those Who Are Free' right on cue, and within moments the crowd had joined in, clapping along in time.

Arthur counted them in as loud as he could, then he and Charlie launched into their encore. Like the night before, Millicent whirled and shrieked and hooted all while Charlie and Arthur played faster and faster. And just like the night before, the song ended when Millicent—spinning out of control—crashed into the group of people closest to the shelter, sending bodies cascading in all directions.

Charlie stepped forward to the front of the shelter and shouted.

"Ladies and Gentlemen, we are the Calver Three! Thanks for coming—it wouldn't be a party without you!"

Amidst the shouting and celebrating, he waded through the sea of people to where he found Millicent lying flat out on her back laughing up at the sky.

"How's that arse of yours?" he asked, offering her a hand.

"If that's the best pick up line you've got," she said, reaching over to collect the bucket, which was now nearly full of coin, "you need to work on it."

"Enjoy yourself?" Charlie asked as they walked back up to Arthur who was packing his bohdran away.

"You know what?" Millicent said, "I think I enjoyed tonight far more than last night. Probably since there's no fear of waking up with a head that feels like it's been split in two."

"You were brilliant!" Arthur said, joining them, and eyeing their takings. "And it looks like we made a decent amount too."

"Who'd have thought," Charlie said, packing his fiddle away, "that we'd be walking away from a gig with a bucket full of coin?"

"Who would have thought that Millicent Hargreaves, soon to be Von Haugen, would have stooped so low, so quickly?" answered a voice he knew only too well.

That was when Charlie realised.

The group over by the edge of the green. Standing in a straight line, clearly out of place.

Clearly out of *their* place.

Millicent stumbled back, tripped over the edge of the shelter and, in falling, dropped the bucket, spilling its contents over the grass.

"I suppose you should get down on your hands and knees and pick up your pennies, you plucky musicians," Roderick Von Haugen said. The other six with him laughed as if this were indeed the funniest joke they'd ever had the good fortune to hear.

"Oh, hi Roderick," Charlie said. "I see you're still a scrote."

Roderick took a step forward and his friends followed suit.

"Ah, yes. The boy from the Backstreets. The overfamiliar and little bit too chummy, Mr. Lightfoot. I see you've got yourself a wonderful thing going." Roderick spread his arms to incorporate the green which was now emptying of people as they made their way home.

"Just entertaining a few people. Providing a bit of joy. You know, making people happy? Who am I kidding? The only time you make anyone happy is when you leave."

Charlie couldn't say why he was provoking Roderick. Obviously, they were outnumbered; obviously, things were about to get very serious very quickly; obviously, winding Roderick up wasn't a very clever thing to do. But—and Charlie was finding this was becoming more and more important to him—he was stuffed if he was going to let anyone barge into his world just because they thought they could.

This was his thing. Not Roderick's. Who did he think he was?

"You want to watch that mouth of yours, boy. Talk like that might hold water on the scum-streets of Lower Calver, but it doesn't work with me. Carry on like that and you're liable to earn yourself a good hiding."

Millicent scrambled to her feet. She had clearly gotten over the initial shock of seeing her betrothed. "What in the hells are you doing, Roderick?" she asked angrily. "How dare you! Just exactly who do you think you are?"

"I, Millicent my dear," he said, lifting his head high, "am Roderick von Haugen—soon to be one of the most powerful men in Middle Calver. And I have come to take you home. This whole charade will make for such an entertaining little story in time, but for now, this nonsense must cease."

Charlie moved forward and stood on one side of Millicent, Arthur did so on the other.

"Is this the man you were supposed to marry?" he said with a slight sneer.

"The one and only," Millicent said, folding her arms.

"Ah, I see," he said. "Well, I believe in doing things properly. I don't believe we've been formally introduced." Arthur extended his hand, which Roderick looked at in the same way someone might inspect an infected boil. Arthur continued regardless. "My name is Arthur Hawthorn. Millicent and Charlie have both told me a great deal about you, most of which appears to be quite accurate. Of course, when they said you were an angular turd, I hadn't realised just how accurate a description that was; your face is literally as if someone shaped poo with a knife."

Roderick was quick; a lot quicker than Charlie expected him to be. With a blur of his backhand, he sent Arthur him sprawling to the floor.

Charlie moved to retaliate but before he could even get close, one of Roderick's friends sent a heavy-booted foot into his stomach. He doubled over and landed in a heap next to Arthur, the wind kicked out of him.

"Roderick! Stop it!" Millicent pleaded and crouched down over Arthur and Charlie.

"Thought… you were winding him up because you had… a plan," Arthur groaned.

"Not really. I was just hoping… to buy us… some time," Charlie replied, gasping for breath.

"Think I've got a couple of loose teeth."

"To be fair, I think it was worth it for the whole poo shaped with a knife thing. Definitely some of your better work."

"It was pretty good, wasn't it?" Arthur said grinning through blood-stained teeth.

Before either could say anything more, firm hands grabbed them by the shoulders and hoisted them upright.

"Roderick, if you even so much as breathe on me, I'll rip your face off," Millicent said clenching her teeth and fists.

Roderick took a half-step back and held his palms up. "Woah there, pussycat!" he said. "Looks like this little trip out of Calver has given you a bit of a feral streak! Don't worry, my love, me and the boys will soon break the wild filly."

His friends all guffawed obnoxiously.

"In the meantime," he said, cracking his knuckles, "we just need to teach smart-talking Mr. Lightfoot and his potty-mouthed friend some old-fashioned manners. Probably an utterly foreign concept to them but from where I'm from, 'manners maketh the man'."

"Problem is," said a voice from behind Roderick, "you ain't where *you're* from right now. You're where *I'm* from."

"Stabby-stabby, leaky-holes time?" said another.

CHAPTER 24

Violent violence.

I N A N A L M O S T practiced synchronicity, the line of Roderick's friends holding Charlie and Arthur each turned to face Hacker John, Ticker the Vengeful, and Steven.

Roderick pushed his forward way through the line.

"Oh, for god's sake…" he said with an air of impatience, "Who the devil are you? Can't you see we're busy here? Clear off!" He waved a dismissive arm in the three mercenary's general direction.

"As much as I'd love to take orders from a posh nob like yourself, I'm afraid we three cannot, and therefore will not, clear off. You see, we've got one of those debts of gratitude thingamajigs we owe those musicians there. Sorry about that, toff-boy."

"Excuse me?" Roderick spat.

"Well, I shan't bore you with the nitty gritty," Hacker John continued, "but let's just say they did a nice thing for us and helped us save face in front of someone we three look up to very much. So, we had a bit of a chat between us and decided to see if we could catch up to them and offer our sincerest thanks. It's the honourable thing to do, after all. By the time we found them, they were already playing in that there shelter. I must say, the three of you aren't half bad."

"Thank you kindly," Charlie said, still in the grip of two of Roderick's friends.

"Don't mention it," Hacker John went on. "Anyways, we just wanted to say thanks once you'd finished playing, but it would appear we might be able to repay you in other ways."

"Erm, excuse me, friend," said one of Roderick's cohorts as he strode up to the Hacker John. He was the biggest of the group, and towered over the mercenary leader. He stood almost eye to eye with Steven, "I'm not entirely sure who you... people think you are but you're meddling in affairs which are none of your concern. You may be able to get away with that kind of thing with the common folk around here, but we seven are anything but. To wit, why don't you just bugger off?"

Hacker John turned to Charlie.

"Did he just say, 'to wit'?"

"Yeah. Folks up in Middle Calver tend to say it a lot," Charlie said.

"I wouldn't expect you oiks to understand," the large friend said dismissively.

"Ha!" said Ticker, launching into his hopping from foot-to-foot dance with a huge grin across his face. "Like being on a farm!" Then he leant his head back and shouted into the night air, "To wit, to woo! Oik, oink!"

Steven started to laugh. It was a slow, low rumble, his shoulders shaking up and down with each snicker.

"This is ridiculous!" Roderick shouted. "I'm dealing with incompetents and mad men!" He addressed his burly companion. "Oliver, hit the big one."

"Oh, I wouldn't do that if I were you," said Hacker John, shaking his head.

Oliver stepped over to Steven and hit him square on the nose.

Steven took a step back, and slowly brought a hand up to his face. He looked confused and pushed his nose flat against the side his cheek.

"Nose not hurt before. Now nose hurt..." he said, squishing his nose flat again. As he brought his hand away, he noticed blood on his fingers, and his brow creased in confusion. He touched his nose again and, once again, his fingers came away with blood on them.

Slowly, Steven's face darkened. His brow lowered and the left side of his mouth drew up into angry, mostly toothless snarl.

"I did warn you," Hacker John said.

Far faster than anyone would've believed Steven could possibly move, he brought his club up from where it had been dangling at his side and thrust the end of it into Oliver's face. Hard.

Oliver too took a step back. But this was after most of his face appeared to explode outwards; first with a loud crack and then a squishing noise. His lips were split open down the middle, and there was now a gap where at least three teeth should've been. Most of his nose was now smeared across his left cheek.

Oliver took another step back. Then another.

"Goh schlit," he said and fell over backwards, eyes rolling up into his head.

"Timber!" Ticker shouted now almost bursting at the seams with glee.

"What are you lot waiting for," shouted Roderick to his men like a spoiled child. "Rough them up!"

He shoved one forwards, who looked back at Roderick; his face a mix of terror and bewilderment. Hacker John folded his arms.

"What's your name, son?" he said looking at the unfortunate friend who'd been nominated.

"M-Marcus..." stammered Marcus.

"I'm guessing, Marcus," continued John, "that you've been in one or two scrapes before. Maybe a spot of fisticuffs after someone got a little out of line? You gave them a bit of a kicking, you and your mates over there, then went on your merry little posh-boy way. Am I about right?"

Marcus nodded timidly.

"Well, what we've got going on here is a little bit different, see? Probably feels a bit different to you too. Does your tummy feel a bit strange? Do you feel a little bit sick?"

Marcus nodded again.

"I understand, Marcus. Mine did the first proper skirmish I got myself into. You see, violence is a strange thing—it comes in many forms and it isn't always the same. Sometimes it's you and your well-to-do chums picking on someone because you can; sometimes it's the very real possibility that a large mercenary is going to break your face with a wooden club. So, you're going to have to make a choice, Marcus—a simple one, really. You can run away now. Run all the way back to the comfort and overwhelming privilege of Middle Calver. Or you can die; right here, right now. And if you think I'm bluffing or just being overly dramatic... Ticker?"

"Yep, yep, yep, that is me! I am he! Ticker, Ticker, Ticker!" said the mercenary in question, whipping around to look at Hacker John.

"Stabby-stabby, leaky-holes time."

Ticker's eyes lit up. A grin spread across his face, one so wide it could easily have touched each ear, and he leapt at the closest of Roderick's friends, who happened to be holding Charlie's left arm. Ticker landed in a blur of motion, latching limpet-like on the man, who squealed as he tried to pull the mad mercenary off. Ticker's arms flapped manically around the man, as if he were trying to put out someone who was on fire, and after a series of dizzying slaps, he leaped off and danced back over to Hacker John.

"W-what the bla—" began the man, before he suddenly stopped speaking.

It was as if someone had asked him to solve a very difficult and complicated problem. He looked from Charlie to Ticker to Hacker John, then he coughed; blood spurted from his mouth. Still confused, he ran his hands up and down his torso, patting himself as if trying to locate a lost key. He brought his hands up to his face and his confused look intensified.

"W-why are my hands re—?" he started, and then toppled forwards, face first to the ground.

"Stabby-stabby, leaky-holes!" said Ticker, spinning the small daggers he held in each hand and slotting them back in his belt.

The remaining friends scattered. There was no thought involved; they just ran in a direction that wasn't where they were, and as fast as they could.

Only Roderick remained.

Charlie looked at him, now alone, deserted by his so-called friends, and it became so very clear just how out of place he looked. He even seemed smaller somehow.

"Right then," Hacker John said, walking over to Charlie. "It would appear that we're just about even."

Charlie nodded and took in the scene before him. "I'd say that just about does it."

"Only one thing left to do…" Hacker John said.

"What's that?" Charlie asked.

"Nightcap," he said, "Know anywhere decent where a thirsty mercenary can get a drink?"

"We're staying at The Traveller's Rest," suggested Charlie. "Don't know what the ale's like though."

"If it's anything like their rooms, I'd be careful," added Arthur, joining them.

"So long as it's wet and strong," said Hacker John, "we aren't fussy drinkers. You can buy us a jar or two. Now that you're highly paid musicians." He slung his arms around Arthur and Charlie's shoulders. Ticker had already skipped off across the grass and Millicent led Steven a few steps in front of them.

"This is not bloody right!"

Arthur, Charlie, and Hacker John paused. They turned around to face Roderick, who was holding what appeared to be a very ornate and quite expensive-looking dagger, which he'd pulled from somewhere about his person.

"You can't just go around… killing people! It's… not the done thing! There must be some sort of repercussions for such unwarranted violence!"

His face, even in the dying light of the lanterns, was very clearly a purplish red. The hand he held the dagger in was trembling; it was hard to tell if it was from fear or rage.

Millicent walked past Charlie, Arthur and Hacker John and approached him. Charlie tried to grab her arm, but she shook him off. She looked her fiancée in the eyes.

"Roderick, it's over," she said. "Go home—*your* home. You don't belong here. Look, we both know that within weeks your family will have found a suitable replacement for me; they're probably doing so as we speak. Can you imagine what it would be like if I returned with you? I'm tarnished—I'm the girl who chose all of this over high society. Even if I came back with you right at this very moment, can you imagine the comments? The snickering behind our back? So go home. Go back to Middle Calver and the life you've had made for you there."

"I…" Roderick began, turning an even deeper shade of magenta, "I… will not be denied!"

Charlie, Arthur and Hacker John took a step forward, but Millicent held up her hand.

"Is this really where this is heading, Roderick?" She shook her head. "Of course it is, how stupid of me! This isn't about me, or marriage or the future or, heavens forbid, love, is it? It's about me turning you down. That's pretty much what this whole thing boils down to isn't it? Nobody's ever said no to you before."

She shook her head again, let out a long sigh, and turned away.

"You… little… whore!" Roderick shouted, the words echoing around the buildings on the edge of the green. "You jumped up little strumpet! You never were good enough for me. You'll never be good enough. No man will ever take you because you just won't do as you're told!"

Charlie saw a look flash across Millicent's eyes that caused him to take an involuntary step back. She spun around, took one step towards an incandescent Roderick, and aimed a kick squarely between his legs, her foot colliding so hard with his nether regions that the man lifted clear from the ground. His breath left him all at once in a loud *OOOOF*, and he crumpled to the floor.

Millicent turned, her face still set in a thunderous glare and marched past an open-mouthed Arthur, Charlie and Hacker John, and over to Steven. She hooked her arm in his, and together they walked across the green and towards The Traveller's Rest.

Charlie looked over at the pile on the floor that was Roderick and winced.

"Reckon he might need to rub his neck to find his scroggs," Hacker John said, also wincing.

"Think I got lucky with just a slap" Charlie said.

CHAPTER 25

Don't bite off your nose to spite your face.

THE NEXT FEW months progressed in a somewhat predictable manner.

The Calver Three, as they now enjoyed calling themselves, moved from village to village and more often than not, played a gig in each one. Sometimes, weather permitting, they'd play outdoors, and these gigs meant they could make the most coin as Millicent could move freely between the crowd and try to get them to fill her bucket. More often than not though, they'd end up at the local inn. These gigs didn't generate as much coin—quite often none at all—but the landlord usually provided them with a hot meal and lodgings for the night at no cost. Only very occasionally would the landlord offer them some coin too.

Millicent, Charlie and Arthur were happy to take whatever came their way. Whilst they knew they could play, and play well, they also knew the adventure they were on was just that—an adventure. As long as they had a roof over their heads and food in their stomachs, they were, for the most part, happy.

There were the odd occasions when the next village was just that bit too far to make the journey in a single day, and in those cases, they looked elsewhere to stay for the night. Most people had a spare room or at the very least a corner of a barn they could offer, and as these instances were few and far between, the three friends didn't particularly mind.

They'd collected their fair share of stories from these travels; like the time they bedded down on the floor of a farmhouse, only to be woken by the farmer and his wife wearing nothing but grins in the middle of the night. The farmer suggested they could all 'get down to a bit of rutting', at which point the Calver Three hastily gathered up their belongings and exited stage left.

For the most part, the three friends made their way into the Kingdom with no real plan and no real need for one. They didn't stray further than roughly a week's walk of Calver; not by organized route, but more by an ambling direction that kept them somewhat parallel to the great city.

It was as they moved into their third month on the road that the niggles began. Like any group of people who spend every waking and sleeping hour in each other's pockets, the disagreements always started small and often ended with either Charlie or Millicent storming out from wherever they were. They were usually resolved by Arthur, and by the time the next gig was about to start. On the rare instance that they hadn't, whatever it was they'd been fighting over was often left in the past by the time the gig finished.

As the three friends arrived at the edge of the latest village—a place called Appleover—another such disagreement was brewing.

"I just don't understand why you want a room for yourself. The landlord will probably charge us extra," Charlie protested.

"Because, dear Charlie, I am sick to the back teeth of your snoring, nail picking, farting, and generally disgusting nature. I would like a nice night where I don't have to deal with a miasma of noxious fumes," Millicent replied.

"I'll have you know I'm a very well-mannered individual! I wear my undergarments inside out before washing them and everything."

"Well, you can both stop bickering now," Arthur said, pointing at the large Inn before them, "we're here."

They'd spent the best part of three days walking to reach Appleover, and last night they'd slept in an old barn, huddled together for warmth.

It had been this which started the argument between Millicent and Charlie, mainly after Charlie had woken Millicent with a blast from what he tastefully referred to as his 'bum trumpet'.

"Crikey, it's bigger than I thought it would be," Charlie commented, taking in the inn before them.

"Yeah, when the guy at the last place said it was big, he wasn't joking," Arthur said.

They'd been told by lots of people they should head towards Appleover and see if they could get a gig at The Ploughman's Folly. At each village they'd visited as they'd got progressively closer to Appleover, someone had suggested they try their luck at one of the largest inns in the area.

Apparently, and according to the locals, The Ploughman's Folly was set on one of the major routes on the way into Calver, and as soon as the three friends arrived in Appleover, they recognised the same double wide cart tracks that they'd initially followed out of the city.

Not only was The Ploughman's Folly the largest inn they'd come across on their fledgling travels, but it was the first to specialise in music. Time and time again they'd been told that at the end of every week, The Ploughman would feature some musical act or other, and it was well known around those parts as the place to go for live entertainment.

It was a strange-looking building as it essentially sat astride the double wide cart track. Most of the inn was on one side; the large building running parallel to the track. On the opposite side sat a second, smaller building, and from the end of the main building rose a third, which reached out over the track and landed on the smaller building on the opposite side. That way, anything passing along the track had to pass under the connecting bridge-like structure of the inn.

Charlie, Arthur and Millicent made their way into the largest of the buildings and managed to secure a couple of rooms and the chance to play that the evening, although they would go on after another band.

With negotiations finalised, Charlie decided he needed a little space. Other than the gigs themselves, he found himself wanting to spend less time with Millicent and Arthur. It wasn't that he didn't like them, it was more he'd spent far too much time with them already and needed a little by himself.

Just like Millicent with her separate room.

He'd always been someone who enjoyed his own company and, if truth be told, he'd previously spent most of his life alone. He didn't have any close friends to speak of other than the two people he'd spent the last couple of months with, and that suited him fine. He supposed it had something to do with being abandoned at an early age and the need to be as self-sufficient as possible.

"I'm going to head out for a bit, see what Appleover's got to offer," he said to Arthur and Millicent after they'd dropped off their things in their rooms and met back downstairs by the bar. "It's the largest place we've been to since we left Calver and I'm sure there must be something interesting around here."

"That's a great idea," Arthur said. "I'll come with you."

"No... it's okay. You don't need to do that," Charlie said hesitantly.

"I don't mind. It might be quite nice to have a bit of an explore—"

"Seriously, you can stay here," insisted Charlie. "Maybe keep Millicent company?"

Arthur looked a little crestfallen. "Oh... okay, sure," he said.

"Don't worry, Arthur" Millicent said, patting him on the shoulder, "we can have a nice drink at the bar and give Mr. Lightfoot some time alone. Clearly, he doesn't want to be around us..."

"No, it's not that," Charlie said, "and I'll thank you not to put words in my mouth,"

"It's fine, don't worry about us," Millicent said, turning away from Charlie as he headed to the door.

He shook his head and turned away.

CHARLIE SPENT MOST of the morning wandering the tangled streets of Appleover. He didn't head anywhere in particular, nor did he do much of anything either; in fact, he spent most of his time wandering aimlessly, never really able to settle on one train of thought or one direction.

He soon discovered that, whilst Appleover was the biggest village they'd encountered since they'd left Calver, it was still considerably smaller than Lower Calver or the Backstreets. As he made his way out of the centre and over to a nearby river, for the first time since they'd left, Charlie found himself missing home.

He missed its familiarity and the people, and he missed the way of life. Of course, these very things were part of the reason he'd left but, right now, at this moment and in this place, he found himself strangely drawn to them.

Most of all, he missed Auntie. Actually, not necessarily the woman herself, but all she stood for. She was consistency and safety and all he'd known for a very long time. Maybe, just maybe, it was time to start winding their way home…

Surely Millicent's troubles were behind her by now and, even though he knew Lady Gwendolyn to be a nasty piece of work, he assumed she would welcome her only daughter home with open arms after such a long absence.

Probably.

There were things which would need to change if he was to return—his arrangement with Dodge for one. He wasn't entirely sure how he'd make that happen, but he was sure he could think of something; once he'd managed to convince Dodge to keep Mr. Lunk from rearranging his body parts as punishment for running away in the first place.

He would also have to find some regular gigs in Lower Calver. With a few tweaks, he had a whole new repertoire of songs to play now and, if he could get Arthur to join him and play at the end of each week, that might open up a whole new audience. After that, who knew? Maybe they could head out beyond the wall every summer.

Actually, that wasn't a bad idea.

They could tour around the part of the Kingdom closest to Calver, play a few gigs in places that had got to know them, then head back into Calver for the winter months and play gigs along the many inns of Lower Calver.

With a new sense of purpose and his mind made up, Charlie headed back to The Ploughman's Folly to talk his plan over with Millicent and Arthur.

CHARLIE TURNED A final corner, stepped out from behind a squat, rather ugly house and was met by the sight of a dozen horses lashed to the rail across the track from The Ploughman's Folly. They were well fed and well attired and the whole scenario didn't feel right at all.

He couldn't say why, but Charlie knew something was very wrong. He burst into a run and slammed through the front door of the inn. Millicent and Arthur were still at the bar. But they were flanked by five King's Guards on either side.

Sat at a table in front of them, laughing together over a jar of ale, was a heavily decorated member of the King's Guard and one Roderick von Haugen.

"Ah, Lighfoot!" Roderick said as Charlie entered. "So very good of you to join us!" He spoke as if Charlie were a long-lost friend. "You'll see that we've already spent a little time with Millicent and Arthur and now, the Calver Three is complete!"

Charlie glanced over at his friends. Arthur's eye had swollen shut and his lip was split and bloody. Millicent had a large red welt on her cheek and her shirt was torn over the shoulder.

"Sit down, why don't you?" Roderick said. He gestured to the chair opposite, and the seated King's Guard kicked it from under the table for Charlie to sit on.

"I'd rather eat my own eyes," Charlie said with a sneer.

"That can be arranged. But for now, you'll sit, boy," Roderick said.

He nodded at the two King's Guard stood closest to Charlie who grabbed him and threw him into the chair.

"So, this is the one?" said Roderick's seated companion. "Doesn't look like much. How did you manage to lose your bit of fluff to him?" He laughed and downed a mouthful of ale.

Roderick flushed but recovered quickly.

"Charlie, this is Commander Pushfoot of the King's Guard. He's about as high up as you can get; certainly when it comes to the region of Middle Calver. You know, it's strange who you end up making friends with when you have an embarrassingly large amount of personal wealth."

"Yeah, as long as the coin keeps flowing," Commander Pushfoot laughed.

Once again, Roderick looked flustered but shook it off.

"Took us a little while to catch up with you," Roderick said, "but when you play in every village along a certain path, you make yourselves very easily found."

"We weren't hiding," Millicent said. "And even if we were, it certainly wouldn't be from the likes of you. Remember what happened the last time you caught up with us—how is little Roderick doing by the way? You remember, don't you, my love? When I left you crying on the grass like a—"

Roderick began to turn the same shade of purple as before. "Shut up!" he shouted but it was already too late.

"You never told me that, von Haugen!" Commander Pushfoot said, leaning forwards. "Did she really drop you?"

"She… she ambushed me!" Roderick practically squealed. "And she had these two, plus three mercenaries with her! If it hadn't been for them sneaking up on me, well then… I'd have… thrashed them within an inch of their lives!"

"We didn't ambush you!" Arthur said. "It was just you and Millicent. You had a dagger and she kicked you square in the–"

"Silence!" Roderick roared. "You there, make him stop talking!"

The guard next to Arthur punched him hard in the stomach. Arthur collapsed to the floor, gasping for air.

"Ah, that's better," said Roderick. "Did I mention how easy things become when you've got an embarrassingly large amount of personal wealth? I think I did mention that, didn't I?"

"Once or twice," Commander Pushfoot said humourlessly, taking another pull on his jar.

"So, you scuttled back home," Charlie said "with your tail between your legs—quite literally—and gathered together this lot, headed back out here, and tracked us down."

"Did you stop off at The Lost Plum?" Arthur managed between wheezes.

Commander Pushfoot spat out a mouthful of ale.

"Are you sure these are a bad lot? They seem pretty funny to me." he said.

"They *are* a bad lot!" said Roderick, thumping the table. "I asked around when I got back to Calver." He pointed accusatorily at Arthur, "That one on the floor is some jumped-up landlord's son,"—then Charlie—"this one plays a fiddle around the Backstreets,"—and finally his fiancee—"and that one doesn't know when to be told what her place is!"

Commander Pushfoot shrugged. "Whatever you say Von Haugen. It's your coin."

"You're damned straight it is." Roderick leant over until his face was mere inches from Charlie's. "And with every breath you take from this moment forward, I want you to remember that it's *my* coin, *my* power and *my* influence that has won out. Not your silly faffing around on your fiddle, or your romantic notions of being a musician, or anything else a simpleton from the gutter could possibly think they could bring to the table. You're not even in my league, scum-boy. And I'm going to make sure that you spend every moment of your remaining existence remembering exactly where your place in life is. At the bottom."

Roderick smiled and patted Charlie gently on the cheek.

Charlie calmly returned the smile. Then he grabbed Roderick by the ears and sunk his teeth into his nose.

CHAPTER 26

Travelling band.

B Y THE TIME Charlie regained consciousness, they were already on the move. He woke up slumped sideways over a horse, tied in place with a rope around his middle. His vision swam into place, weaving in and out at the edges. His head pounded and he couldn't seem to find a bit of him that didn't hurt.

The horse plodded along, jolting his sore ribs with every step. His vision wobbled, his stomach lurched, and Charlie threw up over the side. Once finished, he passed out once again.

The second time Charlie awoke, he was given little choice over the matter. He landed with a thud upon the ground, and jolted awake. There was a brief moment of unfocused bliss—a gap of nothingness where he didn't know who or where he was or what was happening—and then the pain hit him all and everywhere at once. Charlie curled into a ball and hugged his knees to his chest. He screwed his eyes shut in a vain attempt to quieten the pounding behind them but to no avail.

Suddenly, cold water hit him like a hard slap, and he jerked upright, gasping for air. He coughed, then spluttered, then retched.

"Now this is a memory I intend to savour," said Roderick, with the bucket still in his hands. "If I'm ever feeling low, I shall recall this image of the great musician Charlie Lightfoot puking and retching as pisswater drips from his greasy locks. How very pathetic."

"Just as long as you don't get too 'over-excited'," Charlie managed in a coughing wheeze. "Also, that bandage on your nose looks ridiculous."

Roderick kicked Charlie hard, causing him to topple over sideways. "Ingrate," he said, and threw the bucket down on the ground and walked over to where his men were deconstructing a makeshift tent.

Charlie felt hands helping him sit upright. He focused his eyes and saw the familiar shapes of Millicent and Arthur come into view. Once they'd got him sat up, they sat by his side.

"Sorry, that seat's taken," he said to Arthur weakly.

"Sod off, Lightfoot," Arthur replied with smile.

"How are you feeling, Charlie?" Millicent asked, concerned.

"Like I've just been run over by a horse. Wearing hobnail boots. What happened?"

"Roderick had his paid goons rough you up. Pretty badly actually," she said. "They only stopped when we promised to go with them without any further fuss."

"Obviously, I was all for taking them on and giving them a good kicking," added Arthur, "but I didn't want to show you up."

"Obviously," Charlie said.

"Actually, it was pretty scary," Arthur said, turning serious for a second. "We were worried about you."

Charlie winced but managed a smile through teeth that felt loose in more than one place. "Takes more than a few King's Guards to get rid of Mr. Backstreets here," he said. "So, what's happening now?"

"They're taking us back to Calver," Millicent said. "We're about a day's walk away."

"Why are they taking us back?" Charlie asked. "I mean, I can understand Roderick wanting you"—he nodded toward Millicent—"but why us two?"

"He wants you to suffer," she said. "When you wrong someone like Roderick von Haugen, swift retribution is never, ever on the cards. Anyone dares to rise up against the Von Haugen's of this world, then the world needs to know that they've suffered as a result."

Charlie rubbed his head, finding a couple of new and painfully interesting lumps there. Now that things started to shift into focus, he took the opportunity to look around. He guessed they'd taken a more direct route back towards Calver, rather than the wandering one they'd taken on the way out. By the side of a wide track where they were sat, he could see a small village some distance behind them and a series of winding hills up in front. He could just make out the top two sections of Calver in the distance; the thick walls encircling the great hill; and the palace sat proudly at the top.

The rest of Roderick's armed escort were sat by a small fire on the other side of the track, eating what looked like some kind of meat, as well as loaves of bread, a selection of fruit, and a flagon or two of a red liquid Charlie took to be wine.

"Don't suppose there's any of that for us?" he shouted across the divide.

The guardsman didn't stop their conversation, but one of them tossed a bone across which landed at Charlie's feet. It had been gnawed almost completely bare.

Charlie looked down at the bone, shook his head and lay back. He closed his eyes.

"Aren't you scared?" Millicent said.

"Absolutely terrified," Charlie admitted.

"Thank goodness for that," Arthur said. "I was beginning to think it was just me."

"But it would seem there's not a lot we can do about our situation," Charlie continued.

"That's a very relaxed approach to things," Millicent said.

"Right about now," said Charlie, "doing nothing is just about all I'm capable of. The only part of me that doesn't hurt is my spleen and that's only because I'm not sure where it is."

Roderick strutted back over as his men began to load their wrapped encampment onto the back of the horses.

"Right, you gaggle of weary performers—it's time to march ever-onwards towards your unavoidable fate."

"What's he on about?" Charlie asked Millicent.

"It's time to move," Millicent said.

Arthur and Millicent got slowly to their feet and helped Charlie to his. He wobbled and staggered and would've fallen down had they not grabbed him before he did so.

Between them, they managed to support their friend, and as the first half of King's Guards set off on horseback, they followed on foot with the other half riding at their rear.

Roderick took off to ride at the front of the procession like a triumphant warrior returning with his captives.

Commander Pushfoot, clearly wanting to reach Calver as soon as possible, circled back from the front and drew alongside the three prisoners, urging them to quicken their pace.

"You know, if you let us ride on one of those fine horses there, we'd be back a whole lot sooner," Charlie said.

Pushfoot snorted. "There's no way you're going to sully one of the King's Guard's horses. And I'm certain his lordship up front wouldn't stand for it," he said.

"How does that sit with you by the way?" Charlie asked. "You, a Commander in the King's Guard, being ordered around by some tit from Middle Calver."

If Charlie had hoped to get a rise out of Pushfoot, he was mistaken. The Commander simply shrugged.

"As long as he keeps paying me and my lads, he can order me to do a jig before bed each night if it pleases."

"And that sits okay with you?" Arthur pushed.

Commander Pushfoot shrugged again.

"Do you know how long I've been in the King's Guard? Since I was a boy of fourteen. It's all I've ever known. I've helped to keep the peace in the Grand City of Calver for over thirty years. I've fought in battles too—real battles out here in the Kingdom proper. Battles where people try to put holes in you that your insides come out of."

"I didn't know there were still battles to be fought in the Kingdom." Millicent said. "I thought peace had been declared years back."

For the first time, Commander Pushfoot seemed genu-

ENVY

inely interested in what was being said. He leant forward on his saddle and gestured before them with the reigns in his hand.

"Sure, there aren't so many now, but as short a time as ten years ago, there were still quite a few scrapes to get in to. Everything from mercenaries getting just a little too powerful for the King's liking, right through to foreign nations venturing upon our shores, poking around and deciding if they wanted to stay—it was my job to make sure they didn't."

Charlie had never really had much cause to think beyond the Backstreets, and then later, Lower and Middle Calver. The very notion of an entire Kingdom out there, and one visited by people from other lands, seemed as preposterous as Arthur becoming its ruler.

Pushfoot smiled. "Not many people think beyond the walls of Calver, and those who do usually live within a month's ride of the city limits. But there's things out there that would fascinate and terrify you in equal measure. And I've seen it all. Or at least as much as I want to."

He looked out at the city sprawling in the distance.

"Now, I'm stationed back in Calver," he continued, "Middle Calver to be precise. And it's time to settle down. Got my eye on a nice house tucked away on a nice, quiet street near the market district. Got a girl who wants to settle down from a very reputable family, and a girl from the Backstreets who definitely doesn't. But a house and two women doesn't come cheap, and in case you didn't know, nobody joins The King's Guard for the coin."

"Enter one Roderick von Haugen," Arthur said.

"Precisely," said Pushfoot, nodding. He pointed up ahead

at Roderick who was way out in front, sat bolt upright in the saddle as if he had a broom up his back. "He may well be one of the biggest arses I've ever had the misfortune to encounter but that works in my favour. Plenty of people don't like him and there's a whole host of others who he thinks are in his way. Fortunately, I've got the skills and the men to solve those problems, and he pays well—very well."

"What exactly does he have planned once we're back?" Arthur asked.

Pushfoot seemed to lose interest once again.

"Who knows?" he said. "We're to take you to the closest jail to Middle Calver and after that, who cares?" He spurred his horse and trotted off to join his men at the front.

Arthur turned to Charlie. "A return visit to jail," he said. "Who'd have thought?"

"Pretty sure it'll just be a stop off. I wouldn't be surprised if Roderick von Humpergooch has bigger plans for us. One thing's for sure, he'll want everyone to know he's won."

"I'd feel sorry for you," said Millicent, "but I think my fate might be worse. I'm probably going to have to spend the rest of my life with him…"

>>>><<<<

As NIGHT FELL, they finally reached the immense gatehouse leading into Lower Calver. Charlie, Millicent and Arthur were waved through without having to wait on account of their King's Guard escort, and emerged onto the cobbled streets of the city, the wide open expanse of the market place directly in front of them. The street lights lining either side of the King's Pass were lit, causing an effect similar to a winding river of light moving ever upwards, traversing the great hill. The only other light was that of the moon, which was full and hung low in the night sky; its white light cascading down on each and every cobble of the open square before them.

It was hard to say if a city like Calver ever slept. Certain pockets did, but often at different parts of the night and—in some instances—during the day too. There was always something to be done—sometimes for the greater good, but more often for the smaller, slightly more personal good. For the vast majority who called Calver home, simply getting by, making a little coin, and ending the day with a warm meal was all it took to feel like the day had been won.

As the three were led across the marketplace, Roderick brought the precession to a halt. He did this with far more flourish than was necessary; drawing his horse up on its hind legs and whistling loud enough for it to echo off the surrounding buildings. This drew a series of whispered insults from the King's Guards and a weary shake of the head from Commander Pushfoot.

"If he fell off, I honestly think I might wet myself," Millicent said.

"If he wasn't so dangerous, this would all be hilarious," added Arthur.

Roderick trotted back to his captives and, after nearly running them down, drew his horse up alongside Millicent.

"Right then, my betrothed. You shall ride up here with me from here on in," he said, patting the space on the saddle behind him.

"You can fart in your hand and clap if you think I'm

being paraded through the streets with you!" she said.

Roderick turned his usual shade of crimson but laughed and looked to Commander Pushfoot. "You see what happens when you let the fillies loose? They toddle off with the common folk and return with a latrine for a mouth. How very uncouth!"

Pushfoot nodded absently through his boredom.

"Here's how things are going to proceed, young Millicent Hargreaves," Roderick continued. "You will ride with me. I shall present you as the wandering miscreant you are, a veritable slave to folly, who lost herself momentarily, but after I so gallantly rescued you from the clutches of scoundrels and ne'er-do-wells, you came to your senses and now worship the ground I walk on. The city will see that you have very much seen the error of your ways, that you are now so very grateful, and, in addition, you are completely besotted with me. And so on and so on, ad infinitum."

"Roderick," Millicent said, "there are a great, *great* many things wrong with what that little speech. I haven't the energy or inclination to point out each and every one to you, so let's just cut to the chase—the part where I say I'm not doing what you say, and you say what you'll do if I don't. Because with spoilt little boys like you, there's always a threat, isn't there?"

The crack of Roderick's riding whip cannoned across the King's Pass and Millicent fell to the cobbles, clutching her cheek.

"You will be reminded of your place, Millicent Hargreaves," he said, crimson-faced and huffing through flared nostrils, "However long it takes, you will learn how this world—*my world*—works."

Charlie and Arthur launched themselves at Roderick but got no closer than grasping at his stirrups, and were pulled away by the King's Guard. Charlie looked up at Commander Pushfoot who remained on his horse and a little further back from the group.

"Does this sit right with you? A man of the King's Guard?!" He pointed down to Millicent, still on her knees, blood trickling through the fingers pressed against her cheek. "Just so long as you get your coin, am I right?"

Pushfoot looked Charlie hard in the eye. He held Charlie's gaze for a second then smiled and shrugged. "Come on, enough pantomime," he said, riding off towards the front of the group. "It's late, I'm tired and I want my money,"

Roderick circled Charlie and Arthur, now on floor beside Millicent. "You two gentlemen – and I use the term in its loosest sense – will spend some time in Lower Calver's drunk tank whilst I decide what I'm going to do with you. You'll have no food or water, mind you, but you will have a roof over your heads—I'm not a complete animal."

He continued to ride in wide circles around the group.

"In the meantime," he said, tugging at the reins, "and purely for insurance purposes, if any one of you three decides you don't wish to comply, then the others will suffer immeasurably. Understood?"

"Angular turd," Arthur said and spat in Roderick's general direction.

"That's as may be," he said and aimed a kick at Arthur's chest, "but I'm the angular turd who's up here. As opposed to the one someone's just trodden in."

Roderick ordered the King's Guard lift Millicent up to him and help position her behind him. She offered little resistance.

"Right-ho," Roderick said, moving forwards. "Let's get you boys to your accommodation for the next few days."

CHAPTER 27

Lower Calver prison blues.

T HEY MADE THEIR way up the King's Path without
drawing much attention. Those out at that time of night
had places to be. On the occasion someone who'd replaced
too much bravado with not enough common sense approached the column of King's Guards, they were soon sent
on their way; usually with a boot in the face from one of the
Guards on horseback.

They passed the many buildings lining the cobbled path
which ran directly to the gatehouse of Middle Calver and, as
they did so, Charlie's eye was drawn to places like the Flying
Dishcloth and the Watchclock's Hands—inns he'd played in
on a regular basis. They were still full with the sounds of an
evening's entertainment well had, and he found himself
longing for a chance to play those venues once again.

As he shuffled past, he realised that, despite being
bloody, beaten and in many ways a broken mess, he was glad
they'd made the journey out of Calver. Of course, he'd never
wanted any harm to come to Millicent and Arthur, but aside
from that, he felt that, even though it hurt to breathe, and he
knew that going to the latrine later was probably going to feel
like passing nails, he didn't regret heading out on their

musical adventure.

Brief as it was, it had allowed him to glimpse a life be-yond—beyond just playing music in order to earn some coin; beyond being told what to play and when. When he was out in the Kingdom—just the very small part of it they'd visited—he'd played what he'd wanted to play. It had been about the music and that, of course, was when they'd had the most fun.

He smiled to himself as he pictured Arthur beating the living daylights out of his bohdran, sweat flying in all directions as he thrashed his head in time with the beat; as he thought of Millicent, launching herself into the crowd, whirling around, dancing, laughing, completely and utterly free. And he remembered how he'd felt—by the gods, he'd ridden the lightning. They all had. For the briefest of moments, it had been glorious.

"Here we are, your palace awaits," Roderick said, inter-rupting his train of thought. "I don't know why you're smiling, Lightfoot—the remainder of your days are going to be anything but pleasant. I'd try and enjoy your stay in jail because once I work out what I'm going to do with you, your time here will most certainly appear as a highlight."

"The worst you could possibly do is to force me and Charlie to spend any longer listening to your blather," Arthur said. "You are by far and away one of the most irritating arseholes I've ever had the misfortune to come across. And, for your information, I've had piles."

Roderick flushed his trademark crimson and leapt down from his mount. He stormed over to Charlie and Arthur.

"Why won't you two just shut up!" he said, huffing and

puffing. "Don't you know when you're beaten? I could thrash you to within an inch of your life, right here and right now!"

"Actually, *you* couldn't," Arthur said, squaring up to Roderick. "*They* could," he said, pointing in the direction of the King's Guard. "And if you did manage to sum up the courage to try, a bandaged nose would be the least of your injuries."

Roderick held Arthur's gaze for a moment longer and then turned on his heel and marched back to his horse. "Throw them in jail," he shouted. "They bore me and I need to make my triumphant return. Set a couple of men to keep watch at all times. I shall send word when I want them bringing to me."

With not so much as another glance at either Charlie or Arthur, he mounted his horse, turned towards Middle Calver, and rode off. Millicent glanced back over her shoulder, but only briefly.

"That was... incredibly brave," said Charlie.

"Sometimes you've got to say what needs to be said," Arthur said, shrugging.

"When you two lovers have quite finished," said Commander Pushfoot, "I'd like this night over as soon as possible. With that in mind, get your backsides over to the jail."

He ordered a couple of his men to take Charlie and Arthur and ensure they were locked in separate cells. Then, as per Roderick's request, they were to form a rotating watch to guard them day and night.

The guards who had been left behind clearly weren't pleased about it, especially after spending a day's ride to get to Calver. They grumbled and moaned about sleep, about how guard duty at the Lower Calver drunk tank was beneath them, and how they considered it a form of punishment.

Charlie couldn't care less. He was bone-tired, most of him hurt and he just wanted to lie down and get some rest; even if it was on a piss-stained pallet in the corner of a cold, stone jail cell.

As the guards shoved Arthur and Charlie through the main door, the two prisoners crashed into someone being thrown out. They managed to steady themselves by grabbing on to one another, but the evictee bounced off them and landed in a heap on the floor. Instinctively, Charlie bent down to help the man up.

"I'm so sor—" Charlie began as he bent down, but he was hit by a wall of alcohol vapor and gagged on the stench.

"What-ho, Charles!" said Drunk Morgan from his position on the stone floor. "Fancy bumping into you here!"

"Morgan, as I live and try to breathe," Charlie said, unable to help himself from smiling.

"The very same," Drunk Morgan said, wobbling to his feet. "Just checking out for the evening. Apparently, I might have overdone it on the old sozzle-sauce and I'm too far gone to be any trouble to anyone, so these fine fellows are sending me packing."

"Too drunk for the drunk tank," Arthur said, nodding approvingly. "Now that is an accomplishment."

"Perennial overachiever, me," Drunk Morgan nodded modestly. "It's my cross to bear but bear it I do. Didn't expect to see you two honourables back so soon. What is it this time?"

As briefly as he could, given they were blocking the main

doorway to the jail and both sets of guards wanted as little to do with them as possible, Charlie explained why they were heading into the jail once more.

Drunk Morgan shook his head.

"Scandalous!" he shouted waving his finger in the general direction of anyone wearing a breastplate. "The risk-takers and revolutionaries will always struggle against the oppressive nature of the small minded and easily affronted. Stand firm, Lightfoot, and simple yet probably quite steadfast friend. Stand firm, and don't let the buggers get you down."

With that, Drunk Morgan let out a monstrous belch and stumbled out into the night. Within seconds of him leaving there was the unmistakable sound of him falling over with a thud. "All is well, nothing is broken," he shouted back. "Though I may have expelled more than just wind as I toppled. Things are looking a little squelchy in the under-garment department."

Charlie and Arthur, despite their current situation, couldn't help but shake with laugher. The guards pushed them down the corridor and into two adjacent cells at the end. The heavy doors ground to a close and the bolts locked in place.

Charlie took himself over to the pallet in the corner. This one had no straw; no bedding of any sort. It was nothing more than a bare wooden frame nailed together. He didn't care. He sat down, checked it over for any large protruding nails and, carefully, lay back.

He started to form a few thoughts, mainly regarding what might happen when Roderick decided what he wanted to do with him and Arthur, but he was unable to hold any of them in place. Like the early morning ground mist on a soon to be warm day, they swirled beyond reach, then disappeared as he fell into a deep and dreamless sleep.

>>>><<<<

NOISE. LOUD, CLATTERING and intrusive noise.

It battered and clanged its way into Charlie's sleep and, once it had grabbed a hold, wrenched him upwards towards consciousness. Up from the depths of deep and dark rest, it felt like being drawn from the bottom of a well. He tried to fight it but it was no use—he was heading towards waking.

He really didn't want to wake up. Down here, where it was dark and quiet and without meaning, everything was simple. Up there—where it was bright and loud and full of people—life got very complicated, very quickly.

Suddenly, the choice was taken from him. For the second time in only a few days, he was hit in the face with cold water, causing him to gasp and splutter his way upright.

"Morning sleepy-head."

It was the unmistakably piercing voice of Roderick von Haugen.

Charlie rubbed the water from his eyes, spat out a mouthful, and looked up in the direction Roderick had spoken from. The bandage on his nose had gone, although the red welts from Charlie's teeth had not. In addition, he was now sporting two slightly blackening eyes.

"You needn't have put on make-up to see me, von Haugen," Charlie said blowing him a kiss. He twisted his neck first one way and then the other and wondered just how much time had passed since he'd passed out.

"Oh, yes, very funny. I'd missed your wit over these last three days," said Roderick as if reading his mind.

"Yeah, well if wit was snot, you wouldn't have enough to blow your nose," Charlie said and then added, "mind you, if you did, there'd be plenty of space with a hooter like yours."

Roderick looked at Charlie through narrowed eyes.

"You know something, Lightfoot?" he asked.

"I do. Your face makes onions cry."

It was petty and small but by the gods it made him feel better.

"Oh yes, hardy-har. You are such a card!"

The fact that Roderick wasn't getting wound up had begun to bother Charlie.

"What's the plan, von Haugen?" he asked; "You here to take me back to Middle Calver? Give me a public flogging in the town square or something? Maybe leave me out in the stocks?"

Then Roderick did something which really bothered Charlie.

He smiled.

It was the kind of smile behind which lay a whole lot of nasty thoughts, barely concealed.

"Not quite, my good man. Not quite. You may remember that I said I would have you sent for when I'd decided what to do with you and your half-wit friend. And yet, here I am in person."

"Couldn't keep away?" Charlie said, although some of the edge had gone from his voice.

"It's more of a case of wouldn't be anywhere else. You

see, there's a show to be seen, old boy. You like shows, don't you? You are, after all, a showman."

"Roderick, I'm getting bored," Charlie said feigning indifference. "Can't we just cut to the chase and then we won't need to be in the same room for a while."

"For once, Lightfoot, I agree with you. You see, I was going to keep you and your chum around for a little while—some sort of long, drawn out punishment so I could gain as much pleasure out of your suffering for as long as possible. But then I said to myself, 'Roderick old bean, what good would that do? It's time to move on. Clean slate and all that'. Which is why, at noon today, up by the Middle Calver wall—a mere gentle stroll from this very cell—you and Arthur will face the hangman's noose."

Some part of Charlie, a larger part than he would've liked to acknowledge, had known something like this was coming. He didn't know how and he didn't know when, but he knew it was coming. There was no way someone like Roderick von Haugen was going to let this end with Charlie and Arthur simply walking away. Even if it took many years, once he'd humiliated them enough, or gotten bored enough, then it was obvious he would've just disposed of them. He just hadn't thought it would happen so soon.

"You're going to hang us?" Charlie said. "There hasn't been a hanging for years. How on earth did you manage to get that through the palace?"

"With money comes connections," Roderick said, still smiling. "Turns out I went to school with a chap who deals with all the paperwork for this type of thing. Amazing what you can get done in a day or two when you know the right people. Had the gallows knocked up in no time. After that, the whole thing sold itself. It's like you said, there's not been a hanging for ages. There's already a crowd—the buggers have been waiting since first light."

Charlie slumped back down onto his pallet. His mouth felt incredibly dry and his stomach churned over.

"What, no witty comeback? No cutting retort? How very disappointing!" Roderick said. He threw the bucket he was still holding in to the corner of the cell and walked over to the door. As he was about to leave, he turned back to face Charlie, framing him with his hands.

"This is how I want to remember you, Charlie Lightfoot. Broken, beaten, and completely without hope. This is why I came down here myself. To see this. Sure, hanging you means I don't get to see you suffer for long, but my word, it'll be worth it. And for every single person watching, they'll forever know what happens if you cross Roderick von Haugen."

He turned and walked away and for once, Charlie had nothing to say.

CHAPTER 28

Decisions that end badly.

ALTHOUGH IT WAS probably far longer, it seemed mere moments since Roderick had left when two guards appeared Charlie's door.

"How do, Charles?" asked Dave.

"Thought we might come along and, well, make sure you got to see a couple of familiar faces," Frank said, tucking the keys back in his belt.

"Just a shame it had to be these two, hey," added Dave.

Charlie smiled. "It's actually really good to see you," he said.

"Crikey, if you mean that then things really are at a low point for you," said Frank.

"Not entirely sure they could get much lower, Frank," said Dave.

"Dave, you have all the tact and subtlety of a brick wall, you know that?"

"Well there's no point pretending, is there? You've got to be a realist," Dave said.

Charlie stared wide-eyed at the floor. "This is really happening, isn't it?" he said as much to himself as anyone else. "I'm actually going to be led out and hanged in front of most of Lower Calver. Roderick von Arseface is going to win…"

"Don't be like that," Frank said.

"How, exactly, should I be!" Charlie shouted. "All I wanted to do was play my music. That's it. Nothing more! I didn't ask for any of this. I played, and I got good, and I'm pretty sure I didn't plot to overthrow the king or break any laws when I was doing that."

Dave and Frank looked at each other and then the floor.

"I'm sorry…" said Charlie. "None of this is your fault. And I do appreciate you being here; really I do. I'm just scared. And angry…. but mostly, I'm scared."

"Maybe this von Haugen bloke will have a change of heart. Maybe he'll decide this isn't the way forward. Or maybe someone higher up will have got wind of what he's doing and they'll intervene. It could happen, you know," Dave said.

"It could… but it won't," Charlie said defeatedly, walking over to Dave and Frank. "It's done. And do you know what the worst part is? I should've seen this coming. If I'd just stayed in Lower Calver…. or even on the Backstreets—just played my music, earnt a few coins, and been happy with that—none of this would've happened."

Just then the main door swung open and clattered into the wall, followed by the sound of boots stamping down the corridor.

"What's the bloody hold up?" Roderick shouted and threw his thumb backwards. "Crowd out there's getting restless, as am I. I'm like a child on his birth morn; I can't wait any longer!"

He appeared in the doorway to Charlie's cell.

"Come on then you two galoots, let's have Lightfoot out here. Need to parade him before his adoring public. One last gig and all that! And I'm sure you want to put on a good show."

Roderick snorted a laugh, turned on his heel and walked away. As he passed Arthur's cell he banged on the door. "You two, beer-boy. Last orders!" His snorting laughter followed him down the corridor and outside.

"Well… he's a prick," Dave said.

"He tends to have that effect on people," Charlie said.

"A prick he may be," said Commander Pushfoot, appearing suddenly in the doorway, "but, as I believe I've mentioned before, he's a prick who pays incredibly well."

Dave and Frank stiffened. They stood to attention and snapped off a couple of smart salutes.

"At ease, fellas," Commander Pushfoot said, walking into Charlie's cell. "Think we can do without all the pomp and circumstance." He circled the cell, casting his gaze over it, paused by the pallet, shook his head and completed his inspection by coming to a halt in front of Charlie.

"Such a sorry state of affairs," he said. "Shame. Anyway, moving on; here's how things will go. You'll be escorted out of here shortly; not by these two, but by my men—men I can trust. Once outside, you'll be joined by more of my men just in case you get any silly ideas. They'll lead you to the gallows where, no doubt, as well as the hangman, von Haugen will be waiting positively wetting his britches with glee. Your friend next door will go first, then you: Von Haugen's idea. If you decide to try anything, shall we say… heroic, I've ordered my respond with extreme prejudice. If we get a move on, all will be done, dusted and out the way before the shops open. Then I can return to Middle Calver, collect my pay, and forget the two of you ever even existed."

Dave and Frank shifted uneasily.

"Problem, Corporals?" Pushfoot asked, staring hard at his subordinates.

"Carrying out orders is not a problem, sir," Dave said, staring at the wall to the right of his commander.

"And what you do with your money is your business, sir," Frank joined in, also looking at the wall past Pushfoot.

"After all, we all need to make coin, sir," Dave continued.

"And we all have to sleep at night... sir," Frank said.

"Is that so," Commander Pushfoot replied, stepping closer; so close, in fact that he was inches from both men.

"Permission to... speak freely, sir," Dave asked.

"I'd also like to seek that permission... sir," added Frank.

Commander Pushfoot narrowed his eyes. "I'll grant it, but I'd be very careful with the words choose to speak freely with. There's still a couple of spots open on the south side of the wall."

"Understood, sir," Dave said.

"Very well. Speak," Commander Pushfoot said.

Dave slowly brought his fixed stare to his superior. "You, sir," he said, "are an embarrassment to the uniform."

Pushfoot stepped back and folded his arms. "Is that so?" he said and turned to face Frank. "And do you agree with your insubordinate friend's sentiment?"

"Not exactly," Frank said. He too brought his gaze to meet the officer. "I would've added money-grabbing and shallow for good measure."

"Oh, you would, would you? You do realise this means the end of your careers? I'll see to it that the two of you serve the rest of your time pulling night shifts on the south side of the wall. By the time you retire, you'll both wish you'd never joined the King's Guard."

Dave shrugged. "Kind of wish I'd not joined right now. Besides, we're long overdue a change of scenery."

"Yeah, and at least round there we can put in an honest day's graft," Frank said.

"As far as possible away from you, sir,"

"What with you being a money-grabbing, shallow embarrassment to the aforementioned uniform. Sir."

"How very noble," Pushfoot said, arms still folded. "And utterly stupid. All for the sake of your honour. Let me tell you soldiers something; a bit of free advice before you're shipped off to the arse-end of the hill. Principles are expensive things to have. Ask Lightfoot and his friend. They're about to find out the hard way."

He stepped forward again, inches from their face. "Now bugger off out of my sight before I beat you within an inch of your miserable lives!"

Dave and Frank turned to Charlie.

"Gods speed, Charlie" Dave said, and Frank nodded in agreement.

Charlie, completely overcome with emotion, could barely speak.

"Goodbye, you lovely, stupid men," he managed.

"Get them out!" Commander Pushfoot ordered and four of his guards bustled into the cell and escorted Frank and

Dave outside. At first, all that Charlie could hear was the sound of marching boots, then the main door swinging shut, then silence.

Commander Pushfoot stood with his hands clasped behind his back, slightly bent, looking at Charlie.

"What is it with you, Lightfoot?" he asked. "What is it about you that makes people throw their lives away? First that Millicent girl, then your boy next door, and now even two of the King's Guard, willingly destroy their career over… you—a bloody nobody from the Backstreets. Must be quite the burden to bear for you, knowing you've ruined so many lives."

Charlie hung his head. Of course Pushfoot was right. He'd been thinking it himself; it seemed that, once he'd stretched beyond the world he knew, people started to suffer and lives were ruined. How had things gone so wrong? So terribly and dangerously wrong.

Tears rolled freely down his cheeks. He knew he looked weak but he couldn't help it. He didn't feel sorry for himself. He felt sorry for everyone else.

Then a voice spoke up.

"If you're crying in there, then I'm not going up on those gallows with you. There's no way I'm letting you embarrass me up there," Arthur shouted from his cell. "Besides, once you start blubbering, you know you'll set me off too. So, knock it off, Lightfoot or I'm not being your friend any-more!"

Despite himself, despite everything, Charlie laughed. It began as a smile and a shake of the head, but before long he was laughing hard.

"That's better!" Arthur shouted from next door. "Now let's get out there and put on one final show. The best bloody hanging anyone's ever seen in Calver. It's the least we can do. Although, I'm buggered what we'll do if anyone wants an encore."

Charlie was now doubled over, tears of laughter streaming down his face. Commander Pushfoot looked at him like he'd lost his mind, but Charlie didn't care; maybe he had.

"Oh, and one more thing," Arthur shouted. "I heard I'm going before you. Sorry about that. We both know, there's no way you'll be able to follow me. Show'll be over, people will be going home. Good luck with that!"

Charlie fell onto his hands and knees, gasping for breath.

"You two are positively bat-shit." Commander Pushfoot said, completely bemused. He reached down, hauled Charlie to his feet and marched him out of his cell. Once in the corridor, he shoved him towards the waiting guards, then went back to grab Arthur. Their hands were tied behind their backs with thick, coarse rope, which was pulled so tight it cut into their wrists, drawing blood.

"Arthur, you are an absolute, grade A pillock," Charlie said.

"I do my best," he replied. "How are you feeling?"

"Absolutely shitting myself," Charlie said. "You?"

"About the same," he replied. "Well, suppose we ought to go out there and give the crowd what they want," Arthur said.

"Arthur, my friend," Charlie said. "Don't we always?"

CHAPTER 29

Some very insulting alliteration.

C HARLIE AND ARTHUR emerged from the Lower Calver Jail into the bright sunshine of what could, rather ironically, be classed as a glorious morning. The sun cast a softening glow across the tops of the buildings making even the great, thick wall which separated Lower and Middle Calver seem somewhat picturesque. But the raised platform of the gallows, replete with King's Guard and a rather burly hangman took this glorious vision and profoundly stamped it's shining face into the mud.

As their escort ushered Charlie and Arthur along the side of the wall and towards the gallows, it didn't take very long before they were noticed. At first, it was just the odd person but, in a very short space of time, the entire crowd were jostling to get a better look. And what a crowd it was. To Charlie it seemed as if there were at least a couple of hundred people there, with more joining as they piled out of their shops and homes to see the commotion.

He heard murmurs from the crowd but nothing he could discern. As he looked at the faces before him, he wondered if they knew why the hanging was taking place. There hadn't been one for so long; he knew some of them, maybe most of them, would want to know what it was the two of them had done to warrant a hanging.

He thought about shouting out; saying something about how this was all unfair and unjust, that he was about to pay with his life because he simply wanted to play music. But upon looking from face to face, he realised the futility of it. None of those in attendance would pay any mind to what he was saying. It sounded pathetic and pointless when he said it to himself, let alone a crowd of people who were there because—let's face it—they wanted to watch someone die. Did he really think if he made his case succinctly and passionately enough, that they'd all nod their heads, say 'fair enough' and toddle off back home? Or even better—rise up and demand his freedom.

They were led in a crowded hustle along the side of the wall and up the small slope towards the gallows, surrounded on all sides by members of the King's Guard. It was hard to see the faces in the crowd for more than a brief glimpse but then, Charlie supposed that was what Roderick wanted. He could hear people, some talking to each other, some shouting out, but could only manage to catch snippets before he was shoved ever-onwards.

"Who are they?"

"What have they done?"

"Don't know who it is but it must have been bad."

"If they're being hung, you know it's serious."

The guards brought them to a halt just before the first step leading them up to the platform of the gallows.

"Right then, boys," Commander Pushfoot said as he made his way towards them through the wall of King's Guards. "Time to put these on."

ENVY

He held out two, black hoods and Charlie and Arthur must have looked confused because the Commander laughed.

"They go over your heads. The crowd won't like it—in my experience, they like to see a dying man's face before he hits the drop—but von Haugen wants it this way, so this is the way it'll be."

Before either Charlie or Arthur could protest, the hoods were pulled down over their heads and they were marched blindly up the steps. Both stumbled as it was as black as night inside the hoods so, in the end, the King's Guards lifted them up the remaining few.

Two things seemed to happen simultaneously. Charlie felt his head shoved through a loop of rope which was tightened immediately. At the same time, the crowd fell silent.

The only noise Charlie could now make out was that of the blood pounding in his own head. He tried to swallow but the noose was too tight. Next to him he heard Arthur let out a whimper.

"These two criminals," Roderick began as he stepped forward from where he'd been waiting somewhere behind Charlie, "have committed the most heinous of crimes."

There were whispers in the crowd but Charlie couldn't make out any of the words.

"They were apprehended with large amounts of gold, coin, and other valuables on the far edge of the Bloodwastes as they tried to flee out into the Kingdom after bludgeoning to death seven members of an esteemed Middle Calver family. After being disturbed mid-burglary, they resorted to butchery of the vilest kind. Of those killed in this most barbaric fashion, two were children and one was an elderly woman—"

Charlie tried to scream—to shout out that it wasn't true, to make his voice heard—but it was too late. The crowd erupted into a cacophony of anger. It was unintelligible, but the words didn't need to be heard—Charlie felt their fury and their need for violent retribution. He also felt their relief that in attending something as gruesome as a hanging, they'd done the right thing. These were bad men and they deserved to die; it wasn't horrific voyeurism that had drawn them to this place, but to bear witness to justice being served.

He felt a hand upon his shoulder and then Roderick's voice was inches from his ear.

"Pretty bloody good, old boy, wouldn't you say?" he whispered to him, "Do you remember when we first met? Up at that gods-awful shin dig organised by Lady G? My question is: why ever didn't you listen to me when I warned you to keep your distance? Instead, you turned my Millicent against me—you made her into something she's not. I've begun correcting such behaviour, but it'll take some time before I've broken that one's spirit. But break it I will because, as you're about to find out, lad—a von Haugen never loses."

Charlie felt Roderick pat him on the cheek through the thick material of the hood. The thud of Roderick's footsteps moved around and in front him and Arthur, and he heard the crowd begin to quieten. There were still mutterings and conversations and even the odd shout but the fury seemed to have ceased. For now.

"And now, my good people of Calver," Roderick bellowed, "with my heartfelt thanks to the finest members of the

King's Guard for capturing them this morning, these savages will be brought to justice!"

The crowd roared in anticipation, and the boards creaked and Charlie felt Roderick return. "One last thing, Lightfoot," he breathed into Charlie's ear. "Your last moments will not be in darkness. You will not be afforded that final comfort. Instead, you get to see the world from which you are about to depart one final time!"

In a single swift movement, the hood was yanked from Charlie's head despite the rope around his neck. He squinted; the morning light was bright, especially when compared to the darkness of the hood, but he could still make out the crowd gathered before him, the King's Path winding away beneath him, and beyond that, the immense wall of Lower Calver. He saw faces; some he thought he recognised, others he didn't. And he saw Millicent, stood in a cordoned-off area to the side, where the crowd was held back by a large group of the King's Guard. To her right stood Commander Pushfoot, looking as bored as ever. She had tears streaming down her face, but was looking up at Charlie; staring him directly in the eye, determined not to look away.

All of this took place in but a moment. To Charlie, it felt like he saw all of this all at once, but in reality, it was over as soon as it had started. Roderick moved to Arthur, and with an exaggerated flourish, ripped his hood off, and the crowd once again fell silent.

The silence held.

Roderick stepped forwards. He opened his arms wide to the crowd, and opened his mouth, but before he could speak a word, another voice interrupted.

"Oi! You posh, pointy-faced penis! He's mine!"

CHAPTER 30

You've got a bit of person on you.

I T WAS SO out of place, so jarring, that it took a moment for Charlie to recognise the speaker.

"He might be lots of things, but there's no way on the god's green earth that soft wazzock's killed anyone," the voice continued into the now shocked silence.

Charlie looked down towards a figure elbowing its way to the front.

"Dodge?" he said in disbelief.

"How do, Charlie? How's it going? Sorry, daft question given your current sorry state of affairs. Whereas for me, things have been going pretty well, to be honest; making a decent bit of coin, business ventures paying off and all that. Although, come to think of it, there does seem to be a glaring in hole in my finances where certain musician decided to clear off for a jaunt around the countryside... without telling me first, I might add."

"Yeah," said Charlie, "sorry about that, Dodge. It was more of a spur of the moment thing. You know us creatives."

"Bane of my bleeding existence, that's what you are Lightfoot. I take one bag of coin off you—for investment purposes, mind—and what do you do? Run off round the bleeding countryside! Talk about your sensitive type!"

"Erm, pardon me, little rat-man," said Roderick, sneering down at Dodge, "but who the blazes do you think you are?"

"Oh, pardon my manners Lord Poshington. Typical of us lower types to forget our p's and q's, ain't it? My name's Dodge and that right there"—he pointed a grubby finger at Charlie—"is Charlie Lightfoot. He's not a killer; he's a musician. Although, to be perfectly honest with you, I don't know which one's worse. I'm not sure who the other bloke is, but if he's with Charlie, he's probably another soft but generally all right lad, I'd wager."

"Right, wonderful, magnificent," said Roderick, "We've established who you are but what is it you're doing here? I've got a bloody execution to get on with."

The crowd had fallen strangely quiet. They'd been drawn in by the thrill of the gallows and rumours of a just hanging, but now here was this strange looking man, shouting about how the prisoners hadn't done what they were accused of. No one really knew exactly what was going on but one thing was for sure—you didn't pass up a chance to watch a bit of drama like this of a morning.

"Actually, I'm not sure you do have an execution to be getting on with, toff-boy. These lads didn't commit no crime... well, certainly not the one you're accusing them of. And secondly, one of them, at least, works for me. As such, I'm going to need him back and earning. Might as well take his mate too. The end result is, and I'm sorry to disappoint everyone, but there will be no hanging today."

Dodge stood back, arms folded confidently. Roderick stood dumbfounded. Then he began to laugh.

"No hanging today? No hanging today?! Who the devil do you think you are, you scabby little shitbag? No hanging today indeed. What? Think you're going to stop me, do you?" He continued laughing heartily.

"Oh no, sunshine," he said, "I'm not going to stop you. He is."

Dodge put the first two fingers of each hand to his mouth and let out one long, loud whistle. From over to Charlie's left, where a much smaller side street intersected with the King's Pass, the crowd began to part. It didn't seem to be organised in any specific way, it just… split. Then, from behind the corner of the building, at the point where the side street met the King's Pass, came the lumbering form of Mr. Lunk.

He stepped out onto the King's Pass, paused, turned his immense Mr. Lunk-ness towards Middle Calver and the gallows, and began walking steadily forwards. He'd only taken a few steps before the entire remainder of the crowd in his way had shifted and produced a clear path up to Dodge.

"Hello Mr. Lunk," Charlie said, as the giant came to a halt just behind Dodge.

"Hello, funny music man," Mr. Lunk rumbled back.

"What… in the god's name is that?" Roderick said taking a step back.

"My associate," replied Dodge. "Name's Mr. Lunk. He is very good at what he does."

"And… what is it he does?" Roderick asked, clearly not really wishing for an answer.

"Mainly separating people from the daft idea that they shouldn't do what I ask them to," Dodge said.

Mr. Lunk moved another half a step forwards. He rolled his shoulders and flexed his tree-like fingers.

"Oh, mother…" Roderick squeaked. "Pushfoot! Get up here and do something!"

Commander Pushfoot was already on his way. He'd gathered a handful of King's Guards and was currently vaulting the steps. He reached Roderick, shouldered him out the way, and wrenched a lever near the scaffold, releasing the ratchet and causing the trapdoor beneath Charlie and Arthur to swing open.

⇒⇒⇒⚔⇐⇐⇐

THERE WAS A collective gasp from the crowd, a moment of held breath, and then all hell broke loose.

As the trapdoor opened, Charlie felt himself fall and his eyes snapped shut in preparation. He heard Dodge shout something at Mr. Lunk and the next thing he knew, his weight shifted.

But not downwards.

Backwards.

He opened his eyes in time to see Mr. Lunk—every sinew straining, the veins in his neck standing out like pipes—throwing his entire weight into the wood frame of the gallows, sending it crashing backwards towards the wall.

When falling unexpectedly, there is no real way to prepare, unless you're trained in how to fall over properly. Charlie lacked these necessary skills, and even if he had possessed them, with a noose looped over his head and his hands tied behind his back, they probably wouldn't have been much use. Instead he said a quick prayer to any god that happened to be listening and braced for impact.

The gallows crashed backwards, the L-shaped scaffold beams above Charlie smashing into the wall behind, and clattering downwards. Charlie was flung back as the rest of the platform toppled and folded in on itself, and he came to rest in a pile of splintered wood, dust, and rope.

"A-Arthur!" he shouted, pulling his leg free from a broken beam. "Arthur, are you all right?"

There was a cough from somewhere over to his right and then a pile of wood shifted as Arthur pulled himself free of the debris.

"My back hurts a bit but apart from that, I think I'm all right," he said.

He had a piece of wood about the size of Charlie's fiddle sticking out of his left shoulder.

"You've got a bit of wood in you," Charlie said, pointing.

Arthur glanced over at shoulder. His knees buckled and he started to wobble. Charlie quickly waded through the rubble and leant into him before he fell.

"Ooh-er," Arthur said, the colour draining from his cheeks. "Feel a bit light-headed."

"Suppose now's not the best time to make a chip on your shoulder gag," Charlie said, leading him out of the now crumpled gallows.

As they stepped out, Charlie felt hands grab him from behind and before he could react, an arm was tight around his throat gripping him in a choke hold.

"Think me and you might take a walk," Commander Pushfoot said, slivers of wood and dust falling from his uniform. "Don't try anything or I'll poke holes in your liver." Charlie felt something cold and sharp jab his lower back.

"Hey, you can't do—" Arthur started to say but now Charlie wasn't supporting him, he simply slumped down and then flopped over onto one side. As he did so, Dodge came running around the corner of the now ruined gallows.

"Sorry about that," Dodge said, "desperate times call for desperate measures." Then he spotted Commander Pushfoot. "Here! What are you doing with my musician? You leave him alone."

As Dodge took a step forward, Charlie tried to gurgle a warning but Pushfoot's grip around his neck was too tight. The commander drew the knife Dodge clearly hadn't seen from between himself and Charlie and stabbed the man twice, very quickly in the chest.

Dodge stopped in his tracks. Charlie had never seen anyone looking so angry before.

"You-you scumbag!" Dodge raged, blood already filling his mouth. It sprayed over Charlie as he spoke. "You only went and killed me!" He stumbled forwards, tripped over his own feet, and fell over on his side.

Commander Pushfoot shoved Charlie forwards, past Dodge's body, and shoved again as Charlie stopped to look down. And Charlie, eyes fixed on his fallen friend... if you could call him that, walked straight into a wall.

Mr. Lunk looked down at Charlie, then at Dodge. Then, his gaze rose steadily back up towards Charlie, eyes wide and wet. He blinked once, then twice, and then raised his arm up, pointing at Commander Pushfoot.

"*You!*" he roared. The sheer anger and pain in Mr.

Lunk's voice made Charlie jump.

As Mr. Lunk stepped forward, Pushfoot stepped out from behind Charlie, and stabbed once, twice.

Only this time it wasn't Dodge who stood before him.

It was Mr. Lunk.

The blade entered Mr. Lunk's upper leg, but before Pushfoot could withdraw, Mr. Lunk had shot out his hand and wrapped it tightly around both the knife and Commander's own hand. The giant let out an almighty roar and pulled. Commander Pushfoot left the ground and became momentarily airborne, hurtling towards Mr. Lunk, his progress stopped by the latter's massive frame. As Pushfoot smacked face first into Mr. Lunk's midsection, Mr. Lunk reached down and seized the Commander by the neck; his hands so large that they wrapped cleanly around the man's the head at the same time.

Charlie stared up at Mr. Lunk holding Commander Pushfoot. His massive hand covered everything from the neck up.

Pushfoot tried to say speak but his words were lost in Mr. Lunk's grip. The giant grunted once and then everything that was Commander Pushfoot from the neck up exploded. Or rather popped, as it seemed to Charlie.

Bits of Commander Pushfoot splattered across the wall and the ruins of the gallows and even Charlie, and the headless, neckless part him fell to its knees and then flopped onto the floor.

Mr. Lunk wiped the blood and bits of Commander Pushfoot from his hands on the front his shirt. Then he turned to Charlie. He reached out his hand and very carefully, tenderly, once again brushed Charlie's cheek.

"You had some person on you," he said, wiping his hand on his shirt again.

"Thanks..." Charlie said hesitantly. "I'm... I'm sorry about Dodge, Mr. Lunk. I tried to warn him... but there was nothing I could do."

Mr. Lunk looked over at Dodge's body lying on the floor, his eyes full of tears.

"I don't know what to do now," Mr. Lunk said. "Dodge was my friend. He was a good friend. Not so good to others sometimes. Sometimes he made me do bad things. Things I didn't like. But he was my friend."

"Yeah, that's Dodge," Charlie said, wiping scalp from his sleeves. "But at least you knew where you stood with him. You knew at some point it was only a matter of time before he robbed you blind."

"Not all bad," said Mr. Lunk. "Just... not happy with himself."

"And he came through in the end," Charlie said.

He looked out at what was left of the crowd. It appeared that most of them had fled when Mr. Lunk had overturned the gallows. Given that all there was to see now was a pile of wood and a few crushed bodies, they'd realised there would be little more to come, and had headed home, ready to tell others about what happened.

Or wanted to get away before anyone official started asking questions.

"How did you know we would be here anyway?" Charlie asked Mr. Lunk.

"Him," Mr. Lunk said, pointing at a dishevelled figure

making its way towards them, wobbling against the general movement of the crowd. It was the unmistakable gait of Drunk Morgan.

He pin-balled out of the crowd and came to an unsteady stop before Charlie and Mr. Lunk. Charlie started to say something, but Drunk Morgan held up a finger to stop him. From within his tatty cloak he pulled a very battered and very old leatherbound hip flask, unscrewed the lid, and took a long swig. Then, he smacked his lips and slid the hip flask back in his cloak.

"Righty-ho, that's the old cockles warmed," he said. "Positively had to battle my way through that crowd. Not pleasant. Now, before we go any further, I must warn you, I'm not anywhere as inebriated as I'd like to be at this hour of the day. I'm not a morning person; those treacherous times are usually reserved for sleeping off a good one. So, let's get this whole thing over and out of the way; my liver is dangerously close to falling out with me and I need to quell its mutinous notions."

Again, Charlie started to say something and again Drunk Morgan stopped him with a raised finger.

"No doubt, it's an explanation you're after, so here goes. After leaving the drunk tank following our last encounter, I may or may not have accidently bumped into your esteemed associates Dodge and the lovely Mr. Lunk. I also may, or may not, have told them all about your predicament—can't remember, to be honest. And then, as they say, one thing led to another and, well here we are."

He scratched his head, then his backside, and stifled a belch.

"Now if you'll excuse me, there's a gutter around the back of Metheringham's Bakery with my name on it. Or in it. Whichever's the case, the contents of my hip flask calls, and then sleep, until the lure of lady drink come's a-calling once again. It is a hectic, hustle and bustle of a life, but we all have our millstones."

Drunk Morgan turned on his heels, turned some more, bounced off Mr. Lunk and began to wobble away in the rough direction of the marketplace.

"Thank you!" Charlie shouted after him. "I mean it!"

"Thanks are not needed, Mr. Lightfoot," Drunk Morgan slurred loudly without stopping or looking back, "but if it involves you buying me a drink later down the road, then I'll gladly accept!"

Charlie stood for a moment lost in his thoughts, as Mr. Lunk moved over to Dodge's lifeless body. Charlie moved over to Arthur and propped him upright. He gave him a shake but there was no response.

He shook him again and still nothing.

Then he started to panic.

"Get out of the way and let someone who knows what they're doing take a look at him!"

Auntie clambered over the piles of wood and bent down so she could get a better look at Arthur. She reached into her bag, took out a brown bottle with a cork in the top, and stared at the handwritten label. Then she pulled the cork out with her teeth and waved the bottle under Arthur's nose back and forth; just once, but with the desired effect.

"Sweet mother of mercy!" Arthur shouted as his eyes shot open. He coughed and spluttered, but his eyes were open, which, for Charlie, was the main thing. He propped him up against a stack of wood, and then turned to Auntie, wrapping his arms around her.

"Give over, you daft sod," Auntie said, pushing him back. She looked into his eyes, gripping him gently by both arms. "Let's have a look at you, lad. Yep, everything in working order? Well, aside from your common sense, that is. But I see your nine lives are still very much intact."

"It's good to see you, Auntie," Charlie said.

"And it's lovely to see you too," Auntie said, and clasped Charlie's face in her hands.

"Well, I must say," said Blind Watchem as he approached from the remnants of the crowd, "when Morgan told us all about your predicament, I never expected this!" He waved his arms in the general direction of the now ruined gallows.

"Drunk Morgan told you?" Charlie asked.

"Oh yes, we go back a long way," Blind Watchem replied.

Charlie laughed and shook his head. He'd buy the old sozzled fart more than one drink the next time he saw him.

"I must admit, you gave us a bit of a fright," Auntie said.

"I myself was only moderately concerned," said Blind Watchem. "Yet, I can say with all certainty—and I've played some impressive gigs in my time—that I've never literally brought the house down. Well done, Lightfoot!"

"Yeah, thanks," Charlie said. "Probably save the grand finale for a later date though. Much, much later…"

"Quite," said Blind Watchem. "Now where's that lovely young lady you ran away with?"

"Millicent!" cried Charlie, realising he had been so distracted, he hadn't even thought to look for her.

"Oh please, won't somebody come to my rescue. I am but a weak and pathetic rich girl. If only a musician of average height and barely moderate good looks would dash to my aid."

They all looked over to where Millicent had climbed up onto the remains of the gallows and was pawing through the rubble. She'd spoken without even looking over at Charlie.

"Actually, Mr. Backstreets, don't bother. As if I'd need you to save me. You'd be about as much use as a fart in a colander."

"Oh, I'd forgotten how much I like her," Auntie said.

"What are you doing?" Charlie asked.

"Clearly, I'm searching for the remains of my arsehole of a soon-to-be ex-husband, to ensure he's very much, definitely dead."

"Crikey!" said Blind Watchem. "She's a bit full on, isn't she?"

Arthur limped up to Blind Watchem and patted him on the shoulder.

"To be fair, she's been through a bit lately."

"Understatement of the year right there, Arty," Millicent said, still digging. "Ah-ha!" She tossed away a few more pieces of wood, cleared an opening, as Charlie and Arthur clambered up alongside her. Through the gap she'd cleared they could see what was left of Roderick von Haugen. His body was twisted at an odd angle in one direction, his neck in another. As if further proof of his demise were needed, the long metal gallows lever Commander Pushfoot had pulled was embedded deep into his left eye socket.

"Well, I'm no medicine man," Charlie said, wrinkling his nose as he looked down at the body, "but I'd be quite confident in pronouncing him dead."

"I can check for a heartbeat, if you want," offered Arthur, "but I'd be more than happy to follow Charlie's lead on this one."

Millicent said nothing. Instead she made a hawking noise in the back of her throat, and then spat a mouthful in the face of her now very dead husband-to-be.

Charlie looked up at Millicent. Gone was the girl he'd talked to at a party a lifetime ago; this most certainly wasn't the Middle Calver Millicent he'd first met.

"Millicent, dear," Auntie called over, "would you mind coming down from there. It doesn't look too stable and I'd very much like for you to walk me home, if you wouldn't mind."

Her trance broken and, without another look, Millicent scrambled down.

"I'd love to walk you back," said Millicent, looping her arm through Auntie's. "Do you think we might be able to have a cup of tea and a chat once we're there?"

"Oh, I think we've got lots to talk about," Auntie replied. "And plenty of tea to keep us going. Maybe even a slice of cake too."

"That sounds wonderful," Millicent said, and they strode off in the direction of the Backstreets.

Charlie looked from Arthur, to Watchem, to Mr. Lunk.

"Guess that just leaves us then," he said.

Mr. Lunk held Dodge's body, carrying it like a sleeping baby. He gently stroked its hair.

"I shall bury him properly," he said.

"And what then?" Charlie asked.

Mr. Lunk shrugged. He slunk his head. "Dunno."

"Well…" Charlie began, "you're always welcome around Auntie's. Reckon she could put you to good use. Anyone who stands still for too long around her usually ends up with a job of some description."

Mr. Lunk nodded once, then a second time, and then he too strode off in the direction of the Backstreets.

"Feels a bit strange, just… walking away from all of this," Arthur said, as they did just that.

"Well, I for one, have no intention of standing around gawping," Blind Watchem said. "Once the King's Guard get their act together, someone official will want answers. They'll be swarming around here like flies on a turd."

Charlie looked back over his shoulder at the wreck that was once the gallows and the place where he and Arthur had very nearly lost their lives. He clapped Arthur on the back.

"Still never died on stage," he said as they crossed the King's Path and headed towards the Halfway Barrel.

CHAPTER 31

Encore.

THE BURNT TANKARD was, for quite possibly the first time in its existence, packed to the rafters. It seemed to Charlie everyone he'd ever known was crammed into the place.

Trev was his usual stoic self, only this time, it was his usual very busy, stoic self. Auntie had joined him behind the bar, as had Millicent, who had as good as moved in with Auntie. She'd only left once when she'd gone back to her home in Middle Calver to collect a few of her belongings. Charlie and Arthur had offered to go with her but she'd refused.

"This is something I need to do on my own. There needs to be an end," was all Millicent had said.

And end it did.

She'd arrived to find a few of her things already packed into a wooden crate which had been left just inside the front door. Lady Gwendolyn was nowhere to be seen but she'd left word with the maid who'd answered the door. Millicent wasn't to return.

"I've been ostracised," she'd said upon her return. "Cast out into the cruel world and told never to darken the

Hargreaves doorstep ever again."

"That bother you?" Arthur had asked.

"Does it buggery!" Millicent had said, laughing. "Feels like a monumental weight's been lifted!"

Propping up one end of the very crowded bar was Blind Watchem, a cup of rye clutched in his hand. At the other end, Dave and Frank were knocking back jars of ale as if they were going out of fashion. Drunk Morgan held court at a table in the corner, regaling all and sundry with tales from a life spent on the streets. Even Mr. Lunk was there; he'd managed to squeeze his bulk through the back door and was now hunched over, his head touching the rafters above.

Charlie glanced over at Arthur. His shoulder had healed nicely over the past few months. His father had been so pleased to see him, he'd promptly gone out and bought him a new bhodran to replace the one left behind in Appleover.

Charlie whistled over to Millicent. She finished pouring a drink, smiled over at him, and then vaulted up onto the bar. She let out a loud whoop, and began stamping her feet and clapping her hands.

Before long, the rest of the room had joined in.

Charlie looked out at the sea of faces. Smiling, happy faces. Faces of the people he knew. His people.

But also faces of people waiting in anticipation.

Charlie tucked his new fiddle—a gift from Blind Watchem—under his chin.

He looked over at Millicent stamping her way up and down the bar, and then at Arthur; his bodhran already in hand.

"Ready?" he said.

"Ready," Arthur shouted back.

As the opening beat of 'Johan's Battle Axe' thundered across the room, Charlie smiled and let out a laugh.

It was time to ride the lightning.

Acknowledgements.

I can't do the whole Oscar acceptance speech thing. Doesn't work for me. So, here's this instead:

Jack the art dude, Tom the editor dude – the good bits are yours.

To my friends and family – you're all just a bit ace.

Everyone else – thanks for coming. It wouldn't be a party without you.

Oh, and Kirsty. Make your star shine forever bright.

A plea.

If you liked this book, please do me a favour and leave a review somewhere. If you didn't like it, well, there's no accounting for taste, is there?

The socials.

I'm not a fan of social media as such but, in the same way you have to leave the house and speak to people if you want donuts, I do it.

@beedendoesbooks

Printed in Great Britain
by Amazon

20949805R00174